FLIGHT FROM ATLANTIS

by

Virginia Benderly

Wind Song Publishers
P.O.Box 608
Patagonia, AZ
85624

ISBN O-9718159-1-7

Many people have helped me write this book, and I hereby gratefully acknowledge them.

Carol Ann Liaros, who has shown me so many ways to access the subconscious, and to bring into focus the memories we all carry from lifetimes past. Agatha Tutko, who so willingly read the manuscript and cracked the whip so I would finish the book. Thanks, Aggie, I needed that! Jan Hardy, whose expertise in hypnosis made the entire story come together when I had just about given up. Henry Leo Bolduc, for his superb method of training in past life regression, and his delicious sense of humor that made it fun. My editor, Rod Brown, who caught each and every mistake in punctuation and gave me no rest until they were corrected. If there are mistakes, they are mine and not his. Rod, thanks! And for over fifty years of devotion, patience and just plain joy in living, my husband Shaw, who read and re-read, caught my mistakes in spelling and syntax, and without complaint gave me the time I needed to write.

I thank and love you all.

Gini Benderly

Cover painting by Jill Babcock.

Author's Note

Atlantis, at the time of this story, was divided into Provinces. The head of the country was, of course, the King. Under him were the Governors, each of whom managed a Province. Under them were the Judges, who were the law -makers.

The Temples were not what we would call Churches. They were places of learning, where great libraries held the records and wisdom of their world. Each Temple was under the care of a head Priest, and there were both men and women teachers. While Atlantis had public schools as well, many people chose to send their children to the Temples where they would be taught not only the standard curriculum, but the unwritten laws of the Creator they all worshiped, and whom they called simply the Power.

In earlier years, the kings of Atlantis had ruled wisely and well, making their country the most advanced and prosperous in the known world. The laws had been sensible laws, and the Governors and Judges had administered them justly.

Atlantis had undergone at least two great chaotic periods when part of its land mass was lost to the sea, due to volcanic action. Over the years, the Kings, little by little, had become dissolute. They left more and more to the discretion of the Governors and Judges who, in turn, became greedy for the power and wealth that was theirs for the taking. Only the Temple priests tried to hold out against the misuse of authority. They alone knew that Atlantis had very little time left.

Chapter 1

From the rocky path that led up to the highest point above the City, she could look down and see the roof of the Temple. There was the balcony where the great telescope stood; there were the gardens, laid out in formal design; the garden where the children played; the herb garden with the pool, now reflecting the early morning light, where she had spent so many happy hours; and finally, she could just barely see the high walled garden where she had learned things that should have been left, perhaps, to others.

Behind her, the priests came in single file, their sandals making soft hissing noises on the rocks. Her own steps made no sound, but they left a clear trail where the rocks had torn her bare feet. Until it rained again, the path would say to anyone who dared climb it, here, this is the path Fayasas took.

Today, though, there was no rain, no wind, no hint of weather. Just clear blue sky, a gentle sun, the soft Atlantean air; and beside the path, the spring flowers that grew in such profusion among the slopes above the city.

Fayasas breathed deeply of the scented air. Her heart was pounding, and she knew she must slow it before she could face what lay ahead. She thought of the hours of training, and her teacher's voice: "You must have a relaxed body before you can calm your mind. You must have a calm mind before you can direct it to do your will."

Yes, she thought, I must have a calm mind before.... she stopped at the thought that crept unbidden and unwanted into her mind. Her twenty-two years suddenly seemed pitifully short, a mere blink of time. Could she have done differently? For a brief moment, she let her mind drift back, caught herself; then walking more slowly, let her memories take their own direction.

Chapter 2

Faya was sitting on the steps of her house, looking at the new slippers she wore, and thinking that her father, who would be home soon, would appreciate them. He liked to see his only child in red, and her new slippers were as red as they could possibly be. So was the wide hem of her white dress. The short curly black hair was unusual, as were her dark eyes. Most of her playmates had fair hair. Although dark eyes were sometimes seen, most of the children she knew had blue-green eyes. Faya envied them, and had asked repeatedly if her hair would lighten as she grew older.

At the moment, though, she was pleased with herself. The young slave girl had washed and brushed her hair, helped her into her new dress and slippers, and left her sitting primly on the steps with the admonition not to get dirty.

This was her birthday, and she knew her father would swing her up on his shoulder, carry her into the house and give her something he had brought from the City. Faya wiggled her toes in happy anticipation. Soon, now, soon he would be here. Her father, the man who supplied almost everything a small child could want, security, strength and above all, pride in his only daughter. She hugged herself and wriggled because just the idea that he would be here in a few minutes was almost too much to be borne.

Faya squinted up at the sun. It was low in the sky. Where was Father? By this time he certainly should have been home. Perhaps he was detained at his office. He could not have forgotten her birthday! That would have been a blow worse than she had ever known in her short four years.

Forgetting the slave girl's warning, Faya got up and started down the long path that led to the main road her father would ride until he came to their gate. It seemed such a long way. She began to run, then stopped and slipped off the red slippers. There! That was better. It was much easier to run barefoot. The dust was soft underfoot, and she made no sound as she trotted to meet the father she adored.

There he was, just turning into the gate. "Father," she cried,"I thought you had forgotten."

"Forgotten what, my Faya?" The man picked her up as she expected and swung her up to his shoulder. "What did you think I had forgotten?"

"Oh, Father, you know today is my birthday! You are teasing me." No answer. "Aren't you teasing me, Father? You know I am four today, and you promised you would spend the whole week here. Mother and I planned a picnic for tomorrow, and you are going to take me out on the water, aren't you, Father?" Faya leaned forward, still holding the red slippers."What did you bring me for my birthday?" She held on with one hand to the long hair that fell in waves over the man's shoulder, and peered into his face. "Father?"

The man looked up at his daughter intently, then gently disentangled her grasp from his hair and set her down on the narrow roadway. She took his hand, swinging his arm back and forth.

"Faya, I know I promised. But something came up and I must go back to the City tonight."

Faya stopped short and looked up in dismay. "Tonight? But you promised!"

"I know, my darling child, I did promise, and I really meant to keep that promise, but sometimes even...."

Faya broke into wild sobbing. She had never in her short life been thwarted in anything she really wanted, and now she wanted the full attention of her father. He reached down to pick her up again, but she broke away from him and ran toward the house, crying as if her heart was broken. The new red slippers lay in the dust, forgotten. The man looked after her for a moment, sighed, picked up the slippers and resumed his slow walk toward the home that suddenly seemed so far away.

Faya's mother stood in the doorway holding her sobbing daughter. She nodded a cool good evening to her husband and turned to go in, giving the child to the slave girl who waited. Faya was carried off to be soothed, fed and put to bed. Her mother sat down beside a low table, her body tense, and waited for her husband to say something, anything. Faya's disappointment was nothing compared to the apprehension she suddenly felt.

Her husband still stood in the doorway, looking out at an evening sky that promised still more perfect weather for the next day. On either side of the lane he had just walked grew low bushes that were just now coming into bloom. They were cloud-like in their loveliness, and the scent was almost overpowering. Later in the year there would be bright berries that would last for several weeks if the birds left them, for the berries were as sweet to the tongue as the blossoms were to the nose.

Behind them, and following the curve of the house, were fruit trees set in no particular order, for the man had planted them to please his wife's eyes, not for true symmetry. Yet they were a perfect compliment to the entire estate. The thacasca, with its round, ball-like shape and thick leaves large enough to use as dinner plates; the persua; the folata; and underneath them all, the fonta that covered the ground, bearing its lavender flowers. Faya's father sighed again and turned to go in. His wife came up to him and slipped her arm around his waist.

"Must you go back tonight?" she asked. "Faya was heartbroken."

He nodded. "There is a meeting, Kadah, and I must be there. I am expected."

“What are all these meetings, and who are ‘they’? Please tell me. You always shut me out when I’ve asked before.”

“You know very well. The Judges. I am to be one next year. In the meantime, I....”

The woman gasped and broke in. “You are to be a Judge? No! You swore to me when I came to you that you would not!”

“It is a great honor to be chosen. Are you not pleased that you also will be honored? As my consort?” He smiled down at her thinking what an addition she would be to his office.

“Your consort? When you do not honor me by making me your true wife? And what about Faya? You have forgotten her birthday and she has looked forward to this day for weeks. How could you hurt her like this?” Her voice was accusing as she turned away and sat down again on the low stool.

“No, my dear, I did not forget what day this is. I have the best of all presents for her. Faya is four years old today, and while this is a year younger than most children may enter, the Judges have made an exception in her case because she is my daughter. She will enter the School and start her training in ten days. I will be back for her in a week. She will need a few days to become comfortable in a new place. Will you please get her ready?” He smiled at the woman.

She sat frozen, her face a mask of disbelief. “Surely you would not put Faya in that place, with those men? No. I will not permit it.”

“Don’t forget, she is my daughter, too, and it is her right to enter the Training.” He was suddenly angry, knowing he had promised that his children, male or female, would not be forced to enter the Training School. Women just don’t understand, he thought. They don’t know how important to a man’s career an obedient wife is. “Please do as I ask.” He turned and walked into an inner room.

The woman sat very still, her back straight, her knuckles white against the dark blue of her robe. The struggle between love for the man and love for her child nearly broke her for a moment. She took several deep breaths as though to calm herself, then slowly arose and stood quietly for a long moment. She remembered so well the voice of her teacher, "my child, you cannot have a calm mind in a tense body; you must quiet your mind before your body will obey your will." She drew several more deep breaths, forcing her heart to slow and willing her body to relax.

Finally she raised her arms and her face to the painted ceiling and began the Prayer. "To the Power I send my spirit. By this I am renewed." She crossed her arms over her breast. "From the Power I receive blessing. Thus I live in gladness." She dropped her head and closed her eyes. "The Power is within me. I remember, and I am content." She finished the Prayer with her head still bowed, her arms outstretched and her hands open. "Great One," she whispered, "show me the path I must take...tell me what to do."

She did not notice that the man had come back and was watching her from the doorway. She started slightly when he spoke. "You know I have asked you not to use that ridiculous prayer. It has been outlawed, and only the ignorant still believe..."

"You mean you and the Judges don't believe! Why do you think I refuse to let Faya go with you? Judges may legislate all they want, but no one can take away our beliefs."

"There is no use discussing this. I have decided I will not wait the week. I shall return in the morning. Please have Faya ready. She will stay with me in the city apartment until the School opens." He turned on his heel and strode out the door, leaving the woman staring after him in disbelief.

"Wait! Please!" She ran to the open doorway. "Please... you can't take her away from me. You swore you would not."

He did not look back. She watched him walk swiftly away from her, his head high and his step determined. He was a handsome man and her heart was torn between love and despair. They had been together for some seven years, although he had refused to go through the Blessing Ceremony, which in her eyes made them truly Two-in-One. Today he looked unusually handsome. His soft leather tunic reached to his knees and flared slightly over the tight leggings that accentuated his height. She had made the tunic herself although she hated the touch of leather. It was the skin of some animal that also had lived and breathed, and in taking its life for a piece of clothing, she had felt she was betraying the belief that all life was sacred. For love of the man she had done many things that had caused her pain.

She thought of the men, the Judges, who were now in almost complete control of the country. They were wealthy men, for the most part, and felt they had the right to legislate anyway they chose. Some of the Atlanteans were content, but many were appalled at the new laws that took away what they considered their birthright. The schools were in the hands of the Judges who chose the curriculum, and the Prayer was now considered by many to be a relic of the past, and was no longer honored. For the first time in her married life, Kadah had to harden her heart and do the one thing that would forever set his face against her. She turned swiftly, called the slave girl and gave rapid instructions.

Four hours later, just after the moon had risen over the far mountains, she picked up her sleeping child, wrapped her securely in a warm robe and carried her out the back door of the house. With the slave girl trotting at her heels, the woman made her way to the wide stream that ran beyond the fruit orchard. Her husband had given her a small boat, one he felt she could handle alone. It was a sturdy craft, though large enough for only her and the child.

The slave girl laid soft blankets in the bottom of the boat and steadied it as the woman stepped in, carrying her still sleeping daughter. The mild narcotic she had been given held her in its grip; she would not waken for several hours. The woman looked back once at the home she was leaving, then set her mind to the task at hand. She reached down to cover Fayasas more securely, set the small triangular sail, and put her hand to the steering oar. Nodding to the girl to push them off, she whispered a goodbye to the home she had loved.

Would he let her come back? Would anything ever be the same? The boat drifted slowly out on the water.

Chapter Three

When dawn broke, they had left the small stream far behind, and were sailing smoothly down the broad river that made a long loop around the City. In the distance, the woman could see the Temple that was their destination. By now, perhaps, Faya's father would be on his way back to their house, expecting to take his daughter from home and place her among the people the woman mistrusted and disliked with all her heart.

All through the long night, the woman had sent her spirit to her beloved teacher in the old way, and he had answered, "come, my daughter, I am waiting for you."

"You will care for Faya?"

"Of course. But surely you will not go back?"

"I must, Beloved Teacher. I love my...." She could not say my husband, for their union had not been blessed by the Priests. "I love him," she finished. She could feel Asorum smiling. "Yes, I know. Come, we await you."

The woman steered the little boat closer to the bank. The loveliness of the flowering trees that hung out over the water was heartbreaking. She looked down at the child still quietly asleep in the bottom of the boat. "Oh, Faya," she murmured, "what is to become of us?"

Another hour and the boat bumped lightly against the dock below the Temple. The slight jar woke the child. The sun was high in the sky, and the light struck her face like a blow. She murmured and put her hands over her eyes. Feeling the movement of the boat, she opened her eyes just a slit and looked up through her fingers to see her mother's face smiling at her.

Where was she? In the boat. Why? Faya sat up suddenly. Behind her mother, on the dock, stood a man she had never seen. He was taller than her father, and his hair and beard were white. The robe he wore was also white, banded with a wide blue and gold border at the hem that just topped his strange looking sandals.

Faya felt a little twinge of fear. This man seemed to look right into her head, and Faya felt he knew exactly what she was thinking. She started to reach for her mother, but on second look, she saw the twinkle in the tall man' eyes, and a voice inside her said "welcome, my daughter." I am not his daughter, she thought, but again, the laughter in his eyes reassured her.

Asorum reached out to take her mother's hand and help her from the boat. The woman was stiff from sitting so long, and the man had to steady her as she stepped out. Then he held out his hand to the child. Behind him were three more men, also dressed in white robes, but without the deep band of blue and gold. They bowed to her mother and stood aside so the visitors could pass.

For the first time Faya noticed the building that sat on a low hill beyond the landing. She heard her mother murmur, "the Temple, Faya, where I once went to school." Faya looked more intently. The Temple was like no house she had ever seen. It was round, and the pillars that held the deep porch seemed to go entirely around it. There was no door that she could see, but the entrance was wide. The entire structure looked enormous, although it gave a feeling of serenity.

Faya took her mother's hand as they slowly made their way up the sloping lawn to the Temple. Once inside, Faya simply stood with her mouth open. What kind of place was this? They were in a large circular entry hall. To their right was a small pool with a fountain that sprayed water into the air before it dropped back into the basin. To the left was another opening, beyond which she could not see. Immediately ahead were broad stone stairs that led to an open balcony.

“Come, Fayasas, let us see what can be seen.” Asorum took her hand and led her away from her mother, and up the polished staircase. The child went without questioning, but looked back once at the woman who stood at the foot of the stairs. She could not know that this was to be the last time she would ever see her mother’s smiling face.

On the broad balcony, which overlooked the winding river and the far mountains, was the most amazing instrument..

“What is that?” she asked.

“That, my child, is a telescope. Through it you will see the stars and the planets.” Asorum swung the tube around. “That is, of course, when it is dark. Right now you can see the mountains and the City off in the distance. Would you like to look?”

“Yes, please.” The Priest smiled at the polite reply. He lifted the child so she could put her eye to the eyepiece. At first Faya could see nothing. The disappointment showed in her face, and the Priest adjusted some little wheels and told her to look again. This time Faya could make out what looked like tiny insects crawling along a strip of roadway.

Asorum laughed at her bewilderment and explained what the telescope did and how it worked. “Soon,” he said, “you will be studying the heavens. It is a fascinating subject. I mean you will like it.” Even a wise old Priest could sometimes forget and use words beyond the understanding of a four-year old. He didn’t hear Fayasas whisper carefully to herself, “fascinating.”

The two, the small child and the tall old man, spent the next ten minutes or so walking around the balcony, which was roofed, but had only a beautifully designed railing for protection. They looked again through the great telescope. Asorum kept Faya too busy to notice the passage of time, and the fact that her mother had not come up with them. When he finally took her hand to lead her down the stairs, she was chattering to him like the little bird she had once seen caged at a friend's house.

"Did my mother look through the tel...telsope?" she looked up at the Priest.

"Tel-e-scope, Faya."

"Telescope", she said carefully. "Did my mother look through the telescope when she was a little girl?"

"She did, and she had just as hard a time pronouncing it. There are many words you will learn to say properly. The first will be my name. I am call Ah-so-room, with the accent on the 'room'" He pronounced his name slowly. "Try it, Faya."

"Asorum," Faya said. "What does it mean?"

"It means 'One-who-was-called'. Do you know what your name means?"

"Of course I do," she said indignantly. "I'm not a baby. My name means Harp of the Winds. My mother named me that because she heard beautiful music when I was born. Don't you think it is a pretty name?"

"I do, indeed," smiled her companion. "Aren't you hungry after your long trip?" Faya dropped his hand and patted her chest.

"Yes, I am! My stomach is really empty. Could Mother and I have some fruit and bread-cakes?" She looked down the steps with a sudden anxiety in her heart. "Mother! Mother, where are you?"

The Priest took her hand again in time to keep her from hurtling down the broad steps. "Wait, Faya, let us go more slowly." He started to lead her down, but she broke free from his restraining hand and flew down the last few steps.

"Mother?" Faya looked around the great entry, then ran out on the porch. "Mother?" she cried again. She looked toward the dock. The boat was gone. Far out on the broad river she could see a small craft bobbing. Was that Mother? Why didn't she come back? As if her feet had wings, she flew down the grassy slope toward the water, and stood for a moment looking hard at the river, then fell in a crumpled heap on the dock. “Mother, Mother,” she sobbed. She felt hands on her shoulders, hands that made no effort to lift her, only to soothe. Finally she was gently pulled to her feet, and Asorum’s arms were around her. She buried her face in his neck, her tears making runnels down the white of his beard. For the first time, Fayasas felt the love that was to sustain her for the rest of her life.

Chapter Four

The first few days at the Temple became a blur. Faya felt the loss of her mother's presence more than even Asorum knew. They had always been so close. Her father was the one to whom she looked for strength and protection, the bringer of gifts and laughter. But her mother was the deep abiding love that never varied. It was she who taught Faya the values that even a four-year old child should have: truth, honesty and a total lack of fear. Her father had shown her the earth. Her mother gave her the heavens.

The old way of communication, the calling of spirit to spirit, had been practiced by Faya and her mother since the child was able to speak and understand words. The first night she lay wide-eyed on her little pallet, hands open at her sides, her mind struggling to picture the home she had left.

"Mother," she whispered,"Mother, why did you leave me here?"

The answer came gently. "My darling Faya, I have not left you. I will never leave you. Only our bodies are apart. At any time, you can call me and I will answer. Now go to sleep, and I will...."

Faya broke in. "But, why, Mother? Why did you leave me?"

"Faya, I can't tell you now, but it was something I had to do for your own protection. When you are a little older, I will tell you why. Now close your eyes. Shall I sing to you?"

"Yes, please," she sighed as her eyes drooped.

"Faya, little Faya, sleep little Faya. Grow in wisdom, grow in happiness. Sleep little Faya, sleep."

Her mother's voice, singing the familiar sleep-song, had its effect. The long day had been a kaleidoscope of pictures, sounds, new faces, and Faya was desperately tired. She fell asleep almost immediately, the song not finished, but still echoing in her mind.

Faya was left to sleep as long as she liked that first morning. When she opened her eyes the sun was already well over the horizon. She yawned and stretched, then lay quite still for a moment, remembering where she was, and all that had happened the day before.

She was not in her own home, lying on the small bed covered with the soft spread her mother had made. There was no smell of the little wheaten cakes she usually had with her milk, small round cakes baked fresh every morning by the slave girl who had cared for her since she was but a few days old.

Faya lay on her back with her arms at her side, not moving a muscle. Perhaps if she shut her eyes again, she would waken in her own home, with her mother ready to tease her for being such a lazybones. One small tear squeezed its way from the corner of one eye and dripped into her left ear. It tickled, and Faya rolled over on the pallet, sneezed and sat up.

As if her turning had been a signal, the door to her room opened and a young woman entered, carrying a short yellow robe over her arm. "Good morning, Fayasas," she smiled. "Would you like to come with me and get ready for the day?"

Faya stood up slowly, frowning slightly, not at all sure what was expected of her. "What am I to do?" she asked?

"First, a bath. Then dress and have your breakfast. Are you not hungry?"

"Yes, I guess so. But where am I to bathe?" She looked around at the room, empty but for the pallet on which she had slept, a small table and one low chair.

"Come with me. I'll show you where you are to go. In fact, I shall go with you this morning and help you get ready."

The young woman smiled again, her eyes crinkling in the corners like those of the slave girl who had cared for Faya at home. The child walked quietly to the door, determined not to remember, fearing the tears that were still very near the surface would betray her loneliness and heart-break at being left in such a strange place.

She was led down a long passage with doors on either side, doors that stood open, showing rooms exactly like hers. Each room had not one but two pallets. Faya wondered where the people were who had obviously slept there. The young woman accompanying her gently took her arm and steered her into a much larger room. Why, thought Faya, it is almost like our bath place at home!

The floor was polished stone, cool and light. From above, sunlight struck the centered pool and sparkled on the softly foaming water. Faya felt a sense of relief that things were not going to be quite so strange as she had feared.

A second look, though, showed quite a few changes from the rather simple bath place she was used to. There was a round opening in the ceiling that allowed not only light but fresh air to enter. It was framed with many colored transparent stones that broke the light into myriad colors and reflected them in the water and on the floor. Faya put out her hand to let the colors glow on her skin. “It's beautiful,” she whispered to the woman, who smiled, nodded, and indicated that she was to remove her clothes. While the child obeyed and stepped into the pool, her own short dress that she had slept in was exchanged for the new yellow shift.

When Faya had splashed about a few minutes, really enjoying the feel of the scented warm water, the young woman called her out of the pool and wrapped her in a large drying sheet. By then, Faya was quite at home with the woman, and started asking questions. “Who are you? Are you my servant? Will you always stay with me?”

The answers were a little surprising. “No, child, I am not your servant.

There are no servants here. I grew up in this Temple as did your mother, and I will probably stay here for a few more years, until I decide to marry or leave to live in the City. I am simply trying to help you get used to being here. Asorum asked me to do this for you just this one time. Today you will meet girls of your own age, and by tomorrow, you will know pretty well how to manage on your own. They are all very friendly and will show you what to do. Now, shall we find some breakfast?"

"What do I call you?" asked the child, wriggling into her sandals.

"My name is Haindohne, sometimes shortened to Dohnnie. I am a teacher." She smiled as the child took her hand and looked up.

"May I call you Dohnnie? I've never had a real teacher, only my mother." For a moment the loss showed in her face, but Haindohne quickly steered her out the door and down yet another passage. "Yes, you may call me Dohnnie, but not in the classrooms. There I am Haindohne. Will you remember that?"

Faya repeated to herself, in the classroom she is to be called Haindohne. Looking up again, she smiled a rather shy smile and softly squeezed Dohnnie's hand. "Thank you, I will remember."

Breakfast was much the same as she was used to, fruit and small barley bread cakes sweetened with honey. There was plenty of milk, and although she was alone at the table except for Dohnnie, she ate and drank quietly, almost fastidiously. She had never peeled a piece of fruit in her short life, but Dohnnie showed her how to grasp the top of the soft skin of the thacasca and strip it down. The berries in their bright bowl were swimming in milk, the cakes were hot and fresh from the baking, and Faya was a healthy, hungry child. At last, with a sigh of contentment, she lifted the linen from her lap and wiped her mouth.

"Please, Dohnnie, where do I wash my hands? I'm sticky."

Haindohne went to a high bench along the wall and uncovered a basin. "Here, Faya, this is where you rinse off the juice. You must have been really hungry."

"Did I eat too much? Mother always said not to overeat, but I was hungry." She dabbled her fingers in the water, dried them on the cloth Dohnnie handed her, and turned toward the entrance.

"No, child, you didn't eat too much. But what do you do after eating?"

Faya went back to the table, bowed her head and murmured the thanks she had been taught. "I'm sorry; I did forget."

"You won't forget again, because you will be with the others and Thanksgiving is always said in unison. Unison means you all say it together. Now let's go and join one of the classes."

Meeting girls of her own age took away some of the hollow loneliness. There were seven who wore the same yellow shift she now wore. It was short, only just above her knees, and had no decoration whatever. It fell from her shoulders with only a slight flare at the hem. Faya noticed that several of the girls had pinned a flower in their hair; again she wished for the blond hair most frequently seen.

Haindohne introduced Faya to the class, which had started only a few minutes earlier, and seated her on a bench near the door. The teacher was another young woman, who was explaining to the class the meaning of the word joy.

"Which of you knows what joy means?" she asked. Three hands went up. "Yes, Shaleen? can you give us an example of joy?"

The girl beside Faya stood up. "Joy is having something nice when you want it."

"And you, Krola, how do you think of joy?" Krola stood in turn and whispered shyly, "Joy is snuggling down in the covers at night and feeling safe." She sat suddenly as though her words might have given away her secret fears.

“Joy is more than that, although it could certainly make one feel good. How about you, Fayasas; would you like to tell us how you feel about joy?” The teacher smiled encouragingly.

Faya rose slowly to her feet. “Joy is knowing my father is going to spend a whole week at home with me, only he didn’t!” All at once the misery she had been holding in check overwhelmed her and she ran from the room, sobbing piteously.

Haindohne was still in the corridor, and gathered the weeping child in her arms. “Faya. Little Faya,” she whispered, having overheard the outburst. “It will be all right soon. Don’t cry. Your father really loves you very much. You know that, don’t you?

Faya nodded, her head buried in the woman’s neck. “But why did I have to leave home? Was it because I did something my father didn’t like?”

“Oh, my darling child, no! You did absolutely nothing wrong. It was just...did you know that your mother spent part of her childhood here? And she loved it so much she wanted you to enjoy it, too. Did you know that?”

Faya nodded again, this time lifting her face and rubbing her eyes. “Mother said she was here; but I want to go home now.”

Haindohne set Faya gently down and knelt beside her. “You know, Faya, your mother has a very good reason for wanting you to be here. Someday she or Asorum will tell you what it is, when you are a little older and can understand what the word ‘politics’ means. Right now, won’t you please her and try to enjoy being here with the other girls?”

Fayasas smiled damply and nodded. “Will you stay with me?”

“No, Faya, I can’t do that. But I will come for you when class is over. Then we will go outside and look at the beautiful landscape, the gardens, the trees, and I’ll explain them all to you, and you will get to know all their spirits." The woman took Faya's hand and they walked slowly back to the classroom.

The rest of the morning passed quickly. The teacher made a point of including Faya in everything she was telling the others, so the child began to feel more at ease. Several of the girls smiled encouragingly at her, Krola put her hand on Faya's arm and squeezed it, and soon Faya was if not happy, at least comfortable.

As she had promised, Haindohne was waiting when class was over. There was nearly an hour before the noon meal, so teacher and child walked out the great front entrance into the bright light.

Faya was guided around the porch to the back, so she could not see the river and remember how her mother had left her without saying goodbye. She looked only once as they went, but said nothing. Haindohne led her down the steps and through a gate into a walled garden.

"Here, Faya, is where you may play when you are not in class. This is called the Children's Garden. As you can see, there are tables where you may bring your meal and eat, if you had rather be outside; there are swings in the trees, and flowers all around to make your soul happy."

"Mother said my soul was happy when I was born. How did she know that?" Faya was swinging the woman's arm back and forth, much as she had done when walking with her father.

"Faya, what do you remember? I mean from Beyond and Long Ago?" Dohnnie looked serious for a moment.

The little girl slowed her steps, her face sobering. "I think I remember, sometimes, just a little bit, but it is so...so...far off."

"Well," said Dohnnie, "let's not worry about it right now. When it is time, you will be taught how to remember accurately all you need to remember." The woman smiled at her small charge, and Faya smiled back.

There were no more classes the rest of the day for the very young children. Faya and Dohnnie joined them for lunch, which was brought out to the garden. After the meal, and the Thanksgiving, which Faya never again forgot, a circle was formed and the little girls played the games all children learn, Dohnnie and the other teacher joining in with as much enjoyment as the girls.

When the sun was just beginning to redden the western sky, the teacher and Dohnnie gathered up their little ones and led them back into the great entrance hall. Faya looked around in wonder. What was happening now?

The light struck the circular pool through the opening above, just as it had in the bathing room. The fountain sprayed the tinted water, droplets catching the light jewels, and when it fell back into the basin, the sound was sweet and soothing.

From the top of the broad staircase the resident priests descended two by two, each carrying a musical instrument. There were small harps, flutes, tambourines, finger castanets and tiny drums. The children were gathered into a small group on one side of the hall, while from rooms Faya had not yet seen, came young women singing with the music the priests played.

Dohnnie whispered to Faya, "This is the evening ceremony to say goodbye to the day, and give thanks for all we have. You and your friends will learn the songs when you are older." Fayasas nodded, her eyes wide and her attention entirely on the musicians.

Then down the stairs came two more priests, one of them she knew was Asorum, the other she had not seen before. They did not carry instruments, nor were they singing. They stood at the foot of the steps, facing each other, and bowed. Then they turned to the gathered assembly and bowed to them. Finally, Asorum raised his arms in the familiar stance Faya had learned as soon as she could physically manage it, and began the Prayer. The musicians set their instruments down on the polished floor, raised their arms and very softly followed his words, their voices blending with the voices of the women and the children.

"To the Power I send my spirit....." Faya felt the tears welling up, and turning to Dohnnie, buried her face in the woman's robe. Understanding exactly how the little girl felt, the woman did not stop her prayer, nor did she change the position of her upraised arms.

"From the Power I receive blessing...." the picture of her mother standing like this in the bedroom of her home came to Faya very clearly, and she heard without hearing her mother's voice, "Faya, little Faya, can you not join them in the beautiful Prayer to the Creator?"

Faya turned, the tears still streaming down her face, and crossed her arms over her breast. "The Power is within me, I remember, and I am content." The Prayer ended with the two priests holding their arms out to the assembly and blessing them, Asorum adding thanks for the young life they now had in their care. He walked over to Faya, stooped and took the child in his arms. Carrying her back to the foot of the stairs, he introduced her to the others, telling them who she was, and reminding the older ones that the child's mother had been in the Temple when she was Faya's age.

Faya, still in Asorum's arms, smiled shyly and murmured a rather weak greeting to the others. Then Asorum set her down and led the way to a great hall where all the priests, teachers and older girls and boys were to eat their evening meal. Dohnnie showed Faya where she was to sit with the younger children, at a small table in a corner of the large dining hall, then left her to join the adults.

It was a simple meal, consisting of cakes of barley, several vegetables, some of which were unfamiliar to Fayasas, milk for the small ones, and finally fruit. Faya, who had never known what it was to wait on herself, felt a little out of place at first, but the other children were helpful, even though a few laughed when she didn't seem to know how to peel the fruit. For the first time since she had left home, the old assertive manner she had sometimes used when things did not go her way found expression, and she tossed her head and told those who laughed exactly what she thought of them, the Temple, and being where she really did not want to be. A shocked silence made her realize what she had said. Again her mother's voice echoed in her head, bringing more reproof.

"I'm sorry," she whispered. "I didn't mean that." Krola, who had sat next to her in class that morning, got up from her place and sat beside the now frightened child.

"Never mind, Faya, they didn't mean to laugh at you. It was just that we all eat this way, and we thought you did, too. Don't you have fruit where you came from?"

"Of course we do. There are lots of fruit trees all around my house, but I've never had to peel fruit before. The slave girl always did it before she brought it to the table."

Krola's eyes got larger. "Slave girl? Did you really have a slave? By now the entire table was interested and listening intently.

"She was my servant...I mean my mother's...no, my father's... servant...I mean...she took care of me...". Faya was confused, never having had to explain what a slave was, and taking it for granted that everyone had one.

She did not know that her father had brought the young girl to the house, and had told her mother that she was to be in charge of the baby who had been born only a few days before.

Faya's mother was dumbstruck, believing, as she did, that there should be no difference between one person and another, and resenting another taking care of her baby. It was the first inkling she had that the man she adored was not quite what she had thought he was.

He explained that the slave girl had been foraging for herself and needed a home, and for a time that satisfied the woman. In the short years that followed, she learned that the girl was indeed a slave, and to be treated as one. When the man had left the country home for a week, to administer the affairs of the City, the girl became a member of the small family, helping as a younger sister would, taking her meals with the woman, and helping in the care of the baby, Fayasas. When the man came back for a weekend, or a longer stay, the girl again became the slave he expected.

Faya mulled the word over in her mind that night. Oh well, in the morning she would ask Dohnnie. Sleep came quickly.

Chapter Five

Faya's days became full and almost happy. She was a very appealing little girl, and made friends easily. School was so completely new to her that she had little time to mourn her old home, although every night, she and her mother talked in the old way a little while before she fell asleep.

The day soon came when she was moved from her first tiny room into a double, with the same Krola who had befriended her earlier.

At first Faya was not sure she liked this arrangement, since she had always slept in a room alone; but shortly the two little girls became fast friends, and shared the room, their secrets, their hopes and dreams just like all little girls have done since time began. Only one secret Faya kept to herself, and it began to fester in her soul.

She had never quite understood just why her Father was the reason for her having to leave her home. Slowly the memory of the man she had so loved and trusted began to bloom into a resentment. She found it difficult to talk to her Mother about this, because the woman she adored sounded so unhappy herself, that even at her young age, Faya realized there were some things she should not question yet. So she put these things in the back of her mind, and decided to wait. She didn't realize how much older than her years she really was.

Asorum and the other older priests were seldom seen during the school day, but each evening, the same ritual she had witnessed her first day was repeated. Faya grew to love it, and like all the children, looked forward with almost an awe to the sunset, when the priests led them in The Prayer and blessed them for the coming night.

She was almost as much in awe of the Temple itself. The ceiling in the great entrance hall soared up two stories, with a vaulted ceiling, and had a balcony running all around it. There were three floors. The first floor contained the students' sleeping rooms and their bathing rooms, the dining room, the school rooms and the kitchens. The library, a common room for conferences and extra rooms for guests made up a large part of the first floor back of the school rooms.

The second floor, reached by the staircase, led to the balcony. On the right were the priests' rooms. The women who acted as teachers and those who were actually priests in their own right, had their rooms on the left. There were several more that could be used as extra rooms when the Temple was host to a large number of priests from other temples.

On the lower level were the healing rooms. They were small, with room for only one patient and the healer-priest. One room, opening onto a sunken garden in the back of the Temple, was used as a small hospital when needed.

Faya and the other younger students were allowed to go into the rooms only on the first floor. They were forbidden to climb the stairs without permission, and of course they were never permitted to go to the lower level unless there was real need. There was yet another part of the Temple they did not know at all, a place that would in time become very familiar to Faya. But for now, she and her companions had to stay within the confines of the rooms allotted to the students.

Dohnnie saw Faya every day, and frequently took her alone to the Children's Garden, explaining so many things that were new or hard to understand. But even Dohnnie did not know of the growing bitterness in the child she had grown to love.

Things came to a head one day, about four months after Faya's entering the Temple. Dohnnie noticed that the child was obviously avoiding one of the young priests who was in charge of the daily exercises the children usually enjoyed. In fact, Faya had a habit of being late for this class, and hung back, almost as though she was trying to hide herself among the other children. Finally, the woman took Faya aside and asked her bluntly why she disliked the man, or if he had said or done anything to upset her. Faya, to her surprise, burst into tears. “He looks just like my Father”, she sobbed, “and my Father thinks I did something bad so I had to come here.”

Dohnnie gathered the weeping child into her arms. “Faya,” she said firmly, “look at me. And please believe me when I tell you that your Father did not think that. You’ve done nothing bad, nothing at all.”

Faya kept her head down, and hiccuped once or twice. The tears still flowed, but the wild sobbing had ceased. “Then why did Mother take me away? Was it something I did that Mother didn’t like? Was that why I had to leave home?”

Dohnnie thought for a moment, then decided it was time to open and cleanse what had become a festering sore.

“Fayasas,” she began, “there are many things in this world of ours that are hard to explain, and even harder to understand. But I think I can explain this one for you. In the City, there are groups of men who do not believe as we do, as your Mother and those of us who live here in this Temple believe. They are called Judges, because they make laws - rules, about the way people behave, especially in regard to our beliefs. Did you know that in some places they have outlawed the Prayer?”

Realizing that the little girl might not understand the word, she added, “it means they don’t want people to say the Prayer anymore.”

Faya’s eyes grew larger. “The Prayer? You mean it is a bad thing to say?”

“No, child. It is a very good thing to say. It holds all our love and devotion to the great Creator, whom we call the Power, because everything on earth and in the heavens comes from that one Source. But you see, these Judges don’t think that way. They believe that they can do anything they wish to do, without help from the Power. We know better, but they are trying to change the way we live and what we believe."

Faya thought for a minute. Then she looked up at the woman and asked softly, "Did my Father believe the Prayer was bad?" Dohnnie sighed. This was not as simple as she had hoped.

"Yes, Faya, he did. Do you remember how your Mother always said the Prayer when she put you to bed? And how she blessed you and kissed you goodnight?"

"And then sang my sleep-song," added the child.

"That's right. But do you remember ever hearing your Father say the Prayer?"

"No...no, I really don't. Why didn't he? The way Mother said it and held her arms was so beautiful, and I always felt so good afterwards." Faya's tears started again, and Dohnnie quickly went on with her unhappy story.

"Faya, you know your Father was a lawyer, and he had just become one of the Judges I told you about...the ones who do things...differently. He wanted to take you away from home and put you in a school they have for young children, where you would be taught that material possessions were the most important things in the world, and that power, their kind of power, was something to be worked for with all your strength. Their kind of thinking was so very different from what your Mother believed, that she decided to send you here to the Temple, where you would not have any contact with the Judges or their way of thinking.

"It was a very hard thing for her to do, and a very brave one, because your Father has not spoken to her since that time. She is still at her home, but lives quite separate from him. It's very sad, but she was right, Faya, to do this; and as hard as it is for you to be away from her, she felt it was the only way to protect you, whom she loves so dearly, from the influences of the group of Judges who would have tried to make you like them."

“That would have been bad?” asked the child. “Does that mean my Father was bad?”

“No, Faya, he is not bad, not in the way you mean. He loves you very much, which is why he wanted you to go with him. Your Mother felt that you were too young to be with these men. If you had been older, perhaps she would have let you make your own choice.

Dohnnie knew in her heart this was not true, but she felt Fayasas was not ready for more information, so she changed the subject.

“Now let’s talk about this priest you seem to dislike. You say he looks like your Father?”

Faya nodded. “He is not quite as tall, but his hair is the same color, and when he smiles his eyes shine the same way. Do I have to stay in his class?”

Dohnnie sighed. “Yes, Faya, you really do. It would not be fair to the other children to put you in another class and make you special. Here, we are all equal, or trying to be.”

Faya sighed in turn, and reached for Dohnnie’s skirt. “I forgot to bring a wiping cloth with me. Your clothes always smell so good.” She wiped her eyes on the skirt while the woman tried to stifle her laughter. “That’s all right, honey, you may use my skirt...this once. Now, shall we go back?”

Faya shrugged her shoulders in a resigned gesture and nodded. “I guess so. He can’t help looking like my Father, can he?” Under her breath the child muttered, but I don’t have to like him.

Dohnnie had not realized just how hurt Fayasas had been when her Mother left her in Asorum’s care. She decided to confide in Asorum and ask just how much more Faya should be told. She was still trying to sort out the answers to herself when the bell rang for the evening blessing ritual.

"Come on, Faya, I'll race you back!" Letting the child get a head start, the two sprinted for the wide porch of the Temple and entered just as the other children and the priests were gathering in the great hall. Slowing to a more dignified walk, but still rather disheveled, they joined the others. Asorum gave Dohnnie one quick glance, then smiled at Faya. "How would you like to help me lead the Prayer tonight?" he asked the child.

Faya's eyes widened. "May I? Really?"

"Of course you may. We all may speak directly to the Power. You know that. Come, stand here beside me and we'll say the Prayer together." The old priest stood tall beside the little girl, and together they lifted their faces and raised their arms in the beautiful beginning of the Prayer. That moment was Fayasas' true entry into the Temple, one she would never forget.

Chapter Six

Haindohne did go to Asorum to ask about Fayasas. The old priest was quite aware of the conflict in the child's heart, but he had felt that, given enough time, she would begin to be more at ease with the upheaval in her young life. Knowing that her mother had often spoken to her of the Temple, he had hoped Faya would feel more at home here. He paced the garden where the herbs grew in such profusion, the one place he had always gone when trying to think through a difficult problem.

Stooping down to pick a leaf of fonta and holding it to his nose, he inhaled deeply. "Perhaps I should bring her mother here for a few days; no, that would only make it worse when she left." The old man held the leaf between his fingers and stared at it as though it were an unknown species. "Fayasas...of course! 'Harp of the Winds.' Asorum, you are getting old!"

He blessed the leaf he had picked, gently letting it fall back to the earth, and strode out of the garden, and back into the entrance hall. Calling one of the older girls who was arranging flowers around the fountain, he asked which class Fayasas had at this time of day.

"I believe the younger children are learning counting now," the girl smiled. "Shall I get her for you?"

"Please. Ask her to meet me in the herb garden...no, tell her I will be waiting here. The flowers are lovely, and you have made such a beautiful arrangement."

"Thank you. I do like working with them." The girl left and returned a minute or so later, holding Faya by the hand.

"Thank you, child. Please go on with your arranging. Faya, come sit here by me. I have something to ask you."

The child looked anxiously up at the old priest. "Did I do something wrong?" she asked. "I'm not very good at counting yet.

"No, child, you did not. I merely wanted to ask you which of the things you have seen here interested you most. What would you like to do?" He smiled at the young face, which returned the smile.

"Well, I do like the gardens. Do you suppose someday I might learn more about how to use the herbs? Dohnnie..I mean Haindohne.. said they were used for all sorts of things." "Did she tell you how we use them?" "Sort of; she said some of them can make people well if they are sick. Do many people get sick, Asorum?" She, herself, had never had a sick day in her life, and was totally unfamiliar with anyone who was really ill.

Asorum sighed. "Yes, child, there are many who are sick, sick in body and in mind." He said almost under his breath, "and in soul."

"And the pretty herbs can make them well?" Faya reached out for one of the flowers that graced the rim of the pool. "Don't they smell nice!" She stroked the flower gently.

"Yes, they do. But some of them are not quite so nice to smell, nor are they as pretty as these. One of these days I'll tell you all about them. But right now, I want to ask you something else." Faya waited. The old priest sat on the rim of the pool and pulled the child over to lean against him. Faya threw one arm around his neck and leaned her head on his shoulder. The two, so far apart in age, yet so close in spirit, made a picture that Haindohne, who was walking in from one of the classrooms, never forgot.

"Faya, you know what your name means, don't you? You told me your first day here that your mother had heard beautiful music when you were born, and called you Harp-of-the-Winds. It is a beautiful name, but it has a meaning you perhaps don't know about yet."

Haindohne stopped and stood in the shadowy entrance, unseen by either of the two. Her natural curiosity would not let her leave until she had heard what Asorum was going to tell the child she already loved so dearly.

"You know, Faya, your mother lived here at the Temple for many years before she left to go with your father, and while she was here, she learned many things that she never had time to teach you. You were still too young. But now, I think you should know a little more about yourself, and about your mother. Did you know that she was a wonderful musician?"

Faya's eyes grew larger. "You mean she could play music? She used to sing a lot, but we never had anything to play on, like a harp or a water-organ."

"How do you know about a water-organ, Faya?" asked the priest.

"Don, I mean Haindohne, said she had one at her old home."

"That's all right, Faya, you may call her Dohnnie here with me. Only not in class." The priest smiled. "What else did she tell you about it?"

Faya thought for a moment. "Nothing that I can remember. Just that she had one, but when I was going to ask her about it, the bells rang and we had to go into class. I forgot to ask her again."

"I think a water-organ is too large for you now, but I believe I know where I can put my hands on a harp that would fit you. Would you like to learn to play it?" Faya's face brightened. "Oh, yes, I would. Is it hard to play?"

Asorum smiled again. "Yes, my little one, it is one of the most difficult instruments to learn, but one of the most beautiful, and I do believe you could master it in just a few years."

"A few years?" the child said. "Couldn't I learn quicker than that?"

"Faya, do you know how long it has taken Hain...I mean Dohnnie... to learn the names of all the plants she knows? Or how long it has taken some of the other teachers to prepare for classes they teach?"

"I guess I will have to work very hard, won't I?" Fayasas was totally serious, and the old priest had all he could do to keep a straight face. In the shadows, Dohnnie smiled broadly, and made a secret pledge to herself that she would see that no one pressed Faya too hard to learn too much too soon.

"Now run along, and go back to your class. I'll find the harp and we will try it out tonight before the Prayer. It may need new strings, and of course you will have to learn to keep it tuned." "I'll keep it very well tuned, and I'll learn very fast. Thank you, Asorum, thank you for...for...." the child suddenly threw herself in the old man's lap, both arms around his neck, and planted a very wet kiss on his cheek. "For everything," she cried, and ran from the room.

Haindohne, who was still standing just out of sight, walked toward the pool.

"Did you hear everything?" asked Asorum. Haindohne sighed. "Has anyone ever fooled you?" she asked.

"Yes, my dear, I have been fooled more than even I can remember, but not for a very long time." He smiled at the young woman. "I knew when you came in, and I knew you were listening. I'm glad you were, because you are going to have to help me with this exceptional spirit we have been given in trust, and I am not sure just which way to lead her."

"Has she been told very much about her father, what he has been doing?"

Asorum shrugged. "No. The man is not worthy of this daughter, but I have never been able to convince her mother that she should have left him long ago; but, since Fayasas must have chosen this particular pair to be born to, there is a reason. I simply don't know it yet."

Haindohne put her hand on the old priest's arm. "Don't take this blame upon yourself, Asorum. You did everything you could when Kadah was here. Even you could not stop her falling in love with that man."

Asorum nodded. "I know, I know. At the time it seemed possible he would come around to her way of thinking. How could anyone live with that sweet creature and not have some of her goodness rub off on him!"

"He can't be all that bad, you know, not if Faya loves him so dearly, or did. I don't know how she feels now. At first, I believe she felt it was all her fault she was sent from home to live with strangers. Then there seemed to be a bitterness when she thought one of her instructors resembled her father. It's very confusing." The woman sat on the rim of the pool. "Perhaps I can see more clearly if I have some idea of what is in your mind." The old priest walked slowly away from the pool, then back. He stopped, rubbed his chin, and with a rather wry grin said, "I'm not entirely sure what is in my mind, but I rather think her name is the clue I've needed. Fayasas. She seemed to like the idea of the harp, don't you think?"

"She did, indeed," replied the woman. "I gather you will use the harp to enter her soul?"

Asorum nodded. "If I am to help her, the harp just might be the best way of reaching the dark places and letting in the light." "She seems so young to have dark places." Haindohne sighed. "But I know we all have them from past times. Wouldn't it be wonderful if just once we could find someone who had none?" Asorum laughed ruefully. "When we find such a one, it will be the time of the Great Ending. Not in my lifetime, nor yours, my dear." He got up, and stood looking at the doorway through which Faya had left. "I'll start with her lessons in the morning." "Don't forget, you told her you would let her see the harp tonight before the Prayer." Dohnnie smiled at her friend and teacher and added, "You know how children are; tomorrow is so very far off!" They both laughed, and left the hall, Dohnnie to the classrooms, and Asorum back to the herb garden where he could think things out in solitude and peace.

Chapter Seven

As he had said he would, Asorum had the harp tuned and waiting for his small pupil later that afternoon in the great hall. When Faya saw it, her hands went out, then she drew back. Asorum said nothing, just held the harp in his lap. Finally, Faya put out one finger and touched the strings. At the soft sound, her face broke into a smile, and without further thought, she stroked the full length of the strings, slowly, and with extreme care. “Oh, it is beautiful. Is it really for me?” she asked.

“Yes, Faya, it is for you. I have a feeling that you almost know what to do with it already.” Asorum indicated that she should sit down on the first step of the great stairs. “Put it in your lap this way. Now your right hand is on this side and your left over here. This is a very small harp, but a good one to learn on. Later, if you really like it, there are other larger harps that you must stand up and play. But for now, this is the best size for you.”

“Will you be my teacher?” Faya couldn’t take her eyes from the beautiful little instrument. “Why is there a bird up there?” She indicated the post of the harp. “How do you make music with it? Can I sing, too? Will the strings break? They are very little.”

Asorum laughed. “So many questions! But yes, I will be your teacher, at first, anyway. The bird is just for decoration, but I do believe that this particular kind has a rather sweet voice, so maybe that is why it is put there. I will show you tomorrow how to ‘make music’ with it, and yes, the strings do sometimes break, but of course, it can be re-strung when they do.”

“And can I sing with it?” Faya never forgot a question that had not been answered to her satisfaction.

“Certainly you may sing with it, after you learn how to play. In fact, your mother used to sing to all of us when she felt particularly happy, and she accompanied herself on the harp. But now it is almost time for the evening blessing and Prayer. I will put this away until tomorrow." He took the harp and Faya sighed. "Don't worry, little one, you will see it first thing in the morning." That night Faya could not get to sleep. She shut her eyes as tight as she could, but sleep evaded her. All her thoughts were on the little harp. Finally she rolled over on her face, put her hands under her forehead and tried to think of nothing at all. Instead of nothing, music came to her, music she had really never heard, but that seemed so very familiar.

"Mother?" she whispered. "Mother, are you there?" "Yes, darling, I am here, always, when you need me." Faya sighed and turned on her back. "Mother, were you singing now?" "No, Faya, I was not singing. Did you hear something?"

"Yes, I heard some music, but I don't know what it was." She could almost feel her mother's smile. "Faya, my love, there will be many times when you will hear music that you do not know...music that is within your soul. I think perhaps Asorum has given you my old harp. Did he?"

"How did you know, Mother? And was it really your harp once?"

"Yes, I suppose it is the same one. You know, Faya, musical instruments can sometimes talk to you, if you really love them and can listen with your heart. Now try to go to sleep. We will talk more tomorrow night, after you have held the harp and feel its spirit. Sleep, little Faya, grow in wisdom, grow in happiness. Sleep, little Faya, sleep."

The old lullaby worked its magic and before the song was finished, Faya was relaxed and drowsy. "Goodnight, Mother," she whispered, and was almost instantly asleep.

Her mother, so very far away, put her hands over her face and for just a moment her anguish was too much to bear. "Oh Faya, what have I done?" she cried silently. Then she straightened her back and sat quietly in her chair. She knew she had done the only thing possible, but the loss of her beloved child, and the resulting coldness of the man she still loved, tore her heart. In the Temple, Asorum heard the anguished cry, feeling her pain in his own heart. Kadah had been one of his most promising and beloved pupils, and the two had never really been apart in spirit. Yet he knew that so long as she stayed with the man she had chosen, he could do nothing. The Judges were becoming more and more powerful, and the priests, who could not and would not accept their philosophies or their methods of rendering verdicts in trials, were hard pressed to keep what they had built so carefully and so lovingly.

Kadah's husband, and Asorum found he could hardly think of him as such, was ambitious, too much so. The old priest knew that had Fayasas stayed with her father, there would have been a battle royal between her parents. He knew, too, that Kadah had done the only thing she could, but his soul was wrung with pity for them all. He laid aside the book he had been reading and walked slowly up and down his room, trying to think of how he could ease the burden both Kadah and Fayasas carried. Finally his steps slowed as he realized there was nothing at the moment that would help as much as the harp itself. He smiled to himself as he remembered the unborn soul he had 'read' at Kadah's request...music, that was the answer. He knew much more about Faya than he had told her; much more than he had told her mother. In time, he would tell the child, but for now he would let the harp speak for itself. The next morning, after bath and breakfast, Faya walked slowly to her first class, her mind on nothing but the promise of the harp. Her teacher had to call her to attention more than once, but Faya simply couldn't keep her mind on counting, or much of anything else. Even Krola sighed and turned away from her friend when Faya didn't respond to a whispered question. Finally class was over, and Faya's feet had wings when she ran to the great hall to meet Asorum. "Asorum! Asorum, do you have it? May I learn it now?" she asked.

"Gently, my dear! Yes, of course you may learn now, or at least start. Sit here beside me and we'll have a first lesson." The old priest put the harp in the child's lap and showed her how, first of all, to hold it. It was a small instrument, with only twelve strings, but Faya had never had anything so beautiful. There was the small bird on top of the post, and the entire harp was a muted golden color, as though it had once been gilded, but was now slightly tarnished from lack of use.

Faya stroked the strings and listened carefully to the tones. She ran her right hand again over the strings, then looked up at her friend. " How do I make it sing?"

Asorum smiled. "First, Faya, one has to learn what the strings are, and how each one sounds. Here, I'll show you." He took the harp from her and played one string at a time. "See, my dear, each string sings a different note. What you must learn to do is put them together, like this." He played three notes. "When you learn what we call chords, you may then sing with your harp." Faya sighed. "It is so beautiful. Please play that again." Asorum stroked the harp once more, then put it back in the child's lap. "Here, Faya, now play one note, one string, at a time, using the fingers in order." He showed her how to hold her hands, then how each finger was placed.

From that moment on, the harp became a part of the child. Each day when classes were over, Faya would cradle her harp and practice. It was as if she had met an old friend, one who had been absent for a long time, but never forgotten. Even Asorum was astonished at how quickly she learned the technique, and how careful she was with the instrument.

The harp, and the needed discipline, worked its magic, and Faya soon lost the hurt and bewildered look she had sometimes worn. She joined in the games with the other children more readily than before, and even seemed to accept the young priest she had at first so disliked. One day, after classes, she went to look for Haindohne and found her in the herb garden. Faya asked it she might learn something about the plants that grew there. Dohnnie was a little surprised. The child had been so wrapped up in her harp that nothing else seemed to matter. Curiosity got the better of her, and she sat down with Fayasas and took her hand. "If Asorum agrees, I will be glad to start teaching you about the herb garden, but why, Faya? Why are you interested in this? I thought your harp was the most important thing right now." Dohnnie smiled at the child she loved.

Fayasas nodded. "Yes, it is. But you always look so happy when you are out here, and I thought..." She stopped for a moment. "You see, Dohnnie, my mother had a garden sort of like this, and she used to take me out there with her in the evenings, and that's when she looked happiest." Faya didn't actually cry, but her eyes were moist, and she hiccuped once. "I wish Mother could see this garden...I know she would like it, too. It smells so much like ours."

"Honey, you forget that your mother was a student here like you are. She spent many happy hours in this garden, and she, too, asked to learn about the different herbs." Faya looked surprised. "Oh, I didn't know that! Maybe that's why she loved our garden so much? You know, Dohnnie, she could tell each plant and what it was used for, and she used to make pol...polsis...."

Dohnnie interrupted her. "You mean a poultice, Faya? Something to heal a hurt?" Faya nodded. "Poultice. Yes. When the girl had a sore finger Mother took some leaves - big ones - and mashed them in a piece of cloth and wrapped her finger. It got well, too."

Dohnnie sighed. "Faya, you have mentioned "the girl" several times before. Didn't she have a name?" Faya looked thoughtful, then frowned. "I don't know...Mother sometimes called her the little one, but Father, I think he just called her the girl." She looked up at her friend. "I never thought of that before. Maybe she did have a name, but I don't remember what it was."

The woman smiled warmly, realizing that the child was upset at her question. "Don't worry, Faya, perhaps you will remember later. Tell me more about your mother's garden, and I'll try to tell you what you need to know about this one."

The two spent the next hour happily identifying the different plants, Faya keeping up a running "why" conversation, and the older woman trying to keep up and answer as best she could.

Later, Dohnnie went to Asorum to ask just what she should tell Fayasas about the "girl" who had played so large a part in her early upbringing. The old priest sighed. "You know, my dear, that the girl, as Faya calls her, really was a slave and probably one who had been worked over to make her more personable. There is so much pain in the world, and these poor creatures seem to bear the brunt of it."

Dohnnie nodded, and Asorum continued pacing as he spoke. "For now, I think I would not say anything more. She is a little too young to take it all in, and there will be plenty of time for her to learn of this world's injustices."

Chapter Eight

Fayasas was not only very intelligent, she was also very curious about the world she lived in, and had a remarkable talent for remembering what she was taught. In two years, she could name every plant in the herb garden, and its use. She had already mastered her small harp, and was frequently asked to play at the evening blessing service. By the time she was ten, she was helping the older girls care for the youngsters that entered the Temple each year.

There were still many things about the Temple she had not learned; there were rooms the children were not allowed to enter; there were Ceremonies they were too young to take part in. There was one Ceremony, however, that everyone joined in. It was the one Fayasas most loved, and one that occurred every year in the late spring.

For several days before the actual ritual, the Temple was cleaned from top to bottom; fresh flowers were brought in to the great hall, the pools were drained and filled with fresh water, and there was an air of happy expectancy.

From the time she was six, Faya had been allowed to help, and she had felt very grown up, taking her small part quite seriously. It was her place, with three others her own age, to greet the newcomers. For a week they had been practicing the bow required, the reverence given to the older priests and those who came from far distances. Now the time had come, and the four young girls were almost white with excitement and anticipation. Faya heard first the chanting, a hymn to the dawn that was sung only at this particular ceremony. She and her friends hurried to the great hall where they were to wait until time for the Greeting. The music, coming from so great a distance, was hauntingly beautiful, and Faya realized that this was something she had unknowingly waited for all year. Krola, who stood beside Faya, sighed deeply and wiped away a tear she had not known was going to fall. She smiled rather sheepishly at her friend, before she noticed that Faya was not paying any attention to her. Faya was so totally caught up in the music she might have been in a different world. Krola had to poke her rather hard when they were given the signal to go out to the open porch that ran all around the Temple. From there, they waited again, and watched as the priests and priestesses formed two lines and walked slowly up the lawn.

When they reached the small lake that reflected the rising sun, they stopped. Each carried a small round ball that seemed to glow of its own accord. It gave a very soft light, almost as though the sun had lit it from within. Then the two lines split, one to the right and the other to the left. When they had almost surrounded the shining water, they stopped and each laid the glowing ball on the grass at his feet and turned slightly to face Asorum. Faya looked to her right to see the old priest, who was quietly standing in front of a tripod that held a gold basin in which she could just barely see water sparkling. As at a given signal, the celebrants bowed to Asorum, who returned the greeting. He raised his arms in the Prayer, joined by everyone there. When the beautiful words were spoken, Faya felt her breath catch in her throat. She had always loved the Prayer, but this time it was as though the Power to whom they spoke was a real presence. The younger children were not allowed as yet to join further in the ritual, but each one knew in her heart that this was something so special that there were simply no words to tell of it. There was more than one cheek that was wet with tears that morning. Then the most solemn part of the ceremony started. Asorum moved forward until he could look directly down into the golden basin. The hush that fell over the participants was total. Not even a bird was singing. Faya found herself holding her breath. Asorum looked intently into the water in the basin, then closed his eyes briefly. When he looked up again, there was a sigh from everyone there. There was a smile on the old priest's face, and an answering smile from those who participated in the Ceremony.

He nodded to the two lines of priests, and each bent down and picked up his ball of light and held it in both hands. When Asorum again nodded, each priest looked deeply into his own glowing ball, then looked up and nodded in turn. There was agreement, although at the moment, no one knew just what that meant. Quietly, the two lines of priests moved forward to join Asorum, and for a moment Faya lost sight of him. Then the entire group moved forward toward the Temple entrance. Now it was the turn of the children, who had practiced their welcoming greeting for so many days. Slowly and with great dignity, the four girls bowed from the waist, crossing their arms over their knees, then stood upright and extended them, palms up, toward the waiting priests. Haindohne had explained that the open hands symbolized offering the gift of hospitality and even more importantly, the gift of love. Asorum, followed by the others, returned the greeting, and the four girls, standing now straight and as tall as they possibly could, began the Welcome Song. Their young voices, sweet and joyful, seemed to echo the voices of the birds that had suddenly begun singing, as if they knew things were once again in their proper places.

The teacher who taught them singing had carefully rehearsed them, but Asorum, himself, had explained what the Ceremony meant, not only to him and the priests, but to the entire country. The golden basin, filled with pure water, was in itself only a basin, but the intuitive ability of the old priest, aided by the power generated by the others, had allowed a glimpse into the future. For the coming year, there was no great change. Day would follow night, and the seasons would march in their appointed time. Asorum had been greatly concerned about the changes in the country due to the influences of the Judges. His look into the coming year was reassuring. There would be no problems, at least not for the present.

That day and the next were filled with music, laughter, games and a total sense of oneness. Even the older priests and some of the older women gave way to the sheer joy of knowing events would not be cause for distress in the coming year.

Faya and her classmates mingled with the older visitors, some of whom had come from far parts of the country, bringing a breath of adventure that the young students found exciting. Even Asorum allowed some of his dignity to drop from him, and joined in the happy comraderie.

Fayasas was asked to bring her harp into the great hall and play for the assembly. She had by now graduated to a much larger harp, one with a glorious tone, and as she stood beside it, she suddenly felt almost frightened. She had a thoughtful look on her face as she stroked the strings, letting them sigh, then suddenly her fingers found the music she sought, and the harp sang its own song, sweet, rippling notes that flung themselves out into the great room, soaring to the domed ceiling, toying with the water that sprayed from the fountain, and dropping back again in a whisper. It was as though the harp had its own music, and Faya was there only to help it express itself. When she at last stopped and her arms dropped, there was silence in the room; then a great sigh, as though every breath had been held in, lest the magic be broken. Faya carefully stood her harp upright, then walked from the room, almost in a trance. A minute or two later, although she never remembered how she got there, she found herself in the herb garden, always her favorite place of refuge. She was still bewildered and a little unwilling to acknowledge the music that had come from her harp, music she had not known she could play, music that she had never actually heard before.

She sat on one of the low benches and put her head in her hands. “Mother,” she whispered, please help me...tell me what happened. I don’t understand.”

Instead of a reply, there was silent laughter, a joyous ripple of laughter that was felt rather than heard.

Finally her mother’s voice came. “Faya, little Faya, didn’t I tell you that there was music in your soul? Why do you think I named you Harp-of-the-winds? Ask Asorum to explain who you once were, and how you could play that unknown music. He will help you understand. Don’t be upset, my darling child. You have a rare gift, and Asorum will show you how to develop it. I have been so proud of you, always, and now I know it was the right decision to leave you at the Temple.”

“But Mother, why were you laughing?”

“Faya, I wasn’t laughing. What did you hear?”

“I heard someone laughing, and I thought it was you...but it didn’t really sound exactly like you.” She thought for a moment. “I think it was more like the laugh you hear when...I mean it comes from inside...I think, oh, Mother, I don’t know what it was.” Faya was near tears; the experience she had gone through with the harp had been a heavy one for someone so young, and the fact that she still couldn’t grasp the meaning, was a great ache inside. Asorum, knowing that the girl was upset, walked into the garden. He had also heard the laughter, and knew what it meant. He went over to Fayasas, and breathing a silent apology to her mother, took the girl by the hand and led her to a low bench that stood in the midst of the now flowering fonta.

“Faya, I should have told you something long before this, but I was waiting until you were a little older. I see now I was mistaken, because I just didn’t realize how very grown up you are.” He felt, rather than heard, Kadah’s sigh of relief.

"You see, Faya, when a child is born, some of us priests can look into the new soul and read at least a little of what the baby has brought into this lifetime. Even before you were born, Kadah, your mother, asked me to come to her and read you. I was very anxious to do this, because your mother had been a very dear pupil of this Temple, and everyone here loved her. When we knew she was about to give birth, there was both rejoicing and worry. Rejoicing, because we all knew that her child would be a part of her, therefore very special. Worry, because your father, while he was a good father to you, was not of our beliefs, and we were afraid Kadah, who loved him so very much, might allow him to lead you in the wrong paths. This could have happened, and it is why your mother brought you here when you were so young."

The old priest sighed. It was not easy to make a child understand such matters; but then, Faya was not really a child.

"Who was laughing?" Faya pressed him for the answer to the question that seemed to disturb her more than anything else.

"Child, do you remember when one of your teachers told the class about spirits? How each plant, each stone, each tree, and of course, each person has a spirit that is always there, ready to help when needed? Some people call them helpers, or sometimes, guardians. They cannot be seen, but they can be felt, and once in a great while, they can make themselves heard. That is a rare occurrence, and anyone who has this experience is blessed indeed."

"Were my spirits...I mean...those spirits, laughing at the way I played?" Faya looked completely bewildered. "I didn't know the music was coming out of the harp that way. It never did before."

"Oh, Faya, no! The spirits were not laughing at you. They were so joyous that you remembered!"

"Remembered? What did I remember? I didn't know what I was playing until it came through my fingers."

"My dear child, your fingers remembered! They knew that music. It was from a very long time ago, in another place. You were...I told you I 'read' your soul before you were born? You had come from another place. I don't know just where, but you had been a great musician, and your soul was filled with music. That is why your mother named you Fayasas. She knew, too, that you were a very special gift from the Great Creator; she had been given a rare treasure, and a great responsibility."

Faya slowly nodded. The words were understood, but the meaning had not yet been accepted.

Asorum continued. "Think of the words of the sleep song your mother always sang to you: "grow in wisdom, grow in happiness;" they were more than just a soothing way to help you get to sleep. They were a prayer to the Power for her child."

"How did you know those words? Did your mother sing them to you when you were little?"

The old priests chuckled. "No, Faya, my mother sang an entirely different song. Let's not go into that now."

Faya nodded. Asorum continued. "I told you your spirits, or if you prefer, your guardians, were always with you, didn't I? They have always been with you, even from Far Away and Long Ago. When they heard the music, they knew that you had not forgotten your Past. They were simply rejoicing that you had recalled at least a part of it. Now it will be much easier for me to teach you how to remember what you need to remember, why you were born to Kadah, why you could play the harp so well in so short a time, why you are so good with the children, oh, so many things that can help you grow into your full potential. Do you understand?" "Tell me now, please. I do want to know." Faya leaned her head on the old man's shoulder as she had done when she was four years old.

"First I must talk to your mother. Tomorrow, after breakfast, you and I will walk in the garden with the pool, and I will tell you all I can. But it is getting late, and it has been a long day." He kissed her forehead and stood up. "Thank you for playing so beautifully. We all felt a little nearer to the Power tonight." Faya gave a deep sigh. "Thank you, Asorum; I feel better now." The tall white haired old priest smiled and walked toward the door, hesitated, then chuckled silently as Faya muttered under her breath, "but I still don't see why they had to laugh!"

Chapter Nine

True to his promise, Asorum met Faya the next morning in the garden by the pool. Faya looked hollow-eyed as if she had not slept too well. Although she trusted the old priest without reservation, she was still a little bewildered by the events of the day before.

"Good morning, Faya." Asorum smiled at the young girl. "You must have been in a great hurry. I thought I would be here before you."

"I wasn't very hungry. Will you tell me now what happened last evening?"

Asorum sighed. Faya had never yet learned patience, and by now he doubted she ever would. "Sit here with me and I'll tell you all I know about it." The two sat for a long moment watching the morning sky reflected in the water. A small bird, similar to the one carved on Faya's first harp, lit on a branch of the thacasca that overhung the pool. Asorum held out his hand, almost without thinking, and the bird flew to his finger. He stroked the soft breast while he gathered his thoughts.

"Faya, your mother brought you here when you were four. It was such a terribly hard thing for her to do, but she felt she had no choice. I know you and she talk frequently in the old way. Has she never spoken of your father?"

Faya shook her head. "I asked her several times why he was angry with me, but Mother always seemed so sad, and she really didn't tell me anything. I didn't want to make her unhappy, so I stopped asking."

The priest nodded, gave the bird a final soft pat on its head, and tossed it up into the air. It flew up, circled the two people once, then lit again on the thacasca, it's tiny head cocked to one side, looking straight at the old man and the girl. His eyes still on the bird, Asorum continued.

"Your father, Faya, was and still is a very well known person in the

City. He is now one of the Judges - the law-making group. They do not always have the best interests of the country at heart, at least as we see it, and for a long time we were afraid he would try to take you back. Which is why you are seldom allowed to go into the City, and then only with Dohnnie and one of the priests. This is, of course, not exactly what you wanted to hear, but it needs to be said to make sense of your story. Before you were born, your mother prayed to the Power to allow her to have a special soul to care for. She made a promise that no matter what happened, she would do her very best to raise her baby in the Old Way and to protect him or her as best she could. When she knew you were on the way, she came back here and asked me to read you. Do you know about that?"

Faya nodded. "Yes, you told me. You sort of go into a person's mind and find out who they really are."

"Yes, but there is much, much more than just knowing who they are. I have to know, sometimes, where they came from, what their talents are, what kinds of lessons they need to learn, and then I can help steer them properly." The priest sighed again. "It is not always as easy as it sounds. Sometimes what I read can be happy, and sometimes frightening. But when I read you, it was joyous! Both for me, the others in the Temple, and for your mother. We knew Kadah's prayers had been answered, but we also knew there would be great pain for her."

"Because she had to bring me here?" Faya was drinking in every word, her dark eyes fixed on the old priest's face.

"Yes, my dear; that, and because of the rift it would cause between her and the man she had chosen to live with, even without a true marriage. They were joined by the Judges, but Kadah knew in her heart it was not enough. Your father has never forgiven her for taking you away from him, and he has not spoken to her since that time. They live in the same house, but there is such a coldness, such a stony silence between them, that it can never be mended. I had pleaded with her before you were born to leave him, but..." the man shrugged...."she loved him and would not leave."

"But I know my father loved me, didn't he?" Faya, in spite of her earlier resentment and the intervening years, still remembered the man who had brought her presents and swung her up on his shoulders.

"Yes, Faya, he did, very much. And I'm sure he still does." Asorum put his arm around the girl and she nestled against him. "The separation of your parents did not change their feelings about you, my dear."

"Asorum, tell me about the music. You said you would explain why I heard someone laugh."

Asorum smiled to himself. "The music. Yes. You know you play the harp so beautifully and you have learned the technique so easily, that you yourself must know you have played before. I mean before you were born this time as Fayasas." The girl nodded. "I know Mother thought so; she said she heard music when I was born." "I have never known, nor have I asked, just where you were before you were born to Kadah, but I do know this...you had been a great musician, and also..." the priest stopped for a moment. Faya nudged his arm. "Go on, please. Also what?" "You were more than just a musician. You were a great healer, someone who knew the properties of all plants, how to use them to help people. It was a responsibility that you accepted. You were born here this time because you chose to come to this earth and again give of yourself. It was not required of you; it was your own choice. When you played last night, the music was from that other time and place, and the spirits knew then that you remembered, and would do what you had come here to do. Faya shivered suddenly, as if a chill wind had blown over her. "You mean I have to do something that I don't know about yet," she asked.

"I think you do know it, although you may not have the meaning clear in your mind. Didn't you ask Dohnnie not too long ago to tell you about the many plants that grow here?"

"Yes, and I really do want to know about them. Did you know, Asorum, sometimes I think the plants talk to me. Isn't that funny? Plants can't talk...but sometimes I seem to know exactly what they are saying, even if I can't really hear them. Why?"

"Are the plant alive, Faya?"

"Of course they are! They are growing, aren't they?" For a minute Faya didn't understand Asorum's grin, then she laughed and pummeled his knee.

"Oh, you are teasing me again!" Suddenly serious, she looked down at the fonta underfoot. "They haven't any mouth, so they can't talk. But I guess you mean I only think I hear them; is that right?"

"No, child, that's not at all what I mean. All living things have a spirit; a tree, a blade of grass, a plant, even a rock which seems to be a dead thing, has a spirit. We can't see or touch them, but once in a while, if our ears, or I should say our hearts, are attuned properly, we may hear the spirit of that particular plant, tree or rock speak to us. You, Faya, have been so attuned that you sometimes hear the plant spirits tell you things. For instance, if the plant is thirsty, or needs its roots pruned, or wants to be fed, it will tell you so.

"You have heard your harp speak, although you didn't recognize its message. Last night it spoke in a very definite manner, and you responded by allowing your fingers to play what the spirit of the harp wanted you to play. This is how, sometimes, great music is written."

"But how did I know that music? I had never heard it before." Faya slid off the bench and stood up, suddenly very serious. "Will you help me find what I am supposed to do?" Asorum nodded, pointing to the little bird that still sat quietly on the branch above them. “That little bird, Faya, trusts us enough to come down while we are here, because he knows we will do him no harm. When you learn to trust your own emotions, your own feelings of need, when you know in your heart what is right for you, then you and I will go to the priest who tends another garden, and he will start your lessons. In the meantime, Faya, I will tell you only that there is still another herb garden you have not yet seen.” Faya’s eyes grew round with surprise. The priest continued. “It is one of the very few places that children are never, never permitted to enter unless there is some special reason. And then only with proper supervision.”

Faya remembered Dohnnie telling her that there were many more rooms in the Temple, rooms that belonged to the older priests, rooms that were kept for special occasions, rooms where the women lived, rooms which the younger children were not permitted to enter. She had nearly always obeyed, as had Shaleen and Krola, but like all children, they had been curious. She never forgot the scolding she had received when she was six. She and three other children had followed one of their teachers to a part of the Temple they had not seen before. When they were discovered, hiding behind one of the massive pillars that supported the great roof, they were brought before Asorum. He stood at the foot of the grand staircase, his white robed making him seem taller than he was, his eyes stern and his voice like quiet thunder. The words had not mattered so much, but the look in the priest’s eyes was enough to keep the children in line for weeks afterwards. Faya had been crushed. She had also heard a few choice words from her mother that night before she went to sleep, explaining that obedience in small things led to being trusted in larger ones. Never again had she dared look into matters that did not concern her. Now, it seemed, her small obediences were about to permit her to enter a grown-up world, a world where responsibility would be a word that loomed large in her life.

Chapter Ten

Faya sat on the flat rock she had discovered several years before. Her face was lifted to the early morning sun, her eyes closed. This was a place she loved, where she often came to think about things that troubled or puzzled her. The trees that surrounded the rock were heavy in leaf, some of their branches almost sweeping the ground. They had grown from seedlings many years before, and were now tall and regal, almost a small forest; few plants could grow beneath their heavy shade. The ground underfoot was soft and deep, masking any footstep. There, in the very heart of the deep tangle of woods, was the rock, as big across as a table, spotted here and there with moss, offering the only place where the sun could strike a ray through the leaves. To reach her favorite spot, Faya had to bend low, as though in homage to the great age of the trees.

Today she was thinking about the offer Asorum had made, to allow her to learn the secret ways of herbs, to follow what she had known before but had not yet learned to remember. It was a great responsibility, Faya thought, to tell people what was wrong with them and how to fix it. She had seen many people come through the open doors of the Temple, asking for help, and had watched them being led down passages to rooms not yet open to her.They had nearly always come back with smiles on their faces. Haindohne had explained that many of the priests were not only teachers, but great healers; they were known all over the City and even the Judges sometimes came to them for help. No one was ever turned away. Of course, Dohnnie was quick to say, not everyone was healed. Sometimes the patient had come too late, and not even the greatest of the healers could help. Sometimes the patient didn't really want to get better, and they were sent away with little vials of colored water, often with a very mild narcotic in them, to help quiet their emotional upheavals until they could decide for themselves if they really wanted help.

For the most part, though, bodies were made strong, minds were helped clear, and spirits were strengthened. Faya thought it the most wonderful thing in the world to see a back straighten, or watch a child's eyes lose the dullness that fevers bring. Children were her special loves, and she looked forward every day to the time allotted her in the garden where the youngest children were in her charge for a few hours.

Today, she decided, she would tell Asorum she felt she was ready to begin her training. She was thoroughly familiar with the herb garden and its many plants, but now it seemed there were to be more she had not known. She opened her eyes and for just an instant looked straight up through the trees to the sun. It struck her with such force that she was blinded for a long moment. Lowering her head, she put both hands flat on the rock, feeling the coolness, letting the crystal hardness enter her palms. This rock was special, and so far as she knew, hers alone. Not even her closest friends had been there with her.

"Rock," she whispered, remembering that Asorum had told her even rocks had a life of their own, "Rock, can I do this? Can I really become what he told me I had once been, a healer? Can I learn to make people well, will I be strong and steady like you?" Suddenly thinking how silly she sounded, talking to a rock, she got up, brushed the bits of clinging moss off her dress, and held her arms up to the tiny patch of sunny sky. "Thank you," she whispered. Leaving as she had come, Faya walked slowly back to the Temple in time to join the others for the first meal of the day. After they had eaten, Faya sought out Asorum and asked to speak to him. "What is it, child?" the priest smiled at her. The girl looked unusually serious this morning, and lowered her eyes for a long moment before she spoke. Then squaring her shoulders, she looked up and said, "Asorum, I am ready to begin the training."

"Yes, Fayasas, I believe you are." This was one of the few times the old priest had used her full name, and it seemed to put the entire matter in a different perspective. "Come, I will introduce you to your teacher, and from now on, you will be excused from the usual morning classes."

Faya grinned suddenly. "You mean I won't have to memorize those long stories we've had to read?" "To memorize is only one way of learning discipline. It gives you the ability to recall something if you need to, but it is only a technique. Once you have learned it, you can use it or not as you wish. Just remember, those old stories are the foundations of our culture. But no, you won't have to memorize them any more. There will be enough other tasks for you, and you will learn very quickly that recall is most necessary in this new work. They walked down a passage, past the sleeping rooms of the children, past the class rooms already in use, making several turns through an unfamiliar part of the Temple until they came to a door that opened into a cloistered area, surrounding yet another garden that Faya had never before seen. The wide, cool porch area was shaded with a beautifully carved ceiling, supported by slender white columns. There were a few benches placed along the inside walls, with small tables beside each one, but the garden caught and held Faya's attention.

It was laid out in formal beds, each divided by low walls, just high enough to sit on comfortably. The entire garden was surrounded by walls high enough so no one could possibly see over them. Vines grew in profusion, hiding some of the stones, and casting a cooling reflection on the small pool in the center. Flowers floated on the water, some open, some still in bud. None of the plants looked familiar, and Faya had a sudden sinking feeling that there would be many long hours of, again, memorizing the name of each plant and what it was used for.

Asorum seemed to know exactly what she was feeling, and smiled to himself. Patience, little Faya, patience, he said to himself. Aloud, he answered the unspoken question. “Yes, my dear, you will have to learn them. But not all at once. It takes many months, sometimes many years, to recognize each of the many herbs here, but in time, they will become as familiar to you as those in the other herb garden. Dohnnie tells me you know all of them, and what they are for.”

“Yes, but some of them Mother grew, so they were not all strange. Did she come here, too?”

“She did, indeed. Your mother was well on her way to becoming very adept at the mixing of the tinctures we sometime use, but her real love was the other garden, and of course, her music.”

Faya sighed. “I wish I could have heard her play the harp. I never did, you know. But she sang so beautifully. Even my father would sit and listen as long as she would sing the songs he liked. Funny, I never heard her sing any of the songs we sing here.”

“No, Faya, she probably would not because your father would have objected. But let us meet your new teacher.” Asorum quickly steered the girl away from remembrance of the old wounds. They walked across the cloistered porch to a carved door and Asorum opened it and stood back for Faya to enter. The room seemed dark at first, but as her eyes became accustomed to the change in light, she saw that the room, while small, was beautifully appointed. Her own room that she shared with Krola, and the other students’ sleeping rooms, were comparatively bare, having only a pallet, a small table and a low bench with a storage area beneath it. Each girl had decorated her room with vases of flowers and leaves, but there were no curtains at the windows, nor was there any semblance of luxury.

This room had a wonderfully soft rug on the marble floor, and instead of a bench, there was a chair with a cushion and a footstool, a beautifully inlaid table, and silken draperies at the two small windows. The sides of the room were lined with shelves holding scroll after scroll, all neatly tagged with small tassels on their bindings; small figurines of a cool green color stood between some of them, and here and there a stone flecked with shiny bits of silver or gold. Flowers on yet another table filled the room with their spicy scent, while the open door let a soft breeze bring in the warmth of early summer.

Faya simply stared. She had never seen such a room, even though her old home had been very comfortable by the standards of the day. The country house was light, cool and roomy, but there had been few real luxuries. Her father's city apartment, on the other hand, had been much smaller, but filled with pictures, comfortable furniture, and of course the papers and scrolls necessary to a busy lawyer. Faya had been taken there only once, and she remembered very little about it.

The man who had been standing near a window came forward to greet them. He was tall, not quite as tall as Asorum; his hair was dark brown, which made Faya feel better immediately. She still longed for the light hair and blue-green eyes of her companions. How did this man happen to have the unusual darker coloring? "Welcome, Fayasas." The voice was deep and held a hint of laughter. "Asorum tells me you are ready to begin studying with me." The younger priest smiled as Asorum motioned for the girl to make her obeisance. Faya bowed from the waist and then stood as tall as she could, looking her new teacher in the face. She had a feeling this man was going to become very important in her life, and she felt almost awe; but at the same time, she could allow no fear to show.

"I would like to, very much, if you will teach me." For a brief moment her eyes strayed beyond the man's face, to the window which overlooked the new garden, before she could bring them back to the man who stood before her. Both priests realized that she was uncomfortable in the room, and would prefer to be outside.

"You will come here every morning, then, and we will begin at once. You will call me Benai. I believe you are called Faya?" The priest smiled reassuringly. Faya nodded. "Benai. I have not heard that name before."

"No, I am not from your country. My home is...was... far to the east."

"Does it also have a meaning, as our names do?" she asked. Somehow, it seemed important that she learn as much as she could about this new teacher.

"Yes, it does, Faya, but it is not the name I was given as a child. I took this name because I had been sold as a slave when I was five years old, and for several years I was passed from place to place, and became known as Benai, the wanderer.

Faya's eyes got larger and larger. "You were sold as a slave?" she gasped, "When you were a child? How could that be?"

Benai, his mouth twisted into a wry smile, said "There are many things that you, as Fayasas, have not yet learned. I believe you had a slave girl in your old home, didn't you?"

Faya nodded. "Yes, we did, but I don't remember her name."

"And she did whatever she was told to do?" Again Faya nodded. "I guess so. But my mother..." she broke off, looking bewildered. "Did you do something wrong, is that why you were a slave?" Suddenly realizing she had far overstepped the bounds of courtesy and good manners, she blushed and stammered, "I'm sorry. I should not have said that. Please forgive me."

Benai smiled again, and shook his head slightly at Asorum, who had started toward Faya as if to reprove her. "I know, Fayasas, it is hard to understand all the injustices in this world. When we know each other better, perhaps I'll tell you my story. But for now, shall we go out into the garden? I'm sure you would like to see where you will be studying for some time to come." The three left the room and walked out onto the cloistered porch.

Asorum put his hands on the girl's shoulder and said, "Faya, we will see each other soon, but I must leave you here now. Benai will call one of the older students to show you how to return to the great hall when your first lesson is over. It can be rather confusing until you learn your way."

"Recall?" Faya grinned at her old friend. They both laughed, and Faya bowed to him as he turned and left, then stood again to face her new teacher. I wonder, she thought, if Benai can read my thoughts as Asorum can. The twinkle in the priest's eyes answered her unspoken question, and she blushed again. "Fayasas, I see I will have to teach you more than the uses of herbs. Don't you know you can shield your mind from anyone's intrusion? I'm surprised this hasn't come up before. How old are you?"

"Almost twelve," she replied.

"You seem older. But then I don't know when certain subjects are taught in this Temple. Have you learned to communicate at a distance?"

"Oh, yes. My mother and I talk to each other nearly every night. But I knew that before I came here. Doesn't everyone know how to do that?"

"No, my dear, they do not. How did you learn?"

"My mother told me how to just open my mind and let her come in. I don't really know how we do it. It just happens." "Your mother must be a rather special kind of mother," Benai said thoughtfully. "Either that, or..." he stopped for a moment. "Or what, Benai?" Faya looked a little apprehensive. Was this 'gift' something she should not have had?

The priest smiled. "I forgot that Asorum had told me your mother had trained here when she was young. Perhaps that is how she learned distance communication." Realizing that the girl was not satisfied with his answer, he went on, "I did not mean to upset you. It's just that so few people today either can or will make use of the talents our souls are capable of using. They are being taught that only the Judges are able to control the mind, that only the Judges can make decisions, that only the Judges have the power to..." Benai broke off suddenly. "Fayasas, I am truly sorry. I forgot that your Father is a Judge now. Please forgive my rudeness." Faya nodded slowly. "I know, Benai, that my father is a Judge, but I can't believe that he is unkind to people, or that he would control them. Would he?" She raised her face to the priest, her eyes betraying the anguish that still festered in her soul whenever she thought of the man she had once loved so devotedly. Benai was hard put to answer. If he said he agreed with her, he would be telling less than the truth. If he said her father was exactly like all the other Judges, would Faya ever forgive him and be happy studying there? He knew the man was ambitious, almost to fanaticism; Asorum had told him Faya's story and he sympathized with the young girl who had been left in so many ways an orphan.

Faya waited a moment before she repeated her question, "Would my Father really want to control people?" Benai sighed, and knew he had to answer.

"Yes, Fayasas, he would. This is not to say he is a bad man," he went on quickly, "only that he is following the others in their desire to rule the land in their own way. It is not our way, but," he shrugged, "we can do little about it at present. What I started to say was that your mother must have been a very wise soul to have been able to teach you that so very early in your life. I admire her for it. Now let's talk about what you will be studying." Faya nodded, her eyes still on the young man, but willing to put the question aside for now. They walked over to one of the raised beds, where a rather tall plant grew. It had lavender and pink blossoms which ran down the long stem, and drooped toward the ground. Benai reached down and gently touched one of the blossoms. “This, Fayasas, is called ‘trendali’, and it is used for severe headaches. We make a poultice out of the blossoms and bind it on the forehead. The roots we steep in water for a drink that is highly narcotic and helps dull pain. It is a very useful plant, but dangerous if used too often, or if the sufferer drinks too large a dose at once.”

Faya nodded, her eyes on the blossoms, and repeated the name several times. “Asorum told me I would have to remember so many things I learn here. Will I be able to memorize every plant and what it is used for? There are so many.” She looked around the garden almost in dismay.

Benai grinned at the expression on her face, and patted her on shoulder. “Don’t worry...we will go very slowly and in no time at all you will know dozens of my charges. If you learn just one a day, by the time you are thirteen, you’ll know them all so well I will be out of a job!”

The young girl smiled rather sheepishly and said, “well, at least, I know one!”

As Benai had promised, he did not push Faya too fast. By the time of the Resting Period, she had learned the names of three plants, how they were used and whether they were to be handled with bare hands or with gloves. Through the short lunch they shared on the porch, Faya kept up a running chatter, questioning, probing, and allowing almost no time to savor the surprisingly simple meal. They had sat for a few minutes, then, enjoying the heady scent of the garden, but Fayasas was too eager to learn more to sit still for long.

Finally, Benai took her gently by the shoulders and led her back up to the porch. “Hurry makes a person over-anxious and then mistakes are made, Faya. You will have plenty of time to learn all you want to know.

For now, it is getting late, and time for you to go back to your own part of the Temple." When she squinted up at the sky, she realized that it was nearly time for the evening meal. The older student who had been sent for her had been waiting quietly on the spacious porch; she smiled at Fayasas, bowed briefly to the priest, and the two girls left together. Faya was so full of what she had been learning that she was silent on the walk back through the unfamiliar part of the Temple. Suddenly she stopped. "What if..." The words were bitten off.

"What if what, Faya?" asked Ianera, who had also stopped to see why her younger friend was not following. "What if I don't learn all the plants? What if I make a really bad mistake and hurt someone someday? Maybe I should ask Asorum to let me study something else." Fayasas looked back over her shoulder at the passage they had just walked through. "Ianera, I'm scared!"

Ianera laughed. "Don't worry, Faya...Asorum wouldn't let you start something like herbal medicine if he didn't think you could handle it."

"No, I suppose not...but what if..."

Ianera broke in. "Now, Faya, you are only making Shadows. We all do sometimes, but remember what the priests taught us about Shadows?"

Faya smiled a little ruefully. "'Face the Light and the Shadows go away.' You're right, Ianera." They walked on for a few steps. "Oh, I know where I am now. Race you back!" The two ran down the now familiar passage, skidding to a more sedate walk when they were nearly at the entrance to the great hall. The other members of the Temple were already gathering, and the two girls hastily smoothed their robes and moved quietly to their places. Faya grinned at Ianera, then sobered as Asorum took his place at the foot of the stairs.

"Tomorrow," he began, "is the first day of the Festival of Growth. As you all know, it is the time of the year when the growth of plants is at its fullest, when small birds are stretching out from their nests to try their wings, and when all growing things are at their most vibrant period. We celebrate Nature's bounty by giving thanks to the Power, as we always do, but this time, there will be a very special celebration. We are honored to be the host Temple for some priests from a far country. They have already arrived, and will be meeting here with us tomorrow."

There were murmurs from the entire group assembled, but quieted when Asorum raised his hand. "I know you are all anxious to know just what is coming, but be patient, be patient!" He smiled and continued. "These men and women have come to ask our help. They will tell you what they need, but for now, I ask you all only to send your prayers to the Power for guidance. As you sleep tonight, your dreams will help you understand what each of you needs to do to help." For a long moment Asorum was silent, seemingly lost in thought, then he raised his arms and began the Prayer. "To the Power I send my Spirit." He was joined by every voice. The beautiful words rose softly at first, then seemed to gain power until the entire Temple echoed the words. Ianera looked at Fayasas through tears. The younger girl was pale even as she smiled, and felt as though something was to happen that would change her life forever.

Chapter Eleven

Faya wakened early, too excited to stay in bed until her usual time of arising. She looked over at Krola, who was still deeply asleep. Getting out of her pallet, she picked up her dress and walked quietly to the bathing pool. After a hasty plunge, she dressed quickly and walked out to the wide porch that surrounded the Temple. The air was cool, and the sun had not yet risen over the far mountains. The moon was setting in the west, and in the east, the light was beginning to glow on the horizon.

Faya stood quietly for a moment or two, inhaling the freshness of the new day; then abandoning herself to the joy that bubbled inside her, she flew down the steps and ran to the small lake at the foot of the sloping lawn. Kneeling down, she looked at her own reflection in the still water, then cupped her hand and scooped up some of the clear water and drank thirstily. When the ripples had stilled and the lake was again smooth, she sat down on the grass and thought about her dreams of the night before. What had she dreamed? At first, she couldn't remember. Then bits and pieces came into focus and she chuckled at their silliness.

"Asorum will have a fine laugh at these dreams," she mused, "but I suppose every dream really has a meaning...at least, that's what we have been taught." She didn't realize she had spoken aloud until she heard an answering chuckle behind her. Startled, she looked around, and saw a young man smiling at her. She arose quickly, smoothed her dress, and mindful that she had forgotten to put her shoes on, blushed deeply. "I'm sorry. I thought no one was awake yet. Please forgive me if I disturbed you when I came out. I tried to be quiet." She realized she was almost babbling. Something about the stranger confused her. He was not dressed as a priest, and it was so seldom that anyone from the City came to the Temple that she was at a loss to know how to address him.

"I'm Faya...I mean Fayasas. I live here. That is, I'm a student here."

"How do you do, Faya, I mean Fayasas. My name is Rab, I mean Rabithi." Then noting her sudden look of hurt, he took her hand and raised it to his lips. "I'm sorry, Faya; I should not have teased you. You were so serious that I couldn't help myself. Am I forgiven?"

The sudden smile that lit her face was answer enough. "Yes, of course. You must be one of the visitors that Asorum told us about last evening. We are supposed to help you..." She bit off her words, again aware that she had overstepped the bounds of good manners. "I'm sorry. I shouldn't have said that. Will you forgive me?

"Tell you what; let's both pretend that we have never met and we'll just start over. I'm Rab, and you're Faya, and I'm very glad to meet you." They both laughed, suddenly feeling quite comfortable with each other. "Now I believe I heard you saying something about dreams?"

"Yes, we try to recall our dreams every morning to find out what they are telling us. Mine were so silly I think they must mean that I am being foolish about something. But I really don't know what."

"Could you tell me? Maybe I could help you sort them out. I have crazy dreams myself at times, and I've often wondered just why. In fact, I dreamed last night I was going to meet someone very important in my life. And here you are, bare feet, hair a dark cloud around your head, with a name that sings like some haunting music, and the first spark of sun-light catching your eyes." Faya was pleased, surprised, embarrassed and shy all at once. She didn't know just how to answer the young man who had been so free with his compliments. Her first impulse was to run back to the Temple; but she remembered that she had always been told that visitors were to be treated with respect, so she muttered "thank you," and tried to stand very tall. "I will be late for the first meal if I don't return. Will you be eating with us?" Frantically trying to think what she should say to this most unusual young man, she looked about as if to draw some inspiration from the glow of the morning.

Rabithi grinned at her discomfort, then relenting, he drew her arm through his and started back up the sloping lawn to the Temple. “Come on, Faya, we’ll go back together, and yes, I will be eating the first meal with you. We have much to talk to your priests about, and it could be rather serious. But the morning is so beautiful, I did what you did, came out to enjoy the dawn. I won’t tell if you don’t.” He grinned again, and Faya grinned back. When they entered the great hall, it was already a buzz of activity. Many of the women had already eaten and were arranging fresh flowers around the pool. Some of the younger priests were carrying scrolls. Faya and Rab hurried to the dining hall where they separated, each to a different table. When the hasty meal was finished and they all stood for the thanksgiving blessing, Asorum raised his hands for silence .

He turned to a young priest. ”Will you please ask those in the great hall to join us?” He stood silent for a long moment until the others filed in quietly and took their places. Faya caught Krola’s eye and winked. Her friend raised her eyebrows in mock surprise and glanced at the other table where Rab had joined his group. Faya knew they had been seen coming in together, and was also aware that she would have some explaining to do later on.

“If you will all please be seated, I have something important to discuss with you all.” Asorum’s voice was quiet as usual, but his presence was commanding and there was not another sound in the room. “Our guests are from several provinces outside our City, and they have come to ask our help, as I told you last evening. We have spent many hours since then discussing the information they bring, and now it is time to let you all know the problem.” He looked around the room. “Later today, I will ask any of you who had a dream that you feel might relate to what we are about to say, to come to me, or to any of the teachers, and tell us." Asorum had remained standing, and now he leaned forward and put his hands flat on the table and bowed his head as if to gather his thoughts. Looking up he said, "You all know who the Judges are. They are actually the ruling group here in Atlantis, as they make and uphold the laws. Most of them are from old established families, and command great wealth." Faya moved uneasily in her chair, remembering that her father was also a Judge. "Unfortunately, not all Judges are truly concerned with the welfare of our people. You students may not know that we have sent emissaries to many parts of the world, exchanging ideas as well as material things. We have taught some of the less developed countries how to grow better crops, how to store food supplies to prevent famine if there was drought or a bad harvest, and above all, we have tried to be open to any who came seeking our help. Some of the Judges resent this. They prefer to keep the great wealth of Atlantis here at home, rather than sharing with others."

There was a soft murmuring from the gathered priests, and again Asorum raised his hand for silence. "Our guests are here because there have been rumors of a general disruption in our way of life. There are those who would destroy the Temples, do away with the priesthood, and see that no child is ever taught our ways again." The soft murmur rose to a wave of disbelief. Several of the older students looked quickly at the younger children. Faya stood in astonished bewilderment, her mind racing back to her early childhood, when her father, the man she had adored, had forgotten her fourth birthday. That had been the beginning of the greatest change in her life. Over the years, she had tried to put behind her the hurt and feeling of betrayal, but now it was all coming back. The joyous bubble she had been holding in since early this morning, now burst in a wave of denial; her mind and heart were silently screaming against the pain and shock.

Asorum continued. “We are at a crossroads. The Judges wield a great amount of power, but the Temples are still strong, and if we can stop these rumors, we will survive and our lives will go on as before.” He looked around at the assembled students; the teachers, the priests; and finally at the table where their guests were seated. “After the noon meal we will all gather in the great hall for the annual Ceremony of Growth; but in addition, we will be honoring those who are visiting our Temple, especially those who have never been here before. I will ask you older students who are familiar with the gardens and the teaching rooms, to be hosts, and show them around.” He smiled, and there were a few answering smiles, but most of the assemblage looked serious.

Fayasas looked quickly over to the table where Rab was seated only to find that he was looking directly at her. She looked away, but she knew she was blushing, and that her breath was coming faster than usual.” Silly,” she muttered to herself. “Now stop being such an idiot.” But the thought crept into her mind that perhaps he would ask her to be his guide. When the assembled group filed out of the dining hall, Faya found Rab walking beside her. With a grin, he bowed slightly and asked if she would show him the Temple. Very seriously she replied that she would be honored; then the corner of her mouth twitched, and she couldn’t stop the giggle that broke like a bubble.

Shaleen and Krola, walking arm in arm, winked at them as they went past, while Faya tried her best to look dignified. Rab, on the other hand, winked back at the two girls. He said, “Well, Faya, will you show me around your beautiful Temple?” “I will if you will tell me why you are here and where you have come from,” she replied.

They walked slowly back into the great entrance hall, Faya keeping up a running chatter that Rab found both informative and amusing. "You see, Rab, the light breaks up into many colors over the fountain. Don't you think it is beautiful?"

"Yes, it is. What are the stones that are used there?" he asked. "Some of them I have never seen before."

Faya looked thoughtful for a moment. "You will have to ask one of the teachers. I really don't know what they are called, except for the pink one, which is quartz crystal, and the yellow, which is a citrine. I think Dohnnie told me once that they are all members of the crystal family, but I never paid much attention to their names. Come on, I'll show you one of my favorite places."

"And where is that?" asked Rab.

"Come on...I'll show you. Let's go this way...we can get out without Krola seeing us. She's such a big tease!" She took Rab by the arm and led him through a short passage out into the herb garden. "There!" she said. "What do you think of it?" Many of the herbs were in full bloom, their scent mingling with that of the heavy-blooming fonta underfoot, tantalizing the senses. Faya breathed deeply. Her heart was here in the garden where she was always the most comfortable. Rab stood quietly watching her for a long minute. He seemed to feel the undercurrent of sadness that at times crept unwanted and unbidden when memories long buried wriggled like worms to the surface of her mind. But today Faya would not allow anything to disrupt the happiness she was feeling. Suddenly she threw caution and decorum to the wind, and grabbed Rab with both arms, spun him around, laughing with the joy that she could not deny. He answered her laughter, and the two, almost as one person, acknowledged for a brief instant their total dedication to each other, to the sudden blessing of love from one heart to another, and to the great Creator who had brought them together.

Then suddenly shocked by her unwonted behavior, Faya felt her face go crimson. “Rab, I’m sorry. I don’t know why I did that.” She looked quickly away from him, disturbed beyond belief that this young man whom she hardly knew had already begun to mean so much to her. He put his hand on her shoulder and gently turned her to face him. “Faya, you are so very young, but you seem so much older. You know, don’t you, that when I leave here tomorrow, I will remember; and that one day I will come back for you?” Faya looked at him in dismay. “You are leaving tomorrow?” she gasped. “But you just came. I mean, why are you leaving so soon? And where will you go?” The inner child surfaced again, and the old memory of her father’s betrayal loomed large in her memory.

“Faya, I can’t tell you everything, but I can tell you this. I have been traveling around many of the countries outside Atlantis, those that your High Priest mentioned earlier. We, the others who came with me, are also priests, although we do not always dress as such. There are so many reasons I could give you, but I am not free to talk too openly yet. But for now I will just tell you that we are working to keep this country out of the hands of those who would destroy the Temples; and particularly, we are trying to prevent close contact between the Judges and our children, while they are still young enough to be easily influenced.”

He stopped to gather his thoughts, then continued. “Faya, I saw your face at the evening meal when Asorum ...is that his name?...said what he did about the Judges. You looked so shocked and hurt that I wondered then if you had any particular reason to feel so strongly.” It was not really a question, but the girl nodded and answered immediately as if he had a right to know.

“My father is a Judge,” she said softly. “He was the reason my mother brought me to this Temple and left me with Asorum.” “My dear, I’m so sorry. I had no idea it was anything like that. Your mother brought you here? When? Were you very young?"

"I was just four. For a long time I never knew why...I thought I had done something bad, or that my father had decided they didn't want me any longer. But Asorum and Dohnnie told me the real reason, that they and my mother were afraid my father might try to get me back and send me to the school the Judges are running now. I don't understand all of it, but I know I'm not allowed to go into the City alone like some of the other girls do." She looked pensive for a moment while Rab watched her, his face mirroring the compassion that swelled inside him. Finally Faya reached up and almost without thought took his hand. "Come on, Rab, and I'll show you the rest of the Temple grounds. They are lovely this time of year."

Rab looked down at her. "Yes, Faya, show me the rest. But first I want to tell you something. When I first saw you, I knew that we had met before. No," he said hastily, forestalling a question, "not in this lifetime. I don't know when or where, but I do know with certainty that I have known you, and loved you. When you are older, perhaps we will find out. But for now, will you believe that we have been together, maybe many times?"

The young girl dropped his hand and turned away from him, looking back at the pool shimmering in the soft light. For a moment Rab was afraid he had spoken too quickly and frightened her. When she finally turned back to him, the half smile on her lips and the glow in her eyes gave him the answer he wanted.

"Rab, I will grow up as soon as I can." With a shout of laughter at her answer, he shook his head and then solemnly took her hand and kissed it.

"Faya, there could never be anyone like you. Then you will wait for me?"

"I will wait for you, Rab." Faya was quite serious, but Rab had a hard time keeping a straight face. This child, this dark eyed wisp of a girl, was so young, and at the same time, gave such promise of the woman she would someday be, that he wasn't quite sure what to do next. Very wisely, he decided to do nothing. The two walked slowly back through the great entrance hall where people were still milling about, and going out onto the wide porch, stopped a minute to look at the view over the small lake. Trees that lined the walkway of the Temple were hung with fruit, not yet ripe, but promising a heavy harvest in a few months. The air was warm, heady with the scent of flowers from the gardens Rab had not yet seen. They went first into the Children's Garden, where Faya had played and where Dohnnie had given her such comfort in her early years. They sat on one of the benches at a small table, while Faya told the young priest about her early life here. She didn't realize how much she laid bare in a very few sentences, but Rab was so closely attuned to this suddenly dear young girl that he could read between the lines very easily, and understood almost instinctively her hurt, the feeling of abandonment, the despair at leaving her home, and the still bitter disappointment of her father's betrayal. Finally, with a great sigh, Faya got up, smoothed the skirt of her dress and smiled.

"That's enough about me. I want to know about you....where do you come from, why are you traveling around, and where will you go next. Can you tell me? I mean, is it a great secret?"

Rab laughed, knowing that she would continue her questioning until he gave a satisfactory answer. "All right, Faya. I am from one of our provinces far to the north. I have been in the land that is across the great sea that surrounds us, where the people want to learn what we can teach them. They are darker skinned, but beautiful, and they have a language that is not always easy for me to understand. But I am learning." He grinned at the wry face Faya made. "Yes, we have to memorize, too."

Faya looked bewildered for an instance, then laughed in return. "Oh, Rab, do you always know what I am thinking? But why..." she was suddenly serious..."are the Judges trying to influence our children? And what can they do that would be so bad?" Rab stood up, looking away from Faya for a long moment. Then he turned and faced her. "My dear, the Judges, and I realize your father is one of them, are trying to take our beliefs away from the people. There would be no more Prayer, no more praise to the Power, no blessings and no security of soul. If one does not believe in something, what is the purpose in living? I believe the sun will rise tomorrow. I believe the trees will bear fruit after the blossoms have fallen. I believe that there is Something or Someone much greater than I. We use the word 'the Power' because there is no other name we can use, and if this were all taken away, what would be left? Our children must not be deprived of their birthright, and we priests are the ones who must see to it. But we need help...your help, and the prayers and efforts of all people like you."

"What can I do?" asked Faya, almost in tears. She went to stand beside him. "Rab, tell me, what can I do? What must I do? No one has said anything about this before, not even Asorum. I play with the smaller children almost every day, I help them with their lessons when they ask me, and I play my harp for them before they go to sleep. What more can I do?"

"Faya, right now, I can't tell you that. It must be left up to Asorum and the other priests here at your Temple. But you will be told very shortly, I'm certain. There is no immediate danger, but things might come to a head before we are ready, if we are not prepared."

Faya nodded. "When will you be back, Rab?"

"I am not sure, Faya, but I will be back. One day. Shall I bring you something from one of the countries I will be visiting?"

The girl nodded seriously. “Yes, please, Rab, something that I can always keep to remember.” She stopped suddenly.

“Remember, Faya? We will have a lot to remember, but together, not alone.” He slipped an arm under hers, and they walked quietly back into the Temple, joining the others who had congregated in the great entrance hall.

Everyone was busily preparing for the afternoon festivities. The noon meal was eaten hastily, Rab seated with the priests, and Faya at her usual place at the students’ table. When they finished and the Thanksgiving was said, everyone hurried out to the Great Hall.

The younger children were grouped around the fountain, garlands of young green leaves in their hair, and each carrying sprays of flowers. The musicians stood on the great staircase, softly tuning their instruments. Faya’s harp stood at the foot of the staircase, and she gave Rab a quick smile and walked over to the instrument. She knew Asorum would have tuned the harp earlier, since he had sent her out to help visitors see the Temple grounds. She ran her fingers lightly over the strings, then nodded to the children. At the first chord, they picked up the song and their young voices rose in the opening chant. The musicians joined them, and the harmonies began to swell, until the entire Temple seemed to throb with music. Rab stood enthralled, not only at the music itself, but at Faya’s command of her instrument. She played with her eyes closed, her heart leading the way. Her fingers knew instinctively where each chord should be struck, and she seemed to have no need to look at the strings or even at the other musicians. They all blended in that perfect harmony that only those whose souls speak to each other can attain.

Rab found his own eyes wet, and hastily brushed his hand across his face. The chant rose in volume, then softened, then rose again in a joyous peal of devotion. The words themselves didn't seem to be as important as the feeling the music expressed, the offering to the great Creator of the thanks and the love that all who played or sang felt in their hearts. When the music finally died away, those present knew they had been blessed with something magical, so special that it seemed as though it could never be repeated.

It was time, then, for the priests to offer the platters of early fruits, plates of bread-cakes, great mounds of baby vegetables, and pitchers of wines as symbolic gifts to the great Creator. Then they were passed around to the guests assembled, and to the students and teachers. When each person had taken a small portion of each, the remaining food was taken away to be given to the poor of the City. The rest of the day was spent in play for the children, and lengthy discussions among the priests and visitors.

Faya did not see Rab again that evening. He and his friends had joined the others in the closing Prayer, but had not eaten with them. They were still deep in conversation with Asorum and the Temple priests, who had withdrawn to a part of the Temple where students were not permitted. Long after the moon had risen, a sleepless Faya sat on the edge of the circular pool, idly dappling her hands in the water, and trying to concentrate on the reflection from the opening above. The soft moonlight did not cast the colors she could see in the daytime, but its gentle radiance finally worked its spell, and she found herself drowsing. She jerked her head up, and looked around at the empty hall. 'What am I doing here,' she thought. Hastily she got up and ran quietly to her room. Krola was sound asleep, for which Faya was thankful, and she was very careful not to wake her friend as she undressed and lay down on her pallet. But sleep would not come. For the first time, she did not think of her mother as she usually did when she was troubled. All she could see behind her closed eyes was Rab's face. Her last thought was, I must remember my dreams....

Chapter Twelve

That night Faya's dreams were a kaleidoscope of fragmented memories, whirling colors that seemed to mean nothing, music faintly heard and even more faintly remembered when she woke, drenched in sweat and shaking. She had a vague recollection of something terrifying, but could not recall the details. It was so totally unlike any other night she could remember. Her first impulse was to pull the light covers over her head and stay in bed. For some reason, she just didn't want to face the day.

Krola was already stretching and yawning. She grinned at Faya and asked, "Faya, you must have had quite a night! You kept me awake until all hours, moaning and tossing. I never heard you talk in your sleep before."

Faya smiled bravely at her friend, then suddenly burst into tears. Krola was horrified. Faya almost never cried, and the outburst, sudden and unexpected, took her by surprise. She flew off her pallet and gathered the sobbing girl in her arms. "Faya, I'm sorry, I didn't mean...."

Faya shook her head. "It wasn't you, Krola. I just woke up so frightened and I don't know why! I'm still scared," she cried. "I always remember my dreams and this time I don't. Why, Krola? What's happening to me?" She was still shaking, and her friend simply held and rocked her for a few minutes.

"Faya, I don't know. You are usually so happy in the morning. Don't you remember anything at all...I mean, about what you dreamed?" Faya shook her head. "No, just something that seemed so terrible that I was running and running...and I was trying to find my mother...I do remember that...but she kept running away from me, and then there was something big and black that was chasing me, and I think I stumbled and fell, and I was so scared it was going to catch me before I could get up and keep running, and I heard some funny music, at least I think I did, only it wasn't nice music and I just had to get away from it, and the light kept whirling around and around, and then....then I woke up." She hiccuped once and took a deep breath. "I'll be all right, only please don't tell anybody. Promise you won't. I don't want anybody to know, not just yet."

Krola whistled. "Whew! No wonder you were scared! I was, just hearing about it. And you know I won't tell anybody, only I think you should tell Dohnnie or Asorum. They are both very good at translating dreams."

Faya nodded. "Yes, I know they are. Dohnnie has told me before what a dream meant, but this was...this was....oh, Krola, do you suppose it means something terrible is going to happen? I had the funniest feeling last night when we were saying the Prayer together. It was wonderful, and strange, and scary all at once, and I just knew today was going to be a different sort of time."

Krola nodded, looking more serious. "I know, Faya, I felt it too when Asorum told us that some people were here who needed our help. Now how in the world can we help anyone? We're not even allowed to...."

Faya broke in," You mean we aren't old enough? But Asorum told me once that age really didn't matter, so long as the intent was aimed in the right direction, or something like that. I don't remember his exact words, but I think I know what he was trying to tell me." Faya chewed a minute on her lower lip, then rose and stretched. "Well, if we sit here any longer we won't have time for a bath and breakfast, too, and all at once I'm starving!"

Krola grinned. "Fayasas, the human garbage can! But I'm hungry, too. Race you to the bath place. Last one in has to scrub a back!" The two girls shot out of the room and raced down the corridor. Krola was the first in the water, having torn off her sleeping gown on the way, and jumped into the foaming pool, sending up a huge spray of water. Faya stopped to remove her gown properly, but jumped into the pool as near Krola as she could, showering the other girl, and sending the water sliding over the floor of the room. The water was warm, coming as it did from some deep underground springs, a fracture in the earth where hidden fires kept the temperature almost at blood heat. It was constantly flowing, renewing the bathing pool almost hourly.

Krola tossed Faya the sponge and turned her back. "All right, all right, I get the message," Faya laughed as she started to wash her friend's back. Then suddenly serious, she dropped the sponge and fell back into the water, letting the warm scented foam come up to her chin. "Krola, I don't think I want any breakfast this morning." "But Faya..." Krola began. Faya interrupted her."Please, just let me sit here and think a little while. I can't get that dream out of my mind and I want to try to sort things out before I see anyone else. Please?"

Her friend stepped from the pool with a smile and reached for one of the soft drying sheets that hung on the row of hooks on the wall. "All right, Faya. I'll be in the reading room. There won't be classes today, but I want to look up something." She dressed quickly. "I'll see you later after breakfast." Krola looked for a long moment at her friend, then quietly left the room. Faya sat perfectly still, letting the water foam gently around her. The terror she had felt earlier was gone, but questions remained. What had frightened her? Why had she been so terrified? Who or what was chasing her? What did the dream mean? Taking a deep breath, she willed her body to relax. As the tension slowly went out of her shoulders and neck, she stilled her mind. Closing her eyes, she pictured the secret place where she had gone so often to make decisions. Her body remained in the warm pool of water, but in her mind she was under the trees on her special rock. There, she could talk to the spirits of the woods, the beings who surrounded that special place and who had given her such a joyous welcome.

"Help me," she whispered. "I don't know what to do and I'm frightened." Slowly, the peace she always felt here seeped into the fabric of her being, and the music only she seemed to be able to hear once again worked its magic. Her mother had told her it was music from Long Ago and Far Away, but Faya had never really understood. Now, she decided, I will just listen and not try to analyze; maybe I'll learn what this is all about.

+ + + + +

Above her, the small bit of sky that shone through the heavy leafy canopy was warm and sunny. The moss under her hand had crept over the rock until the hard granite was softened; birds flew from branch to branch, busily carrying food to the young fledglings who demanded with wide open mouths. Their chirping blended with the unheard but very real music until Faya was not entirely sure which was which. Her mind, now calm and open to whatever came, was filled with the wonder of her world, the scent of the air, the vibrant colors of the leaves, the feel of the moss, the brilliance of the rock when the shaft of sun lit it. The music swelled until she felt she must burst with the beauty of it.

Then the pictures formed, swirling at first and ethereal; they reminded her of a column of smoke she had once seen in the distant City...form that had no form. But slowly, they began to take a more solid shape. Her closed eyes saw men and women running; she heard children crying; there was a fire that suddenly burst forth in angry redness, consuming everything in its path. Water, angry, swirling water, met the fire and the billowing steam rose so far above the horizon that the scenery was blanked out. Even her beloved rock place seemed to be in danger, and without thinking, Faya cried out aloud and started violently. Immediately, she opened her eyes and found herself in the bathing pool, again shaking with fright, and a little disoriented.

She stood up, stumbled, caught herself on the rim of the pool, and stood there for a moment, trying to shake off the sudden dizziness. She stepped out and groped blindly for the drying sheet. Wrapping it around her, she left the room and ran back to her own sleeping room, where Dohnnie found her half an hour later, huddled on her pallet, still wrapped in the sheet.

"My dear, whatever is the matter?" The woman took the still shivering girl in her arms and rocked her gently. "Krola sent me to find you;. She was worried. We all were. What frightened you so? Can't you tell me?" Faya could only shake her head and burrow deeper into the safety of the woman's arms. "All right, Faya, I'll stay here with you for a little while. It was probably only a dream...Krola wouldn't tell me what it was, only that you had been crying. But a dream can't hurt you, not if you know it is a dream." Dohnnie started to hum softly, and soon she felt Faya begin to relax.

Finally she gave a great sigh and sat up. "Oh, Dohnnie, I'm so ashamed, I never meant to be such a baby, and after Asorum gave me permission to start the new studies. And after we were told to help the Visitors. What will he think of me!" The woman smiled. "The same as he always has. Everyone has something, sometimes, that frightens them. But Faya, you know how to handle dreams. They are only...." Faya interrupted her. "But Dohnnie, it wasn't the dream that frightened me so much, although it was pretty awful. I saw a terrible picture when I was in the bathing pool - not a dream - I wasn't asleep at all - it was much worse than the dream I had last night. I saw such a picture of horror" She shivered again.

Realizing that the girl was still in the grip of a waking nightmare,

Dohnnie knew it was time to go to Asorum. Only the older priests were trained to go into another's mind and cleanse the sickness that could lie hidden until the body became too ill to cope with reality.

Chapter Thirteen

Faya walked slowly through the entrance hall onto the porch which wrapped around the great Temple. It was early afternoon, and she had eaten nothing at all this day. The two hours she had spent with Asorum and another of the older priests were not entirely clear in her mind, but she felt a great sense of relief. But why couldn't she remember what had just been said? It was as if she were trying to grasp a shadow in her hand, and as all shadows do, this one simply wouldn't stand still to be held.

Sensing rather than hearing someone behind her, she turned to find Dohnnie smiling at her, and carrying a bowl in her hands. "Here, Faya, I've brought you some of the soup we had for lunch. You missed the noon meal, and you must be hungry. Let's take it out to the Children's Garden, shall we?" Without giving the girl a chance to reply, the woman led the way down the broad steps and around the side of the Temple. Entering the open gate of the garden, she set the bowl down on a table and pulled a bench up for seating. Faya stumbled slightly, then caught the edge of the table and lowered herself onto the bench. The bowl was still steaming, and hunger suddenly took over. She lifted the spoon and began to eat greedily. Dohnnie sat quietly until the first pangs had been satisfied.

"Are you feeling better, now?" she asked. Faya nodded, "yes, thank you. I didn't realize I was so hungry. What time is it?" She squinted up through the trees at the sun. "Is there something the matter with me? I can't seem to remember just what happened. I know I was talking with Asorum and Basliri, but for some reason, I can't remember what it was about. And why did I miss the noon meal?" Realizing that the young girl was still upset, Dohnnie pushed the now empty bowl aside and folded her arms on the table. "Faya, you had a very unhappy experience last night. Do you remember anything about it? Your dreams, I mean, and the vision you had this morning when you were in the bath?"

Faya shook her head. "No, I can't . I mean I think I do, but when I try to, it goes away. I just remember being frightened."

Dohnnie nodded. "You had a right to be frightened. It was a hard thing for anyone to go through, but it's over, and you need not ever have to remember it again."

"Dohnnie, what did happen? And why did Asorum and Basliri take me into one of the healing chambers? Am I sick? Please, Dohnnie, tell me what happened to me."

The woman sat silent for a long minute, then took a deep breath. "Child, I asked Asorum if I may talk to you about this, and he said to use my own judgement. I believe you are perfectly able to understand what I am going to say. You had a vision, a waking dream, if you choose to call it that, of an occurrence that has not yet happened. You know that sometimes Asorum or one of the older priests may 'read' a person's mind when there is a physical ailment that cannot be addressed simply through our medicines." Faya nodded, her eyes on the woman's face.

"Well, this time, there was something in your mind, something that you had seen or dreamed, that was hurting you physically. Remember, I found you curled up on your pallet, shaking with fear. That was totally unlike you, so I knew that since no one had actually hurt you, there must be something in your heart that the average healers here could not help. So I went to Asorum and asked his help."

Faya frowned slightly, then grinned, her old bounce already beginning to come back. "I guess if I am going to ever become a healer, I have to go through something like that. Is that why?" "No, honey, that is not at all why. I know that your music is often played without your actual remembrance, but this was the first time that you have shown us that you have another gift, that of being able to foresee something that may happen in the future. Many of us can do this, but usually not without training. You've had no training along these lines, so this is a true gift that you will learn to perfect. It's called 'clear seeing.' What you saw may or may not really happen, depending on what we can do about changing the shape of destiny. Nothing is written in stone, but predicted events can and do take place when nothing is done to alter their probable course. Do you understand at all what I am trying to tell you?"

Faya got up from the table and walked slowly over to one of the flowering shrubs that covered part of the wall. She absently picked a flower, inhaled its scent, then went back to the table.

"Yes, I think so. I 'saw' something that might happen. I don't remember exactly what it was - it's all sort of fuzzy - and the priests thought it might make me sick. Is that what you mean?" Dohnnie sighed. This was not going to be as easy as she had hoped, not without giving away more than she cared to.

"Not exactly, Faya. It was simply that the memory of a bad experience might cause more nightmares, and that would, of course, make you feel unhappy and frightened, and that is something Asorum would not permit. So he helped you relax and sleep for a bit, and gave you the suggestion that you would not remember it any more."

And that, thought the woman, is as far as I'm going to go today. She had no intention of letting the young girl know the immensity of tragedy that might possibly come if Faya's vision became reality. It would have been too heavy a burden for such a child to bear, so after Asorum and Basliri had discovered the entire sequence of events Faya had seen, they suggested she forget the incident and replace it with a more pleasant experience. She had obviously accepted the suggestion, since she both trusted and loved her mentors.

Faya gave one more deep sigh, then shrugged as if to leave the whole discussion right there on the table. “Thank you, Dohnnie. I feel all right now. Do you suppose there is any more soup? I’m still hungry.” They both laughed as Dohnnie gathered up the bowl and led the way back to the Temple. Later that afternoon Dohnnie sought out Asorum and learned the entire story. She felt her skin tighten and her heart beat fast as she listened to what Faya had really seen. Fortunately, the child had not remembered the details when she was awake, but under the wise old priest’s skillful and gentle probing, had painted a picture of such destruction that it was all the woman could do not to cover her ears. Her country, her world, gone mad, and her people facing a death worse than she could ever have imagined. When she and the priest were finished talking, Dohnnie’s face was streaked with tears, and her knees were shaking.

“Asorum, tell me, will this really happen? And why will it happen? And how can we prevent it? We must...we must stop this insanity.”

“Yes, Haindohne, we must stop this insanity,” the old priest repeated, “But at the moment I have not the least idea how it can be done.”

“But you do believe that what Faya saw was a true picture of what we are headed for?” The woman was still shaking, and her voice quivering as she spoke.

“I not only think, I know that the child is a true clairvoyant and her vision was absolutely correct. I have also had visions that were so close to hers that it is impossible for her to be mistaken.”

Dohnnie gasped. “You’ve seen the same thing? When? How long ago? Why wasn’t anyone told of this? Asorum, I can’t believe... oh, please, tell me. What have we done? Have we abandoned the Power? Has the Power abandoned us? Why must this happen?” She put her trembling hands over her face and slipped to the floor on her knees, rocking back and forth in pain and despair. Asorum leaned forward and gently took her hands.

"Dohnnie, look at me. We will do everything possible to avert this disaster, but I had to tell you. That's one reason the other priests were here at this time. They also had their seers who can see into the future, and while some of their visions were not quite as clear as Faya's, the ending was always the same. Destruction of our world; by fire, by earthquakes, and finally by flood." The old priest was quiet for a long moment, staring at his clasped hands. Finally he shook his shoulders and got up from the bench, leaving Dohnnie still on her knees on the floor. The woman was silently weeping, but Asorum walked past her, out into the open air. He stood looking at the far distant City, the white buildings shining in the clear bright air, the graceful towers spiraling upwards as though holding their arms up to the Creator, and the sparkle of the lakes shimmering beneath the late afternoon sky. Farther in the distance, he could see the great palace, where the king, nominally the head of the country, spent his days in unheard of luxury. He had his women, his great wealth shining around him, and the animals that had been brought from other countries for his pleasure. The king had abrogated his power and left Atlantis to be governed by the Judges.

A deep sigh tore a ragged breath from Asorum's chest, and he covered his face for an instant. "What can I do, Great One, to prevent this terrible thing that must happen? Help me, help me!" He didn't realize he had cried aloud until he felt a small hand reaching up for his arm. Looking down, he met the smiling face of one of the youngest students, who had been at the Temple only a few days. She was tiny, coming not much higher than the tassel that fell from his belt.

"Do you want to go down the steps, Sir?" asked the child. "I'll help you. Hold on to my hand." The tears he had been holding in so rigidly suddenly spilled, and he knelt down, put his arms around the child and buried his face in her hair. In an instant he had himself under control again, and stood, holding the little girl, and smiling sheepishly at both her and himself.

"Thank you, child. I really did need some help. These steps can be difficult when you reach my great age. But I believe I can manage it now. Would you like me to carry you down?"

"Yes, please. I really could do it, but it's a little bit hard, you know. I fell down yesterday and hurt my knee. Want to see where the blood came?" She wriggled around to lift one leg, showing a tiny almost healed scratch on one knee. "It really did hurt. But I didn't cry, at least, not very loud."

Asorum chuckled. "I'm sure you are a very brave little girl. Here we are. Did you want to go into the Children's Garden? I believe there may be some one there for you to play with." He set her down on the grass and patted her arm. "Run along now, your little friends are waiting for you." She gave him a delicious smile, bobbed a quick curtsy and ran off happily, the tiny hurt on her knee quite forgotten. 'Oh if we could all solve problems this easily,' thought the old priest. 'Well, no matter. We must do what we must do.' He turned to go back in, then stopped for one last look at the distant City. Once more he whispered, "help me, please, for her sake," then walked slowly back up the wide steps.

Chapter Fourteen

Faya was on her knees in the herb garden with Benai, carefully pulling aside the warm brown loam to expose the underground roots of a plant she was studying. Her hands were encased in thin white gloves, and she moved with caution.

"Benai, is this how this herb grows, with those awful looking white roots? They look sick." Her teacher smiled at her serious face. "Yes, Faya, they do look sick, but I can assure you, they are anything but! They are deadly. If one were to grind even one of those roots into a paste and apply to someone's skin, it would soon cause paralysis of the part it touched. Shortly after, a coma, and the lungs and heart would cease to function. Death would come slowly but surely. There is no known antidote. Please be careful...you must not ever, ever, touch that plant's roots without wearing gloves."

"But the plant itself is so pretty. Are the leaves and the flowers poisonous, too?"

"No, they are not. That is one reason it is so dangerous. It looks innocuous, and you can quite safely handle the plant. But never the roots. Study it carefully, Faya. We want no accidents." The girl nodded, still intent on memorizing the way the white tendrils crept just under the soil, their lack of color, and the way they spread. The plant was confined in its own bed, with a deeply imbedded border of stones around it to keep the roots within bounds.

The two had been working for several hours and Faya realized the sun was high in the sky. "Isn't it time for the noon meal, Benai? I'm hungry."

The priest laughed. "Yes, my little one, it is indeed time for the noon meal, and I have a surprise for you." Faya stood up, removed her gloves and waited expectantly. "We are going to have a picnic today, over by the pool." Almost on cue, two of the young students arrived bearing trays and pitchers of the special wine Benai loved. "How old are you, Faya?" The girl looked startled, then laughed delightedly. "Oh no! I had forgotten. Today is my birthday. Is this a party for me?"

"Yes, it is. You've been with me for over two years now, and you have applied yourself so well that I decided you needed a small reward. So, we are going to have a picnic, with everything I know you like best."

"Even wine?" she asked mischievously.

"Even wine," he answered.

Faya led the way past the garden beds they had been working in to the small central pool. Benai had had two chairs placed for them to relax on, and pulled up a small table between them. "Your glass, madam," he said grandly.

The girl held the goblet out to be filled, and as she took her first sip, a delighted smile spread over her face. The wine was slightly sweet, heady and smooth. Faya knew she had been given a special honor, and raised her glass in salute, as she had seen the older priests do at special meals. Benai answered with his, and as the two slowly sipped the drink, she knew the long hours she had spent grubbing in the dirt, learning characteristics of plants, and the longer hours of study when her body cried out for rest, had finally been recognized.

She sighed. "Benai, I never had anything that tasted like this. May I have some more?"

"Certainly not! Eat your lunch now, or you won't be able to hold your head up this afternoon. This is a one-glass celebration, because you are still only fourteen, you know. When you are sixteen, I'll give you another taste." They both laughed, and Faya's healthy appetite made short work of the lunch.

"Benai, tell me more about your life before you came here. You always said you would, but we never seem to have time just to sit and talk."

The priest nodded. "I know I promised I would tell you about the land where I was born. Where shall I start?"

"When you were born," said the practical Fayasas.

"No, I think I had better start a little later. You know, of course, that I come from a land that has been called by various names. Black Land, Red Land, Land of Sand, and a lot of other names not so nice. It is very hot there, with little rainfall, but there is an area that is fertile and green, a beautiful place. Not too far from where my home is, or used to be, there is a very large figure of a lion with a human head that stands as though guarding a great secret. Faya, it is so enormous, so huge, that one cannot imagine it. It looks with blind eyes straight ahead, as if it were waiting for something or someone; and when the dawn light strikes it, one knows without doubt that the great Creator must have blessed its use. Who actually carved it I do not know, but it has been said that your people may have had a hand in it; perhaps teaching the mathematics of its structure, perhaps actually showing my people how to carve the stone, and where it should be placed on the bedrock. It is a very ancient Being, and it keeps its secret well." He stopped for a moment and took another sip of wine.

"Please, tell me more. I have never been anywhere but here, and I would love to see more of the world." Faya's eyes were intent on Benai's face, and she was drinking in every word. "When I was a child, a very small child, I used to help my father make little figures of mud. I didn't actually mold them, because I had not at that time had the training I would have needed, but I did carry trays of mud from the canal banks, so he would not have to walk so far. He and I would sit with our backs against the wall of our house, and he would tell me stories of the times when he was a boy. My mother had died when I was born, so there was just my father to take care of me." He looked across the garden for a long moment and Faya knew he was seeing with his mind, or perhaps with his heart, the father he had loved.

"Go on, please. How long did you stay there? You told me once you were sold when you were a child. Did your father die and leave you alone?" Faya's curiosity vied with her compassion, and she leaned forward so she could rest one elbow on Benai's knee.

"I don't know when my father died, but I can just remember a terrible year when our big river didn't rise as usual, and people had very little food. We had sold everything there was to sell, which wasn't much at that, and there was no way to feed me. So my father, may his soul live forever, offered me to the man who owned our house as a payment for rent, assuming that the landlord would train me to be a useful servant. Instead, the man in turn sold me to some traders who bought young boys, and took them out of the town where they lived. I never saw my father again."

Faya's eyes were wide with shock. "Oh, Benai, I never dreamed anything like that could happen. Where did you go? What happened to you after that?"

She was so distressed that the young priest decided to soften the story as much as he could. The life he had been forced into was not something he wanted this young innocent to hear, and indeed he wished he could forget it, himself. So he merely shrugged and said, "I was passed from one 'owner' to another, each making me work very hard, until I was old enough to escape from my bondage, which I did, by hiding on a ship and sailing out of my country forever." He took another sip of the wine, held the goblet up, admiring the color. "You know, Faya, this wine is very much the color of some of the wonderful materials I have seen in the bazaars...soft silks, rich brocades and the most beautiful gossamer shawls in the world. Someday, you must go to these places and see for yourself."

The girl nodded. "Yes, someday I would like to do that. But tell me more. Where did you go after you escaped? Did you ever have a chance to go home?"

Benai just shook his head. "No, Faya, I never went home again. There really wasn't any home left for me anyway. No family, no friends, so I drifted for a few years, making a living by my wits, and not a very good one at that, until I met a wonderful man, who saw a bitter, struggling young boy and took pity on him. He took me into his own home, taught me to read and write, taught me mathematics, then sent me to a school run by some of your own priests. Not here," he said hastily forestalling more questions. "It was in another part of the country. There I showed an aptitude for working with plants, so I slowly began to study these beautiful things that have come to mean so much to me. My teachers taught me what I am now teaching you. I was at the school for about ten years, then received my degree as a Healer."

He took another sip of his wine. "I can understand why you sometimes feel you are getting nowhere. I felt that way, too, at first. My teachers (and I had several) made me work very hard, but slowly I understood what they were trying to pound into my thick skull." He laughed ruefully. "I was much more rebellious than you could imagine, because I could not forget what had happened to me when I was younger."

Faya nodded. She could remember the betrayal she felt when her mother had brought her to the Temple. Benai continued, "then one day, my teacher sat me down and gave me a good talking to. He said that even though I had worked so hard to become a Healer, it was all going to be wasted. When I asked why, he said because I had not yet learned to forgive, and until I did, the bitterness would gnaw at my heart until I could no long function as a Healer for other people."

Faya frowned. "But how could he expect to forgive the man who took you from your father?"

Benai smiled gently. "That's what I said. And do you know what my teacher did? He made me sit before him on the floor, cross legged, and form a picture in my mind. I had to look at the face of that first man, the one who bought me, and smile at him. I had to hold that smile until I really felt it inside. Then I had to ask the man to forgive me."

Faya gasped. "Forgive you?" she asked, "but he was the one who should have asked...."

Benai stopped her. "I know, Faya, that's what I thought, too, at first. But I came to realize that what my teacher meant was that the man, brutal as he was, had also been made by the Creator, and if I believed that we were all made by the same Creator, I was a part of that man and he was a part of me. Does that make sense to you?"

"I don't know," she said slowly, still frowning. "That would be a very difficult thing to do."

"Yes," Benai answered, "it was hard. Very hard. But once I could do that, I was never again able to hold resentment or bitterness against any living person. What I was actually doing was forgiving myself for feeling such hatred for so many long years." He stretched and gave a big yawn. "Are you finished with your lunch?" She nodded. "Then let's get back to work."

They both rose, Faya again donning her gloves, and picking up the small trowel she had set down on the rim of the bed. Kneeling once more by the plants she had been studying, she patted the earth back over the area she had uncovered. "I wonder," she said over her shoulder to Benai, "if this plant knows just how dangerous it is, and what damage it could do. You told me it could kill, but can it also help someone?"

“Yes, Faya, there are times when this particular plant is most useful, to control spasms, for instance, providing the Healer knows exactly the dosage, and how to apply it. I have a long description of it with its use in an old book. I’ll get it out for you later if you’d like to read it.”

“Yes, I would. There’s so much to learn,” she sighed.

Chapter Fifteen

Several weeks later, Faya was in the Children's Garden, where she often took her small harp to play for her young charges. They were clustered around her, begging for more songs, and she was glad to oblige. She did not have a great voice, but it was clear and sweet, and well suited to the types of songs children like to sing. The tiny girl who had offered to help Asorum down the steps had cuddled as close as she could without interfering with the harp. She had become very attached to the older girl, and was the first to run for a kiss and a hug whenever Faya was given the care of the children for part of the afternoon's playtime.

Faya loved the times she could spend with the children, and willingly played for them. She taught them the songs she had learned, and often sat for an hour explaining the different plants, the birds, and the small furry animals that crept into the garden. This was a place of sanctuary, where no danger could come, and no fear existed. This was where Dohnnie had eased her pain when she was first at the Temple, and where she always felt closest to her mother.

The herb garden with the pool was a place for meditation and finding inner peace. The garden she worked in with Benai was fascinating, but she never felt quite at ease there. But here, in the Children's Garden, Faya was content to become a small child again, and to join her heart with the innocence of the little ones who needed and loved her. Today seemed like so many others. Music, laughter, the joyous knowledge that in this one place there was no need to pretend to be other than what one actually was. What was different? Why was there just a slight twinge of apprehension? Faya began another song, her fingers automatically playing the music she had started, but there was a small nagging question in the back of her mind.

“You play beautifully.” The voice came from behind her, and Faya swung around in surprise. She had not heard anyone come into the garden.

“Oh,” she said. “I’m sorry, I didn’t know anyone was listening; I sing only for the children.” She looked in wonder at the two men who stood watching her. They were dressed as priests, but she had not been told that there were visitors expected. She rose to her feet to make the usual bow, handing her small harp to one of the children. “Will you be seated, sirs? This garden is for the children, and I don’t want them to be deprived of their playtime.” She indicated a bench, and took up her harp again. The two men sat down and leaned back as if they intended to stay. Faya was a bit nonplused, but she started the song again, and the children, looking a little wary, picked up the melody. When the song was finished, Faya laid aside the harp. She was uncertain just what to do. This was the first time any grown-ups, except the teachers, had ever come into the Children’s Garden, and she wasn’t sure quite how to handle their intrusion.

“Would you like me to show you into the Temple?” she asked. “I”m sure Asorum will want to welcome you properly; or have you already seen him?”

The older of the two priests smiled and said, “There is time for that. We really were most anxious to see what you teach the children here. You see, we are from a southern province, and our temples are not so grand as this one. Our teachers cannot be quite as well paid as I’m sure yours are, so we want to upgrade our staff if we possibly can.” Faya noticed that his hands were covered with rings, which none of the Temple priests wore, and his robe was just a little too rich looking.

“Upgrade, sir? I don’t understand.”

“What he means, my dear,” the younger of the two broke in, “is that we need to see how your teaching staff compares with ours, and what the curriculum is...what classes you teach, how long your pupils are in school during the day, and especially what the very youngest students are taught to begin with."

Faya's anxiety increased. There was something about these two men that bothered her. She didn't at all like the way the men kept looking at the children, nor the way the children responded by gathering around her as if they were uneasy. A tiny element of fear had entered the garden for the first time.

She was saved from any more questions by the arrival of Haindohne, who had come to bring the usual snacks at this hour. Faya introduced her, not knowing the priests' names, but merely telling the woman where they were from. She was greatly relieved when Dohnnie explained to the men that this garden was sacred to the children, and she would appreciate their leaving and coming into the Temple proper. She was polite, but firm, and the men rose at once. They said they could not stay, but would come back at a later date and go through the Temple and the class rooms. When they had left, Dohnnie stood looking pensive. "Faya, what did these men want? They are dressed as priests, yet something tells me they are not. What did they ask you?" Faya, too, was upset. She had felt there was something not just right, but she was not able to explain even to herself why she felt that way. She sat the children at the tables and gave them their snacks. Then she and Dohnnie moved over to another quieter place in the garden where they could talk without upsetting the younger ones. "Dohnnie, I really don't know why, but I don't like them. They said they were priests, and they must be from a poorer community, because they told me they couldn't pay their teachers as much as we do, but did you notice all the rings one of them was wearing?"

"Yes, Faya, I did notice. And you are right, I'm sure. They either were not really priests, or they are from some group we know nothing about. None of ours would have acted that way. They should have gone first to the Temple proper and asked for either Asorum or the head caretaker. What did they ask you?" Faya thought for a moment. "They wanted to know what we were teaching, how long the children were in classes; things like that. But I didn't tell them anything." She put her hands on her hips and said, "What gave them the right to come into the Children's Garden and act as if they owned the place!"

Dohnnie laughed briefly at Faya's reaction, then sobered. "I think we had better find out more about these men. Were the children frightened?"

"I think they were, just a little. They didn't seem to want to go near them, and they stuck pretty close to me while the men were here."

"Well, my dear, let the children finish, then bring them in. I know it's a little early, but they won't realize it, and we will see that they get more play time tomorrow." She picked up the tray she had brought the food in, and walked back to the Temple, going immediately to Asorum. When she had told him the whole story, he looked at first puzzled, then more serious than usual.

"You are saying that neither you nor Faya think they were really priests?" he asked.

"I'm not at all sure. I only saw them for a minute or two. They left right away when I asked them to, and nothing was actually said that gave me the impression they were not true priests. But," she stopped then continued, "for some reason, they just didn't ring true. Faya noticed that they were wearing a lot of jewelry. Not that there's anything wrong with that, but they had said their temple was poor." She sighed. "It's a puzzle. Who are they, and what did they really want? And why the children first?"

Asorum looked grim. "I can think of several answers to those questions, none of which I like. How old is Faya now?"

"She's just past fourteen. Why?"

"How long has it been since she has seen her father?" Dohnnie looked bewildered for a second or two. "Oh, no, surely he wouldn't come here. It's been ten years, she was just four when her mother brought her to the Temple."

Asorum shook his head. "No, I don't really think he would take such a chance, but he might well have sent someone to find out about his daughter, and to judge whether the children could be reached. If you remember, the group that was here two years ago said the Judges were trying to convince the people that their children should be sent to a public school (run by them, of course) and at the same time, trying to discredit our way of life." He heaved a great sigh. "Well, Haindohne, it is up to us and our people to see that this can never happen. Faya is very perceptive, and she must be warned that there could be a real danger here. I don't want to frighten her. She's still such a child, but she does have a way of getting information out of me! More than I want to give her sometimes. Let's not say anything about this to any of the students. I'll talk to the men and women here, and we'll all keep an eye on things. But for now, there really isn't anything we can do. We don't know enough at present."

He patted her shoulder and left her, shaking his head at the thoughts that crept into his mind. Dohnnie went back to the Children's Garden, to find Faya picking up the empty plates. "I came back to give you a hand, but I see you're ahead of me." She smiled at the girl and gave her a hug. "Don't worry, child, everything will be all right. I've told Asorum what happened, and he is going to look into the matter as best he can."

Faya returned the hug and the two walked back to the Temple,

Dohnnie to teach a class, and Faya to practice an hour or so before the evening blessing.

Chapter Sixteen

Working, studying, practicing, and learning all she could about the healing herbs kept Faya busy for the next few years. For months after Rab's visit she had watched every visitor who came to the Temple, but had not seen any who had been with his group. Several times she had asked Dohnnie or Asorum if there had been any word from him, but neither could give her the news she waited for, that Rab would be coming back. She had entirely forgotten the two men who had come unbidden and unwanted into the Children's Garden, nor had either Asorum nor Dohnnie mentioned them again.

One early spring day, Faya was asked to come to the lower level of the Temple where the healing rooms were. She had not been there since the day Asorum and Basliri had helped her sleep, and had wiped the memory of her terrible vision from her conscious mind. She was met at the foot of the stairs and led to a room she had never seen. The priest waiting for her was one who taught a class on the medicinal herbs, but since she had been studying only with Benai, she had not really known this man. He held open the door and indicated she was to enter.

"You are Fayasas?" It was a question rather than a statement. The girl bowed briefly and straightened up.

"Yes, sir, I am."

"And your mother was Kadah, who was a student here at one time?"

"Yes, sir," Faya replied.

"I am called Ranoi. I have heard how you have progressed with Benai, and I asked permission to have you study with me for a while. Please look at this." he said, indicating a strange looking piece of equipment that sat near the wall.

Faya looked where he pointed. There was a stone bench, about four feet wide and deep enough to use comfortably as a seat. On it, driven into the stone itself, were two thin silver rods, about an inch and a half apart, each about the width of her little finger. They were curved slightly, and extended about two feet above the stone seat. Attached to the rods were two wings that flared out a little more than a foot on each side, made of the same metal as the rods, and strung from the top of the wings to the bottom were very thin wires.

Faya looked at the priest questioningly. “Sir, what is this?”

Ranoi answered with a smile, “Faya, suppose you sit on the bench, and lean back against the two rods.” She did as he suggested. The rods were curved to fit the curve of her spine. She wriggled a bit until she felt comfortable, then asked, "Like this?”

Ranoi went behind her and picked up a thin metal wand. Without answering, he struck one of the wires that strung the wings, and Faya felt an electric tingle run through her body. She sat forward in surprise. Ranoi laughed gently at her startled look and began to explain.

“Faya, this instrument is used to re-tune the body. You know everyone has ‘centers’ in their bodies that respond to emotions. When these centers are out of balance, when the emotions are out of control and the body feels ill, sometimes the medicines we make here are not what is needed. Sometimes we have to help a sick person sleep so the mind can be helped. Sometimes we have to soothe the physical body, and ease the emotional turmoil that can cause illness. Generally it can be done with the herbal oils massaged into the skin while music and incense are used as additional aids. But there are times when a stronger, more intense modality is called for, and this instrument is very helpful.”

Faya turned on the bench and ran her fingers across the wire strings. “It’s very like my harp, isn’t it?” she commented.

“Yes, very like it, and the results are surprisingly similar. You know how often you have been asked to play when someone is ill. Well, the use of this instrument simply augments the response the human body feels when a string on the harp is plucked at the correct tone. Did you know that your harp music was a great healing aid?"

"Dohnnie told me the sick people like it."

"It's much more than just liking it. There is something about the vibration of a string that is amplified when the back is held against the rods here. It is like your sounding board; if you put your hand on it when the harp is being played, you can feel the vibrations go through your hand, can't you?"

Faya nodded. "And sometimes up into my arm." The priest smiled. "That's the whole idea, my dear. This intensifies the vibrations and the body is very quick to respond. I would like to teach you to use this, because you already have a command of the harp, and this is so like it. Not everyone is as sensitive to vibratory sounds as you seem to be, so would you like to be my pupil for a while?"

Faya looked down at the floor. Then she slowly looked around the room, which she had not really examined. In the corner was a small fireplace, which had no fire in it at the moment. In another corner was a brazier on a tripod, a hook on the wall that held a robe, and a ewer standing beside the brazier.

Her mind was whirling, her body still slightly tingling from the touch of the rods when the wire had been struck, and she wondered if this was something she could handle. Ranoi did not press her for an answer, realizing that the idea would take a bit of getting used to. Finally she looked up at him and asked, "Why did you ask about my Mother?"

"Because she was also studying with me just before she left to go with your father. You two are so very much alike. I think you will do very well with this."

"But I am not at all like my Mother. Her eyes are blue and she has light hair. And she...." Faya stopped suddenly, as if she had just realized that she had not seen her mother in so many years, and her memories might not be as accurate as she would have liked.

Ranoi smiled. "I didn't mean that you looked so much like her, although you really do, you know. You have the same shape face and smile. But you are alike inside. She was a splendid musician, and very gentle with children. I have watched you for some time, and again I tell you that you and your Mother are very much alike."

Faya suddenly smiled at him, and her face lit up. "If you think I am like my Mother, I would like to study with you. I haven't seen her since I was four, and I have often wondered if I remembered her as she really is. She was so beautiful, and she always smelled so nice."

Ranoi laughed. "I'm sure she is still beautiful, and I've noticed that women who find a perfume they like seldom change it. But to more prosaic matters; if you will come here every afternoon, I believe you could soon learn to handle this instrument. I know you work with Benai in the mornings, and this will leave you very little time for recreation, but you will enjoy it, I'm sure, knowing that you are helping those in need."

Faya smiled again. "Yes, I think I will. But how does anyone know just which string to strike? With the harp, I can hear what I play. If I were to hit the wrong string here, would I hurt the patient?" It was the first time Faya had ever used that word, and it slipped out so easily that Ranoi smiled to himself. She is already a healer, he thought. I was right to ask for her.

"This is something that you will learn as we go along. There is so much more to healing than just making the patient feel better. There must be a deep probing to find what is really wrong. We have priests whose talents allow them to do just that. Some of the women priests are skilled in finding the lives their patients have lived before, and bringing the problems out from under the dark cloak that we all use to hide things we don't want to remember. You will not be asked to do that for a long time, but you will be taught to follow the instructions of those who can put their energies into finding the right strings, as you put it." Faya sat rather suddenly on the stone bench. She didn't lean back, this time. "Can I really do this?" she whispered, feeling as though she had been offered a gift but almost afraid to accept it.

"My dear, I would not for a minute ask you to study a field too hard for you. I know how hard you have worked with Benai, and I also have asked Asorum about your progress in other fields, the touch you have with children, your music, your stubbornness when you set your mind on something...."

Faya interrupted him indignantly. "I'm not stubborn!" "No?" he asked.

"Well, not very," she grinned. "It's just that sometimes I want to do something and other things get in my way."

"Yes, I know. I think they often do, particularly when I am trying to treat a patient who needs help but won't cooperate. You'd be surprised how many people want to be healed, but are unwilling to really work at it. They are the ones who expect us healers to do everything, while they eat the wrong things, drink too much, forget to give thanks for what they have, and are just generally like spoiled children." He sighed. "We get all kinds here at the Temple, but we have to remember why we chose to work here, to do the very best we can for those who ask our help."

Faya nodded. "You won't let me hurt anyone, will you? You see, when I am learning about the herbs from Benai, I am not actually doing anything with or for anyone else. If I were to eat one of the poisonous herbs, I would be hurting only me. But if I don't know exactly which vibration would help a patient, I might do more harm than good."

Ranoi took her hand and held it while he looked her in the face. "Fayasas, I assure you, you will not be expected to go beyond your knowledge and experience. Now don't worry about it any more. I will expect you tomorrow afternoon." He dropped her hand and indicated that the interview was over. Faya bowed and left the room, feeling as though she had been swung out over a chasm on a rope that just might not hold her.

As she usually did when she was troubled, she lay on her pallet that night and silently called her mother. "Am I getting into something too deep for me?" she asked.

The answer came, as she had expected. "Oh Faya, why do you question your abilities? My darling, you are perfectly able to do anything you really want to do. You are such a very special person, and I have no doubt at all that you will be very good as a healer."

"But Mother, you always tell me that. I mean, that I can do anything. But you're my Mother...."

"Child, listen to me." The interruption was firm. "When I knew you were in my womb, I asked the Power for the privilege of raising a special child. Somehow I felt that I would have only one, and when you were born, I knew in my soul that you were a rare gift from the Creator. I also knew I must do everything I could to see that my gift was given every opportunity to grow to its full potential. I have always tried to guide you, even if we were apart. Faya, I know you. I know what you can do. I also know that right now you are feeling bewildered, that events have happened very quickly, that you are unsure of yourself. But Faya, I tell you that you are quite able to tackle this new challenge, if you really want to. You will never be forced to invest your time and energies in something that you are not suited for. So go to sleep, ask for a dream to help you decide, and in the morning, you'll find you have made your decision and it will be the right one."

Faya sighed again, and whispered aloud, "all right, Mother." Krola, who was trying to get to sleep on the other pallet, turned on her side facing her friend and muttered sleepily, "Faya, who are you talking to??"

"No one, Krola. Go to sleep."

"But I heard you say something. Are you having bad dreams again?"

"No, Krola, I'm fine. I was just talking to my mother."

Krola sat up in alarm. "Faya, what are you talking about? Your mother isn't here. I'm going to call Dohnnie." She slid off her pallet and stood up.

Faya laughed and reached out for her. "Honestly, you are the biggest worrier I know. Lie down and go back to sleep. I always talk to my mother at night, only I forgot and spoke out loud. I'm sorry, I didn't mean to scare you."

Krola stared at her. "You mean you can talk to someone who is not here? Really?"

Faya nodded. "Yes, but only my Mother. She and I have always done this, only I don't usually forget and speak so anyone can hear me. I try to remember that others don't always know how to communicate silently. Sorry I startled you."

Krola shook her head, lay back down on her pallet and then raised up on one arm. "Faya, do you ever wish you had a room to yourself? I mean, am I in your way here?"

"No, of course not. You're my best friend, and you know it! To be honest, I have always felt that you were my sister. Remember how you stood up for me when I first came here? I was so scared at being in such a strange place, and I didn't know why my mother had left me. You were so good to me."

"Oh, Faya, I knew what it was like, too. I was only a year older than you, and both my parents were dead, so you meant as much to me as I did to you."

"I've never asked you, but how did your parents die? They must have been so young."

Krola lay back down and put her arms under her head. "Well, I can barely remember them, but I know they died in a fire. Our house was on a hill, I believe, and one night it was very windy. We had several servants and one of them spilled something in the kitchen and it caught fire. The wind was so strong it whipped the flames over the house before they could be stopped. My father got me out and he and mother went back to try and save my older brother. But they didn't get out in time. I was taken in by a neighbor and then brought here. I've often wondered what he would have been like, my brother, I mean."

Faya gasped, "Oh, Krola, I had no idea you had gone through such a tragedy. I'm so sorry I asked."

"Don't be, Faya, I don't really remember my family and I have had so many wonderful years here. You all have become my family, you know." She sat up suddenly. "How did you learn to talk to your mother like that? Can anyone learn?"

Faya said slowly, "I honestly don't know how I do it. I just sort of open my mind and my Mother comes in. Benai seemed to think that one could be trained to talk silently, but I never asked him how. I know both he and Asorum can. I've caught them reading my thoughts more than once." She chuckled. "And sometimes, I wish they couldn't. Rab could, too. When do you suppose he will come back?" Krola rolled over on her side.

"Rab? You haven't mentioned him in such a long time I thought maybe you had forgotten all about him."

Faya said seriously, "Oh no, Krola. He promised he would come back, and I know he will someday, whenever he can."

"I hope he will, Faya." She yawned. "I'm sleepy. Talk to you in the morning." She was almost immediately asleep, but Faya lay awake for some time, reviewing the day, still a little worried about taking on a new duty, and not at all sure of her ability to become a proper healer. Finally she decided to ask for a dream to help her decide. Once she had made the request to her subconscious, she relaxed and in a few minutes was sleeping soundly. If she dreamed, she did not remember it upon waking, but felt strangely peaceful and sure of herself.

Chapter Seventeen

That next morning she bathed, ate breakfast, and presented herself to Benai at the earliest moment she could, anxious to tell him of her new teacher and to describe the strange piece of equipment she was to learn how to use. She found to her surprise that Benai already knew of his pupil's new studies, and was familiar with the instrument she was to learn to use.

"Oh, Benai, can't I ever surprise you?" she grinned at him in mock despair.

"Well, I will be surprised if you even remember your name today. I know it's always exciting to start a new project. But you must not neglect your other studies, and I've been meaning to ask you: how much exercise are you getting these days? Besides crawling around on the ground looking for herb roots?" He grinned back at her, knowing how little regard Faya had for getting really dirty if it meant finding out something she didn't know. "Plenty," she answered. "You try taking care of small children who insist on your doing everything they do! Really, Benai, I do get enough exercise, and I take long walks by myself sometimes. I have a special place. I go there when I want to work something out in my mind, and it can be quite a hike. It's through the woods back of the Temple, but I won't tell you anything more. It's secret."

"Then I won't ask you anything more," he replied with a smile."I know all about secret places, too. I also have one, and I won't tell you anything more, either." They laughed together, then sobered while Benai explained the properties of a herb Faya was studying. The morning passed quickly, as did most of the hours they spent working together. Benai had become so much a part of Faya's life that she could not imagine a day without his company. They were a team, teacher and student, but also friends. From then on, the mornings belonged to Benai and the afternoons to Ranoi. The few precious hours Faya could take with the children became more and more dear to her. The youngest one, whose name was Ceki, became her shadow. When the time came to go out to the Children's Garden, Ceki would hurl herself at Faya, demanding to be picked up and hugged, chattering away like a young birdling just learning how to chirp. The laughter, the songs and the play time became Faya's release from the heavy study load she carried.

She was fast maturing into a lovely young woman, never as tall as she would have liked to be, and to her sorrow, hair and eyes staying the same dark color. But on the whole she was fairly well pleased with the way she looked. She carried herself well, her back straight, and she had a habit of looking directly at the person she was talking to, not at all aware that this could be a bit disconcerting to some. She was completely herself, not a selfish bone in her body, willing to give of her time and energy whenever she was needed, but always keeping a part of herself separate from the rest of her world. Even Krola, her closest friend, did not know of the torments Faya sometimes faced when sleep would not come and the memories crowded in. Shaleen probably came the closest to understanding her friend, but even she was not allowed past a certain barrier Faya had thrown up for protection. She had slowly learned the stories of her friends, why they were at the Temple, and who would eventually go home and who might stay. Dohnnie had told her that she had come as a teenaged girl, because she loved teaching, and intended to stay at the Temple until she married. With a grin that was almost a self-mocking grimace, she qualified that statement by saying she would marry if and when she found the right man.

Shaleen had been left at the Temple by a mother who could not care for her baby when her husband died suddenly, leaving her with very little for herself and the child. She came to visit her daughter whenever she could. Faya had envied her friend the personal contact with her mother, and Shaleen had tried to include her friend in the few visits her mother made. She, more than any of the others, understood what Faya had gone through.

Most of the students would leave when they had finished their schooling. For a long time, Faya could not understand why they were allowed to go to the City on special occasions, while she was not. Haindohne had tried to explain without bringing Faya's father too much into the story, but finally had to ask Asorum's help. He had told Faya when he felt she was old enough to understand, and she seemed to accept his explanation, but for some time she felt set apart.

As much as she loved her work and her studies, she sometimes felt restless, without knowing why. More and more she found herself thinking about the young priest who had promised to come back for her one day. When the restlessness became intolerable, she would go to her special place and try to reason things out. And it was there that Rab found her, on a summer day when she was 17, huddled on her beloved rock, her arms cradling her head, and swaying softly back and forth as if in pain. At the sound of his steps she raised her face and looked at him blindly. She shook her head slightly, then again buried her face in her arms. He stooped beside her and put one hand on her arm.

"Faya," he said softly, "it's really me. I told you I would come back. Please, look at me." At his touch she shuddered once, then looked up into his face. Her own face crumpled and she burst into tears.

"Oh Rab, I waited so long!" Then she was in his arms and he was holding her, murmuring endearments and trying to calm her almost frantic gasping for breath.

All she could do was cry his name over and over. He just rocked her for a moment or two until he could feel her body relax. “Honey, what is it? Are you so unhappy?”

“Oh, no, Rab, not now! I was just...I was....” she stopped, trying to find the right words. “I don’t know, Rab. I sometimes come here when I’m lonely, I guess.” She sat up suddenly and pushed his arms away. “Rab! How did you know where I was? Nobody knows this place but me. Not even Krola. I never told anyone about it.”

The young man laughed. “Faya, my little innocent, you forget that we think as one. Didn’t you ask me years ago how I could know what you were thinking? I merely tuned in to your thoughts until I came here.”

Faya grinned up at him. “That’s cheating! Do you mean that I could never keep a secret from you? It’s not fair!” Then she sobered. “Really, Rab, I’m so glad you are here. I’ve wanted you to see my special place. Are you going to be here a long time? Please say you are.” She pulled his arms around her again and nestled against his shoulder. They settled down on the rock, the moss soft beneath them and the one stray beam of sun lighting Rab’s red-gold hair. For the moment words were unnecessary, both content just being together. After a long moment, Rab turned her face up and kissed her gently. She drew back for a startled instant, then sighed, “Again, please.”

The second kiss was much more satisfactory, long and lingering. Rab moved his lips to her eyes, her cheeks, her throat and again to her mouth. Knowing that Faya had never been intimate with any man, Rab held her gently away from him. When she moved to come closer, he smiled and said, “Wait, Faya. I promised I would bring you something. Don’t you want to see it?”

“You remembered? Of course I want to see it. What did you bring me? Is it from your part of Atlantis? I mean up north where you live?”

“No, darling, it is not from Atlantis at all. It is from a place far to the east of here, where some great mines are." He reached into a pocket of his robe and pulled out a string of blue polished nuggets, each one separated from the next by a tiny gold rondel. The clasp was also of gold, intricately woven into a double knot. She gasped. "Rab, they are beautiful! I've never seen anything like this. But I don't know the stone. What is it called?"

"The people who mine it call it the sky stone. They say that the tiny bits of black matrix represent the stars while the blue is of course the color of the sky. I found it in a bazaar, and knew at once it was yours."

"Put it on for me, Rab." She held it out for him, then turned her back so he could fit the clasp. When it lay around her throat, she again snuggled up to her young priest. "Thank you, Rab. I'll always wear it."

"And one day, Faya, you will give it to our daughter. And she will in turn give it to her daughter, and then to her daughter, so down through the ages that blue necklace will speak of the great love Rab the priest had for a young girl named Harp-of-the-Winds."

Faya nodded, too content for a minute even to speak. Then his words sank into her consciousness and she sat up. "Our daughter? But...."

"Faya, don't you know, haven't you always known, that you and I are going to be married and live a long, long life together? We will travel and see the wonderful world that is out there, waiting." Faya shivered suddenly. It was if a cold wind had all at once blown across her, and she was shaken. "What is it, Faya?" Rab asked. "Did I say too much? I've been wanting to tell you that ever since I first met you, but you were so young, and I knew I was to be gone so long."

"Oh, Rab, it's nothing. I don't know why I suddenly felt so cold. I'm really all right. Please tell me more about your travels, where you've been, why you were gone so long, and how long you will be here. And tell me about the great mines where my necklace came from."

"Questions, questions! All right, let's see, first the necklace. There is a city where artisans work in gold and colored stones. They have bazaars where these things are sold, as well as many other objects. You've seen some of the lovely things in Benai's rooms, haven't you?"

Faya nodded. "Yes, I have. Go on, tell me more."

"The stones are mined in great sheets, and then cut and polished by hand. It is painstaking work, and the artisans are truly gifted. They start as small children, which is not always such a nice thing to have happen to you if you are the child, but as they grow older, some places allow them to make a living cutting the stones. But unhappily, sometimes they are kept in bondage so long that they really never have any life of their own. I have always made it a practice never to buy anything from those who keep children as slaves."

"Benai told me once a long time ago that he had been sold as a slave," Faya said slowly, "but I don't think I ever truly realized that children are forced to work like that."

Rab sighed. "My dear, there are much worse lives led by some of these children. They are sold into all kinds of trades, some I will never tell even you about. That is one thing we are trying to stop, without much success, I'm afraid. Girl babies have a particularly hard time in some of the eastern countries. Many are abandoned by their mothers or fathers who want sons. These girls are sometimes taken by traders, but more often, just left to die. Our priests have set up places in many of the countries where children are raised under at least a little more humane condition, and married to decent men when they are old enough."

Faya shuddered. "What a terrible life they must have. I mean the ones who are sold. I'm so lucky that my Mother had the Temple to bring me to, even if I thought for a long time I had done something really bad so my father didn't want me at home." She hastened to add, "Asorum told me why, so it's all right now. Only I still wish my Mother could come here. Or that I could go home once in a while."

Rab gathered her more closely and started rocking her gently. "I know, Faya, I know. But for the time being, at least until we are married, Asorum doesn't dare let you go into the City alone, not even with the other students, because there is always the possibility that one of the Judges will find out and manage somehow to take you to your father."

Faya grinned up at him. "You said...do you mean that after I'm married no one can touch me? I mean, no one can make me do anything...I mean...oh, Rab, hurry up and marry me."

"Just so you can go to the City? Fine reason to get married!"

"You know very well that's not what I meant. You are trying to confuse me!"

He laughed. "Faya, it's always a temptation to tease you because you take things so seriously. Honey, I want to marry you this very minute, but I have a feeling that Asorum and your mother may have a few things to say about it first."

Faya heaved a great sigh, then snuggled against Rab again. "I suppose I will just have to be patient. But Rab, can we at least tell them? I want everyone to know what a wonderful, handsome husband I will have."

Rab made a mock face. "So now you are marrying me just for my looks. And here I thought it was for my upstanding character. Sure it isn't for the blue beads?"

She punched him hard in the ribs with her elbow and when he winced, she gasped. "Oh, Rab, did I hurt you? I'm so sorry...I didn't mean to...let me see...are you all right?"

He laughed, but it was a choked sort of laugh. "Faya, I'm all right, just a little sore. There was a slight altercation yesterday." She interrupted,

“A what?” He smiled ruefully. “An altercation, a fight, and I didn’t get the best of it. In fact, if it hadn’t been for some of my friends, I might not have been here to give you that necklace. No, honestly, I’m fine now.” Faya was trying to pull his robe open to see where she had punched him. He was trying to fend her off with one hand and keep his robe around him with the other.

Finally in exasperation, she said, “honestly, Rab, you forget that I’m studying to be a healer. Now let me look and see what’s hurt.” He relaxed and let her open the robe. When she saw the ugly gash running across the lower ribs, she blanched. The wound was raw and oozing, and she knew what pain he must have been in.

“We are going to the Temple right this minute. I can at least dress that and make it more comfortable, and one of the Healers will help it to get well very soon.” She stood up and pulled at his arm. “Come on, Rab, the sooner we get it fixed the better.” The old imperious manner she had tried so hard to overcome suddenly took over, and Rab shook his head in disbelief. “I thought I was marrying a sweet young thing that would let me be the boss, but I see I was wrong.”

She was impatient. “Oh, Rab, not now. I want to get that rib looked after, then you can tease me all you want.” She began to hurry along the path through the woods, and he caught up and put one arm around her. “My darling girl, not so fast! Another few minutes won’t make any difference, and I do want to be sure we are right in telling anyone what our plans are, such as plans go, since we really haven’t made any.”

She stopped so suddenly that he nearly fell against her. “Rab, tell me you really love me and want to marry me.”

“Faya. I’ve always loved you, and I’ve wanted to come back here as quickly as I could, but I had to let you grow up a little first. I would have been taking advantage of a child if I had come any sooner. You are what, seventeen?" She nodded. "And I am twenty-four. Not a great age difference, but I've been so many places and done so many things that sometimes I feel a million years older."

"And you will tell me all about it one of these days, but right now, I want you to see Ranoi. He's one of my teachers and a great Healer."

They were by now on the sloping lawn that led up to the great entrance of the Temple. Faya ran on ahead to alert her teacher that he had a patient, a very special patient, and Rab walked more slowly after her. When he had arrived at the Temple he had gone at once to look for Faya, forgetting that he had not eaten since the night before, and at the moment was a little weak from loss of blood. Now he was feeling tired and sore. He was met by a young woman whose sympathy shone in her face, and led down to one of the healing rooms. Faya was already there, spreading a clean cloth on a bench so he could stretch out, and Ranoi was just coming in, his hands full of a mixture of dried herbs. The young woman helped take Rab's outer robe off, and he lay down on the bench with a sigh of relief. Faya stood back to give Ranoi room to work, but her eyes never left her beloved's face. Ranoi motioned his helper to pour water in a basin, and began to shred the herbs, adding them to the water and stirring them around. When they had soaked a minute or so, he took them from the water, shook off the excess, wrapped them in a cloth and placed it over the wound on Rab's side. Putting his two hands on either side of his patient's head, he closed his eyes and Faya saw his lips moving. In a very short time, Rab's own eyes closed, and he slept. Ranoi covered him with a soft blanket and motioned Faya and his helper out of the room. "Leave him now. He will be much better after he has slept a while. The wound is not too deep. Did he tell you how he got such a gash?"

Faya shook her head. "No, Ranoi, he did not. I didn't even know he had been hurt until I...." she stopped in confusion. How much could she say? "I mean, he did tell me that he was in a fight, but I don't know any more about it."

Ranoi looked at her closely. "It is unusual for a priest to fight. We go out of our way to avoid conflict. There must have been a very serious reason for this. Well, tomorrow he will be feeling much better. I know Asorum will want to know all about this." He smiled at the two and walked away quickly, leaving Faya and the young woman alone in the passageway. Faya was reluctant to leave, but she knew better than to disobey a teacher, so she went slowly up the stairs after thanking the woman for her help.

Chapter Eighteen

That night her prayers were more halting than usual. She prayed for Rab and for his healing, but her thoughts were scattered and she had to struggle to concentrate on calming her mind. Why had there been a fight? Who were the opponents? Where had Rab been in the years since she had seen him? Why had he come back at this particular time? Who had attacked him? Why? Why?

Finally she rolled over on her stomach and buried her face in her hands. "Mother," she whispered, "help me."

The answer came almost before the words. "Faya, I'm here. I know what you want to ask, and I can tell you part of the answer. There has been such a lot of unrest in the City, and the Judges are getting stronger every day. Your father...." here she stopped, her voice breaking just a bit. "Your father," she finally went on, "has forbidden me ever to leave this house, so I can't get out and about as I used to. But I can tell you this; if there was a fight, Rab and his friends didn't start it. The Judges have allowed gangs of rough men to roam the streets, and if they are caught beating some helpless person, they are never punished. They are actually urged to report any so-called irregularity and it is becoming almost impossible to know whom to trust. Even friends and neighbors are looking at each other in fear and mistrust."

"Oh, Mother, I didn't know. We haven't been told that things were getting that bad. I have noticed that Dohnnie has been going more frequently into the City, but when I asked her once why she was away so much, she said it was on business."

"Dohnnie came to see me about six weeks ago. Did you know that? Asorum had sent her to see if I was all right. I have had to close my mind when he called to me, so I wouldn't have to tell him how impossible things are here. He knew something was wrong, though, so he sent Dohnnie. She's a dear, and we had a lovely visit."

"What about Father? Has he changed so much?"

Her mother sighed. "No, dear, he hasn't changed. Not really. He has always been a very ambitious man, and now that he is a Judge, he is even more anxious to become one of the Governors. I never wanted you to know, because you loved him so when you were a baby, but I am afraid I have said too much not to finish the story."

Faya turned on her back, her arms at her sides, and her jaws tight. "Tell me, Mother."

"Faya, little Faya, I will tell you, but not tonight. I'm suddenly so very tired. We can talk again tomorrow night. Now go to sleep, and don't worry. The Priests are still strong, and things will work out. Ask the Power for strength for yourself, my darling, and never, never forget that I love you more than anything in this world."

"I love you, too, Mother. You've always been my guide even though I can't quite remember if your eyes are blue or green." She gave a little chuckle.

"Grey-blue, Faya. Good night, my love. Sleep well." Her voice seemed so far away that for an instant Faya was frightened. Then she remembered that there was a great distance between them, and her mother had said she was tired. "Night, Mother," she murmured drowsily, not knowing that she would never again hear her mother's voice.

The news came the next day that Kadah had not waked from her sleep. Asorum was the one to tell her daughter and hold her while she sobbed.

Since Kadah had been a beloved student at the Temple, Asorum insisted that her body be brought back and given the honor due one who had been so staunch in her beliefs.

Somewhat to his surprise, Faya's father made no great objection, except to send word that he would be unable to attend the ceremonies, which he said he considered improper for the wife of a Judge. He would have preferred that she be cremated in accordance with their rituals, and he hoped Asorum understood that he was bowing to the wishes of the priests only for Faya's sake.

Kadah's body was brought into the great entrance hall on a bier of green branches, and covered with fresh flowers. Faya had seen several funeral services since she had lived there, but had never actually taken part in the ceremonies, since she had not been a member of the deceased's family. Today, she was to act as the only family member, and lead the ceremony.

She stood white faced but calm at the foot of her mother's bier, her white robe, belted with a broad blue sash, fell in graceful folds to her bare feet, and a wreath of fonta leaves crowned her head. In one hand she carried a lighted torch made of a sweet smelling wood, and the smoke billowed softly up toward the ceiling where the circle of translucent stones let in the morning light. In the other hand she held a scroll, on which was written the family name and the ancestors of the woman who lay on the bier. The scroll would be kept by her descendants so the generations would never be lost.

Rab had asked to be allowed to stand with Faya, but she had refused his offer. She needed his courage, but she knew this was one thing she must do alone. Laying the scroll at her mother's feet, Faya handed the torch to a priest who stood by, waiting to bless the body. She went to her harp, which had been placed by the circular pool, and bowed her head briefly. Then she started to play. It was a simple melody, the same lullaby her mother had sung to her so many times. The words were so soft and low that those assembled could barely hear them, but Asorum and

Dohnnie knew she was singing only to her mother. “Sleep, sleep, grow in wisdom, grow in happiness, sleep, my mother, sleep.” She finished the song, stood her harp carefully upright, took again the torch, and bowed to the priest who stood at the head of the bier.

Two women carried in a small brazier filled with incense, and placed it before Faya, who lighted the small amber balls with her torch. As the scent arose, the chanting began, a song of exultation for a spirit that was now free. The priest at the head leaned over Kadah’s face and touched her forehead with his fingertips, murmuring his blessing. Asorum, as the elder priest who had read the woman’s soul, gave it permission to seek its future as it chose, knowing that Kadah’s life had always been one of self denial and love, and that it would continue in that pattern.

Faya, her part of the ceremony finished, stepped up to the head of the bier for one last look at the mother she loved so dearly. For one long moment she looked down as if to sear the memory into her heart forever. She leaned forward and kissed the calm face which seemed almost to wear a slight smile, then turned, handed her torch to a priest, and left the room. Rab hurried after her, knowing she would head for her special place and wait there, while her mother’s body was carried up the steep hills back of the Temple to the place where it would be sealed in a small cave. Many of the people of Atlantis chose cremation, but to those who followed the old laws, the body was a sacred gift from the Creator, and they would not destroy it.

Asorum slowly took the scroll Faya had left and smoothing it in his fingers, he gave a final blessing to the woman he had taught and loved, and whose daughter’s soul he now had in his care. He shook his head slightly, feeling suddenly very old. “Kadah,” he whispered softly, “I would have spared you this early death if it had been possible. I promise you, I will watch over Faya as if she were my own daughter. Go now to the freedom you have so painfully earned, and live again in the light of the Happy Spirits as they joyfully receive you." He bowed to her, then turned and walked out of the Temple into the bright sunshine.

Chapter Nineteen

For several weeks Faya looked drawn and pale. Even the beloved harp could not lift her spirits. Finally, Asorum went to Basrili and asked his help again. He felt that he was too close to the girl, himself, to be really effective, so in asking for the other priest's help, he indicated how worried he really was. He knew that Faya mourned her mother, but nothing seemed to help lift her out of the depression that was eating away at her very soul. Even Rab could do no more than just be there, waiting for Faya to let him in to her life again.

Basrili talked to Faya but could not break through the barrier she had thrown up around her. He did not want to use more persuasive methods just yet, so he suggested to Asorum that they simply give the girl more time. It was Ceki who worked the necessary magic to bring Faya back from her pain and despair.

The tiny girl was so young that no one would have suspected her of holding so much compassion in her small body; but she seemed to know instinctively when someone was in need of help. She would run to Faya whenever they met and hurl herself into Faya's arms, hugging her tightly, prattling away about nothing in particular and everything in general, her joyous acceptance of life bringing smiles in spite of pain.

Slowly the torn part of life began to heal. Faya could not be with Ceki more than a few minutes before she, too, began to smile; the small child would climb up on Faya's lap, demanding a kiss, then a hug, then a story about "when you were very little". Frequently Faya took Ceki with her when she practiced a new piece of music on her harp, and the little girl sat quietly, her eyes never leaving the face of the surrogate mother she had come to adore. When the music ceased, both would heave a deep sigh as if they were finding themselves back in the real world after a journey to another place, another time. The black despair slowly lifted from Faya's soul, and though she would always grieve for the mother she had lost twice, her youth and natural buoyancy began to bring a measure of peace and acceptance.

She was in the herb garden one afternoon, just before time for the Blessing, when Rab, who had patiently waited for the healing to bring her back to him, found her there and hesitantly put a hand on her shoulder. Faya turned, looked at him in wonder, then melted into his arms. "Oh, Rab," she whispered, "forgive me, please forgive me." The tears she had held in so long came in wrenching sobs, shaking her body but completing the healing. Rab held her quietly for a long moment, then turned her face up and began to wipe the tears that were still welling from her eyes. He grinned down at her.

"Faya, my darling Faya, will you tell me how you can cry and still look so absolutely beautiful?"

She hiccuped once or twice, then managed a shaky smile. "Do I?" she asked. "My nose must be red and I know my eyes are swollen. Do you have to look at me? Couldn't you just admire the garden and let me put some water on my face so I don't look so...so...so weepy."

"Well", he said slowly and deliberately, "I suppose I could. I could also just pretend you are someone I don't really know and am not sure I want to see again. I mean any woman who looks like you do right now would have a hard time attracting a husband, wouldn't she?"

Faya stared at him, shocked into speechlessness, then caught the wicked light sparkling in his eyes. Putting her hands on her hips and looking him in the face, she drew herself up to her full height. He mentally braced for the tongue lashing that was coming, but her face suddenly crinkled and she began to laugh. Sheepishly, he grinned, and then they were in each other's arms, swaying back and forth, their laughter uncontrolled, laughter that slowly turned to caresses, first his, and then her answering touch on his face. Suddenly the passion both had held in for so long broke the last barrier, and Faya clung to her love, her lips warm and moving under his. He held her for a moment longer, then he lifted his head.

"Faya," he murmured against her hair, "I can't take much more of this. Can't we tell Asorum we want to be married right away?" She pulled his face down to hers and sought his mouth again. The kiss she gave him was not the kiss of a young inexperienced girl, but one from a woman who knew exactly what she wanted, and made no effort to deny it. When he could draw a breath again, he turned her smartly around and gave her a little push. "We are going in right this minute, and you and I are going to be married this very night."

"Wait, Rab," she laughed with a little quiver in her voice, "I am not at all sure that is possible. I mean, there are plans to be made, I don't have a wedding robe, you haven't formally asked if you might marry me, and I'm sure I can think of a dozen other...."

He interrupted her excuses. "No, I don't think it is possible. I know it is possible. Now let's go find Asorum. Dohnnie can be the stand-in for your mother, and the priests will marry us and bless the union. Then, my girl, we can take up where we left off." The wicked light that shone again in his eyes was answered by the mock obedience she showed as she began to trot along the path in the garden that led to the Temple. Somehow Rab knew that he would never be able to force his will on Faya; then he thought with a wry inward smile, why should I ever want to? She is exactly right as she is, and she'll never change, thank all the happy spirits!

They went first to Dohnnie, asking her to be the go-between, an old custom that was seldom used in these modern days, but one that Faya thought her mother would have approved. The woman, after one startled gasp of surprise, agreed, and went to look for Asorum. He was in the library, reading one of the thousands of scrolls that lined the walls. He looked up when she entered and bowed.

“Dohnnie, I’m glad you are here. I want to discuss something with you.” He indicated the scroll open on the table. “Do you know that the ancients foretold the possible chaos that could occur in our country if the power sources were overloaded? I’m worried. There has been too much talk lately, especially in the City, about raising the capacity of the generators, and now it seems...” He stopped and looked closely at the woman. ”What’s wrong, my dear? You so seldom come here, and I get started talking about something you probably aren’t interested in hearing. I’m sorry, Dohnnie. Now tell me, did you want something of me?”

Dohnnie smiled, then went over and stood before him. “I am here, Asorum, to ask formal permission for Fayasas and Rabithi to be married according to our custom. We need your blessing, and request that you perform the ceremony.”

Asorum blinked once or twice, then asked mildly if they were really serious. Dohnnie nodded emphatically. “I would prefer you saw them together yourself, Asorum. Fayasas is headstrong, and when she sets her mind to something, she never stops until she gets what she wants. Rab is a likable young priest, well schooled in our principals, and has traveled over much of the world. He met Faya several years ago, and evidently has never changed his mind about wanting to marry her. When she grew up,” she added hastily. “And no, there has been nothing between them you would have not approved.”

She stopped for a moment. “I know Faya is very young. Just seventeen. But she is much more mature in some ways than most of the students here. She has worked very hard, learning everything she could about the healing arts, and she is emotionally older than her years. Her mother's death was a hard blow, and Rab has been a strong arm when she most needed it."

"Did he, by any chance, give her that string of blue beads I've seen her wearing lately?"

"You don't miss much, my friend. Yes, he brought it back from some eastern country."

"Was he sent there, or was he just roaming around the earth?"

"He was sent with about fifteen others from several of the provinces to determine if there could be other lands that might be safe, if and when." She stopped, wondering if she had overstepped the bounds of good taste in reminding Asorum of something he was already all too concerned about.

The old priest sighed, then got to his feet, laying aside the scroll. "Haindohne, you and I have skirted this subject several times. I suppose it would be just as well to sit down and talk it out. Although," he smiled, "this doesn't seem exactly the proper time. Now, about Fayasas. Do you really think she is mature enough to take this step? I know her work because both Ranoi and Benai have given me excellent reports about her dedication to her studies." He thought for a moment. "I wonder if her mother had not died so short a time ago if Faya would have been so ready for marriage. They were so very close, and I know the child depended on her mother to a far greater degree than even she knew. They talked together almost every night, and Faya took Kadah's advice seriously. Is this young priest merely taking her mother's place, and will it be a true marriage? Could Faya be needing someone older to take the place of the father she never really had? Dohnnie, you know the child, and being a woman, perhaps you can see this more clearly than I."

Asorum began to pace the room, hands behind his back, his eyes on the floor. Dohnnie watched him a minute or two, then went over and gently put her hand on his arm.

“My dear friend, trust the great heart of that child. Faya has never once wavered in her belief that he would come back for her, and when he did, it was like two souls blending. Rab is a good man. He will take care of Faya, and she will make him entirely happy. And he loves her so.”

Asorum smiled at her earnestness. “Dohnnie, why have you never married? I think any man would be proud to call you wife.” She merely smiled back and shook her head.“Will you perform the ceremony, then?”

“Of course I will,” he answered. “Tell them to come to me tomorrow. I only wish Kadah were here to see her daughter married. Well, perhaps she is, after all. We don’t really know where the spirit goes after it leaves the body. I rather imagine Kadah will not be far away.”

Dohnnie gave him a grateful smile and left him to his reading. Faya and Rab were waiting for her, and all they needed was the smile still on her face.

Chapter Twenty

Shaleen and Krola were white with excitement. They had never seen a wedding ceremony, and that was enough to keep their adrenaline high, but this was not just any wedding. It was the uniting of a very dear friend to her chosen mate, and they were both to take part. Krola would carry the ceremonial torch, and Shaleen would carry the basin of incense. Both girls would wear a new white robe with a broad band of green at the hem, and green ribbons binding their hair.

Faya's wedding robe was of light silvery green, also with a broad band of darker green at the hem. Green was the color of spring, of new life, of young tender buds, and as such, was the most suitable color for a wedding robe. It represented the beginning of a new life and a prayer for the children most couples expected would come.

In spite of his hope for an immediate wedding, Rab bowed to the customs of the Temple. He would not deny Faya the joy of a proper ceremony, nor the entire student body the pleasure of seeing their friend become a wife. It was with a rather deep but resigned sigh that he allowed one of his own friends to take him in hand and provide the proper outfit for a groom to wear.

His robe was the color of dark amber, signifying strength. It was the light of the sun, the deep glow in late afternoon that is the promise of tomorrow's sunrise after the dark night; the warmth that would surround their union; it was the color of joy.

Asorum and the other older priests would wear their usual white robes, some with a deep gold band, others who had not served in the Temple so long, would have no color on their hems. Dohnnie, taking Kadah's place, would wear red, signifying the life blood that had fed her baby in the womb, blood that had been shed when her baby was born.

Both Ranoi and Benai had offered to take her father's place, but Faya did not want anyone to represent him. There was no longer any bitterness, just indifference.

The great entrance hall, where so many ceremonies had been held, was swept, washed down and filled with flowers and ringed with small torches. The circular pool was banked with yet more flowers, the herbs that Faya had worked with so long taking the place of honor. Their musky, aromatic odors scented the room, vying with the other blossoms.

Faya dressed carefully, helped by several of her close friends. Krola and Shaleen had already taken their places at the foot of the stairs, giving mischievous glances at a very nervous Rab, who stood straight and tall carrying the outer robe he would give his bride, the symbol of the warmth and safety he would provide. He looked neither right nor left, but Krola could see the muscle on the right side of his jaw twitch. She gave him a conspiratorial wink, and he managed a rather weak grin back. Then he looked properly solemn as Asorum, joined by his fellow priests, walked slowly down the stairs.

Each of the musicians carried their light instruments as they did each evening for the Blessing. The women followed, carrying small wreaths of green herbs mixed with yellow blossoms, representing the two who were to be married. Asorum raised his hands and everyone fell silent.

The early evening sun struck the openings over the pool and cast a jeweled glow over the assembled people. Rab's red gold hair caught a stray beam and seemed to have a life of its own as it fell over his shoulders. Asorum lifted his arms and began the Prayer. "To the Power I send my spirit." The people answered, "By this I am renewed." Crossing his arms over his breast, he continued, "From the Power I receive blessing." And the people replied, "Thus I live in gladness." And as one, they all bowed their heads for the final words, "The Power is within me. I remember, and I am content." Asorum stood silent for a moment. He looked at his people, smiled and said, "We invite the presence of the Power to bless us this evening, and to help us join Rabithi and Fayasas, making them Two-in-One. Is the man here?"

Rab stepped forward, bowed and answered, "I am come to uphold my part in the fulfillment of a promise."

"Is the woman here?" Asorum asked.

From the doorway the voice of Dohnnie answered. "The woman is here." She and Faya walked slowly across the marble floor to stand before Asorum. Faya bowed and said, "I also keep my part of a promise made."

Dohnnie stepped forward and kissed Faya on the cheek. "I take the place of her mother, who bore her, who nursed her, who taught her to be obedient to the Power. As such, I have the right to say to Rabithi, Fayasas is my child, the gift of the past ages, the hope of the future years. She will now walk in your steps, with love in her heart. Be gentle, be kind, be always faithful to that love." She stepped back and Rab took her place beside Faya.

"And I, Asorum, your high priest, tell you this, Rabithi. Walk in the Light; remember that you are a child of the Earth and also the Infinite. I charge you, do not forget to give your thanks to the Power for each gift, especially this one who stands beside you."

Rab and Faya turned to face each other. "Fayasas," said Rab slowly, "I offer you all that I have, and as a symbol, I give you this robe with all my love. Will you accept it?"

Faya smiled at him with such complete trust that Dohnnie wiped away a tear and even Asorum was heard to clear his throat.

"Rabithi, I accept the robe, and in return," here she reached into one of the long sleeves of her own robe and took out a small rolled parchment, “I give you this song I have written for you, with my love. Will you accept it?”

No one had expected the woman to give the man a gift, but Rab took the scroll and kissed it. “With all my heart,” he said, his own voice a little husky.

Asorum again raised his arms and the musicians took their instruments in hand. “When one is one, there is loneliness. When two become one, there is joy. As your priest, I now say you are Two-in-One. Rejoice.” The musicians started the music and the singers began the hymn of joy that was the signal for Krola to bring her torch and give it to Faya. The new bride took it, and as the music soared, she walked slowly around the great hall, lighting the small torches set in holders around the room. This was the woman’s part, the symbol of bringing light to her home. When all were burning, Shaleen brought the small basin filled with balls of incense and Faya lit it, and handed her torch back to Krola. As the sweet smoke rose up to the ceiling, Rab took Faya in his arms. Their love was such a clear shining joy that no one could doubt that their union would be blessed.

Chapter Twenty-One

There was feasting after the ceremony was over; platters of fruits and vegetables, small barley cakes dripping with honey; the special wine that Benai had once given Faya was poured freely, watered for the younger children; with milk for the very young.

Only one person did not join the festivities. Ceki stood by the pool, her eyes downcast, and her face closed. She mutely shook her head when Ianera offered her a barley cake.

"Aren't you hungry, Ceki?" asked the woman. "These are specially good today. Nuts in them. And the honey is from the fonta flowers. Please take one." The tiny girl merely shook her head again and turned away. "I don't want anything," she said. "I want to go home."

"But you are home, little one." She held out the cake again. The child, in a fit of temper, slapped Ianera's hand and the cake fell to the floor. Leaving it where it fell, the older girl tried to pick up the now sobbing Ceki, but she broke away and ran toward the sleeping rooms. Dohnnie, who was coming in from the porch, saw her just as she stumbled and fell. She and Ianera ran to the child who was now screaming in pain, and Dohnnie picked her up.

"Ceki, Ceki child, you are all right. It was just a small tumble. Here, let me see your leg." The blood was running slowly down where the knee was scraped; Dohnnie knew it was a very minor injury, but Ceki could not be quieted. By now everyone in the hall was only too aware that a child's shrill voice could pierce through any music, and several of the women started toward Dohnnie and Ianera, who were trying without success to soothe the little girl.

Dohnnie asked one of the younger students to bring a soft cloth. She carried the still crying child over to the pool and sat down on the rim, holding Ceki as best she could while the little girl squirmed, trying to get free. "Ceki, let me see your knee. I'll wash it and we'll get it nice and clean, then I'll put something on it to take away the pain." A soft cloth was handed to her and she dipped it in the clear water and began gently to wipe the blood off. Ceki still sobbed, but it was more for effect than real pain. "Hush, darling. You don't want to spoil Faya's wedding, do you? You two have always been such good friends, and this is her happy day. If you will stop crying and listen to the beautiful music, it will make you feel better."

"No it won't! I don't like that music, and I hate Faya." The sobs broke out again and Ceki slapped at Dohnnie's hand as she attended the scrape which by now had stopped bleeding.

"Ceki! You don't hate Faya. You are always so happy when you're together."

"But we won't be any longer. She's going to go away and be with that man. I hate him, too. I want my mother."

Ianera and Dohnnie looked at each other. They knew that Ceki's mother had placed her in the Temple school for much the same reason Kadah had left Faya there. The only difference was that Ceki's father had agreed, and there was no bitterness between the parents. The Judges were becoming more outspoken against the old beliefs, and many of the young girls were sent to the Temple for their own protection. It was not a physical danger, but a spiritual one, and as such, much more damaging. "Tell you what, little one, we'll go fix that knee and tomorrow we'll ask your mother to come for a visit. Will that be all right?" Dohnnie smiled as the little Ceki stopped crying; her face was still a thunder cloud, but her body was relaxing.

"I guess so," she muttered, still glowering at the crowd of happy people who had gone back to their feasting.

Dohnnie carried her out of the room, dressed her knee and put her to bed after promising that in the morning Asorum would send her mother a message that her daughter wanted to see her. Returning to the great hall, she joined with the others in wishing Faya and Rab a long happy life together. She was disturbed at Ceki's outburst against Faya, but she realized that the child thought that Rab would take Faya away and she would never see her again. Abandonment was one of the worst things a child could suffer, and although she had been content when left at the Temple, it was Faya who had taken the place of her mother whom she saw infrequently. "No wonder she was angry and hurt," Dohnnie mused. "I'll have to tell Faya to let Ceki know that she is not going away at all, and there won't be nearly as many changes as she fears.."

Rab and Faya had been given a large room near the one Benai lived in. It had its own small bathing room, and Rab had added some of the artifacts he had picked up in his travels. He had not yet allowed Faya to see it, wanting instead to have everything in readiness for his young bride. When they walked across the threshold, and Faya knew for the first time that she was no longer alone, the love she felt for Rab swelled to such a degree of happiness that her soul could hardly contain it. She could not stop the small gasp of delight as her eyes went from the soft rug underfoot to the silken drapes at the two windows that looked out on the garden; then back to her husband, who stood quietly watching her. "Are you happy with our own place, Faya?" he asked. "Oh, Rab, it is so lovely, I think...I think I'm going to cry." "No, my darling, you are not going to cry. You are going to smile with me and drink one more glass of Benai's special wine, which he left there on the table for us; then for the rest of our lives, you and I are going to be the two happiest people in Atlantis."

He poured two small glasses of the wine and they pledged their love to each other and to the Power that had brought them together. As Rab took Faya in his arms, a sigh of a breeze brought the scent of the herbs she loved so well; her echoing sigh was a surrender to the warmth of his kiss and of the devotion shining in his eyes.

She thought briefly of the words Asorum had spoken, “when two become one, there is joy.” Then the passion both were so capable of flamed, and there was no more need for words.

Chapter Twenty-Two

Faya and Rab were left alone for the customary week. Food was brought to their room each morning and evening; otherwise they were allowed the privacy newly married couples need to become accustomed to living as one instead of two. Faya was happier than she had ever dreamed was possible. She still missed her mother, and once in a while the turn of a phrase or a lightly hummed tune would bring a sharp pain. She would always feel for her loss, but Rab was aware of how devastated she had been, and made every effort to keep his young wife happy.

The garden was especially sweet to them both. Faya, of course, had studied there for several years, and she took a great delight in showing her new husband the different plants, what they were used for, and how much good they could do for the sick or injured. Rab, on the other hand, loved the garden for its many scents, the peace that wrapped them both as they strolled along the paths, and the almost hypnotic sound of the water as it fell from the fountain into its basin.

Their days of solitude were over entirely too soon. They had come to know and delight in each other. Rab was a gentle and tender lover, and Faya was a willing pupil who soon learned to throw caution to the wind and accept her husband with a passion equal to his. But almost as fascinating was their understanding of each other's place in the scheme of living. They knew with certainty that they had been together many life times before, and Faya's one great desire was to be sure of their continued togetherness.

Faya spoke often of the daughter they would have. When Rab asked why she was so certain their first child would be a girl, she reminded him that she had to give the blue beads to her daughter, so of course, there would be a girl. "Of course," smiled her husband, knowing that Faya nearly always got her way when she really wanted something.

When their first wonderful week was over, the newly-weds rejoined the other members of the Temple, slipping back into their usual duties, Faya to her studies and Rab to a discussion with his own group about a planned voyage to a far country. Some days later, Faya looked up from her work in the garden to see a small forlorn figure standing in the open doorway that led from her new room to the porch. She gasped in dismay.

"Ceki, what are you doing here? How did you get here?" She stood up hastily, brushing off the dirt that clung to her robe, and walked swiftly to the child who was still staring at her without making a sound. "Ceki, darling, you aren't supposed to be here, not in this part of the Temple." When the child made no reply, Faya knelt down and tried to take Ceki in her arms, but the little girl pushed her away.

"Ceki, what's the matter? Are you all right?"

The child just stood and looked at Faya with a heartbroken expression on her face. Finally she gave a sob and cried, "You don't love me any more. I thought you loved me, but you don't."

"Oh Ceki, of course I love you. Why in the world would you think I don't?" Faya was still trying to reach out for the little girl, who kept her at arm's length. "I will always love you; aren't we friends any more?"

The child shook her head. "No."

"Why Ceki, of course we are. At least, I'm your friend and I will always be your friend. What is it, honey? Why are you so unhappy with me?"

"Because you came here to live and you don't play with me like you used to."

Faya rose to her feet and took the child firmly by the hand. "Now you and I are going to sit down here on the porch and I am going to tell you why I can't play with you every day." They walked over to one of the benches and Faya lifted Ceki to her lap. "You see, my darling, when people get older, they do things that they didn't do when they are younger."

"Like what?" Ceki muttered, still on the verge of tears.

"Well, for one thing, I met someone I loved very much - no, not more than I love you, just in a different way - and I wanted to be with him. You like to be with your friends, don't you?"

Ceki nodded. "Yes, but that isn't the same. They can't play the harp and sing to me like you did, and they don't know how to make up stories, or tell me secrets about the trees and the plants. Faya, can't you come back and stay with me instead of that man?"

Faya almost chuckled aloud. "Darling, that man, as you call him, is my husband. When a man and woman get married, they want to live together. Your mother and father live together, don't they?" Ceki nodded. "Well, it's the same thing."

"But you're not a mommy, so it can't be the same thing." Ceki felt she had explained it very clearly. Mothers were one thing, but her friend Faya was quite another.

The chuckle that Faya had been holding in suddenly erupted and she laughed so hard that Ceki almost fell off her lap. "Oh, Ceki, Ceki, wait until you are grown up and in love. Then come and tell me it can't be the same thing." Her laughter was infectious and the little girl began to smile. Then she threw her arms around Faya's neck and snuggled close.

"Faya, please come back with me. I won't ask for stories, just play the music like you did before."

"Honey, I'll play for you just as soon as I finish my work here. But now you must go back. Do you think you can find the way alone? And Ceki, you must promise me that you will never, never come here again. This garden is full of plants that could hurt you, and anyway, this is my room and people don't go into a room without asking permission first. Will you promise?"

Ceki nodded. "All right, I won't come here again. But I don't think I know how to get back. Will you come with me?"

"Yes, darling, I guess I had better take you back, just as soon as I tell Benai where we are going." She spoke briefly to the priest who had been working in another part of the garden, and had heard the whole thing. He nodded his permission, and the two walked swiftly back to the part of the Temple where Ceki should have been.

"Now will you play your harp for me like you promised?" Ceki was very much like her older friend; she never forgot a promise made. Faya grinned and gave her a quick hug.

"Yes, I will play for you, just for a little while. But you know, Ceki, I have work to do and I can't stay very long."

"All right, just one song." The child was happy now she had her adored foster mother back where she belonged, with her. Faya had left her harp in the great hall, ready to be played if asked for at the evening Blessing. She tuned it and started her song. Ceki stood quietly, her eyes fixed on Faya, and her ears drinking in every note.

"That's nice," she sighed when the music stopped. "Will you play another one, please?"

"No, Ceki, I told you just one. I have to go back and work in the garden. But I'll see you this evening, and maybe I'll be asked to play again. Now you remember your promise, never to go to that part of the Temple again without permission." She stooped, gave Ceki a kiss and ran swiftly back to her own room.

When she told Rab about it later that evening, he chuckled and said, "I think, my dear wife, that you may be going to have a problem with that little girl. You did neglect her for a whole week! And a week is a very long time when you are that age."

Faya nodded, entirely serious. "I know, Rab, and I don't know what to do about it. I can't be with her as I used to, and I don't want her to think I've abandoned her. What do you think I should do?"

"I haven't the faintest idea. I only know what I think you should do right now."

"What?"

"Come here and I'll show you." The old wicked light suddenly shone in his eyes, and Faya meekly cast down her own eyes and said, "Yes, my lord," then flew laughing into his arms.

Chapter Twenty-three

The first year after their marriage was a busy time for Faya. In addition to her mornings with Ranoi and her afternoons with Benai, she was asked several times to stop her work and bring her harp to one of the healing rooms. There she would find one of the healer priests, who asked her to tune her heart and mind to the patient lying there. At first, she did not know just what was expected of her, but as time went on, she found it easier to make the soul connection, and allow her hands to strike the right chords. She didn't quite understand how her music could heal, but Ranoi explained that the vibrations of the harp strings were much like the winged instrument he had taught her to use. Little by little, Faya became more adept at playing just the particular needed melodies, and she became known as the woman with the magic hands. Asorum was immensely proud of her, as slowly her fame spread throughout the City. She, herself, was unaware of how well she was known. People came to the Temple just to ask Fayasas play for them when they were ill physically, or emotionally upset, and her work brought not only healing, but a certain status for the Temple itself. That brought it even more to the notice of the Judges.

One morning Faya awoke with the instinctive knowledge that something was different. Rab had been away for several days and she expected him back that afternoon. He could not always tell her where he was going or why, but she suspected it had a great deal to do with the unrest in the City that she kept hearing about. When asked, Rab simply told her that he and the group of priests he had traveled with for a number of years were working to convince the populace that the Temples were a necessary part of Atlantean life, and that the Judges had no right to impose their will on the people. She never knew just how dangerous his part really was.

This particular morning, Faya was impatient for Rab to come home. She paced the great Hall, knowing that she might be summoned to attend another person who needed her healing music, but unwilling to go down to the healing rooms until called for. She couldn't understand why she felt the way she did. She tried to sit quietly, but found that impossible. Walking didn't seem to help, either. She wanted to laugh, and she wanted to cry. She felt as though she would explode if Rab didn't come back soon. What was wrong with her!

Dohnnie, coming in from the teaching rooms, saw the young woman she loved so dearly, and walked over to her. "Faya, I haven't had a chance to talk to you for a week. How are you? You look well. Is Rab still away?"

Faya looked at her for a second or so as if she wasn't sure who Dohnnie was, then suddenly started laughing and grabbed her friend around the waist and swung her around. "Oh, Dohnnie, I don't know why, but I am so happy I ...." She stopped suddenly and her face became as woebegone as Ceki's had. "Dohnnie, what's the matter with me?"

Dohnnie looked closely at the young face now wet with tears, then she held her away and her eyes went over Faya from head to foot. She began to smile. "I don't think there is anything wrong with you, my dear. In fact, I believe everything is completely right and as it should be. Come with me, Faya. I want Asorum to confirm something." She took Faya's hand and led her swiftly out to the herb garden where Faya had always gone when she needed to think. Dohnnie knew Asorum walked there in the mornings. It was such a peaceful place with the dawn light waking the birds, and the scent of dew covered herbs flinging joy over all. Asorum was just starting in when the two women stood blocking the doorway.

"Asorum, Faya is in need of your council," the older woman said.

The old priest looked at both of them questioningly. “My council? I am flattered. What is it I can tell you?” He smiled at them both, and motioned them to a bench that was placed near the clear pool. “How can I help you?”

Dohnnie looked first at Asorum then at Faya. The priest caught the look on her face, turned his own gaze on the younger woman, stared hard for just a second, then turned back to Dohnnie and smiled again. “Yes,” he nodded, “you are correct. And she doesn’t know yet? Well, it’s very early. But, yes, she is.”

Faya, entirely bewildered, asked “I am what, Asorum?”

Both Dohnnie and Asorum began to laugh. “Oh, nothing very much, my dear,” said the priest. “After all, a baby is just one of those things that happens every so often, you know.”

“A baby? What are you talking about? What baby? And what have I got to do with...ohhh...you mean...my baby? I’m going to have a baby?”

“Yes, Faya, I rather think you are.” the priest said dryly. “But it’s nothing to get excited about. Babies are born every day, you know.”

“Nothing to get excited about? Asorum, how could you say a thing like that! A baby is special! A baby is the most precious gift the Power can give! And mine will be...” She broke off, seeing the laughter that was almost choking her two friends. “Oh, Asorum, you are a terrible person! And Dohnnie, you are no better! How did you know when I didn’t? To tease me like that! A baby. My baby!”

“Well, I somehow think Rab may have had something to do with it,” laughed Dohnnie. “We knew because we can read your soul. At least, Asorum can. I just knew, but really I don’t know how I knew.”

Asorum patted Dohnnie’s hand. “You knew, my dear, because of the great love you have in your heart for this child.” He smiled fondly at Faya. “Do you remember the first time you came to the Temple? You were only four. And now you are a married woman, about to bring new life into this place. Your mother would have been so happy to see this day." The priest sighed. "Kadah; I think of her so often you know. She was very dear to me."

Faya threw her arms around her old friend, much as she had when she was a little girl. "Asorum, how can I ever tell you how much I love you? You have been both mother and father to me for so many years, and I hold you so dear to my heart. You, too, Dohnnie. If you hadn't been here when Mother left me, I think I would have died."

"Probably not, my dear." answered Dohnnie. "But I've always been so happy that I could be here when you needed me. Has Rab come back yet?"

"No, he will be here sometime this afternoon. I only wish he and I could talk the old way, like I did with my mother. But somehow he can't get the hang of it. Oh, wait until I tell him! We're going to have a baby! When will she be here, Asorum?"

"She, Faya? Why are you so sure it will be a girl? Perhaps you and Rab will have a boy first."

"No, Asorum. It will be a girl. I already know what her name will be, and she will have the red-gold hair Rab has. Not dark, like mine."

"Faya, you don't know how very attractive you are, with those dark eyes and hair. So unusual here in Atlantis. Be glad you are a little different," Dohnnie told her. Faya made a small face at her friend, then patted her stomach. "She will have light hair and blue-grey eyes like my mother's."

"What will you name her, Faya," asked the priest smiling at her.

"Her name will be - is already - Mai-dwar. And I will write a song for her and sing it while she is growing inside, so she will already know me when she is born. Mai-dwar. And she will wear the blue beads when she is older."

Dohnnie and Asorum looked at each other and the old priest shook his head. "Such a to-do over having a baby. Blue beads, indeed. She will have to wait a long time for those, I'm afraid. It will be another eight months before she is here, and then she has to grow up, you know, and...."

Faya put her hand on his knee and grinned up at him. "Laugh all you want, but I know this baby is special. Very special. You tell him, Dohnnie. You will be the stand-in for the grandmother, and Asorum will hold her and speak her name so the Happy Spirits will know who she is. And Rab will acknowledge her as his own, and add his blessing so we will become a true family. Asorum," she said suddenly, "when I was born, did my father acknowledge me?"

"Yes, child, he certainly did, but not here at the Temple. He wouldn't let the marriage be blessed by the priests, which made Kadah so unhappy, but you were surely his child and he loved you."

"Yes, I remember," she said slowly, "how he would swing me up on his shoulder when he came home from the City. But..." and she stopped. "I don't want to think about that anymore. Oh, why doesn't Rab come home!"

"He will be home soon, my dear, and in the meantime, I think Ranoi has someone waiting for you. Yes, and you will need your harp." Asorum stood up and took Faya's face in both hands. He kissed her forehead and smiled into her eyes. "You know you have my blessing, and your daughter will be as dear to me as you are. Now go along to the healing rooms. You are needed."

Faya bowed to him and ran quickly into the Temple hall, where she lifted her harp and carried it gently it down the stairs. Ranoi was indeed waiting for her, and that day her music was especially sweet. The patient who lay waiting for her relaxed almost instantly and soon drifted off into a healing sleep while Ranoi applied the herbal oils that unknotted the tense muscles and brought relief.

When Rab came home later that afternoon, Faya was on her knees in the herb garden while Benai instructed her how to gather just the right part of the plant she was studying. "Too far down on the stem, Faya, you will find the leaves much too coarse and bitter. You want only the very tender young tips." Faya nodded and carefully picked the leaves he indicated. "And these will be sweeter to taste?" she asked. Benai smiled. "Nothing is going to make those leaves really sweet, but you can add honey to make them at least a bit more palatable. They are useful when a child has a bad cough. I have found them to ease the congestion in the lungs very quickly."

"What does one do with them, make a tea?" she asked.

"Yes, they can be steeped for about ten minutes, then strained and the water blended with honey and perhaps a spoonful of thacasca juice for flavor. Then give about a half cupful every two hours." Benai finished his instructions and rose to his feet.

Rab, who had left his outer robe and street sandals in their room, slipped his feet into a lighter pair and walked out into the garden. "And what kind of medicine do you offer to a man who is tired, hungry, and aching for the sight of his wife?" he asked. Faya, startled, looked up into her husband's smile and hastily got to her feet. She rubbed her hand across her forehead to push back her wayward hair, left a smudge of dirt on her face, and ran to his arms.

Benai shrugged, grinned at them, and turned to go back to his own room, muttering to himself, "no use to try for more instruction this day!" Neither of them heard him leave.

"Oh, Rab, I have the most wonderful news. Mai-dwar is on the way!"

Rab looked at her in bewilderment. "Who is Mai-dwar? Are we having company?"

She laughed up into his face. "Mai-dwar, you dear idiot. Our daughter. You know, the one we have been waiting and praying for. She has finally decided to come to us."

Rab looked first incredulous, then slowly a smile spread across his face, and he lifted his wife up and carried her to the porch. Setting her down gently he asked, "Are you sure? Is it really true?"

"Yes, Rab, it is really true. Asorum and Dohnnie told me."

"You mean you didn't know? They had to tell you?" he teased.

"I'll have you know, sir, that I have never had a baby before, so how was I to know! But seriously, Rab, isn't it wonderful? She has chosen us, and now we will be a true family."

"Darling, we have been a true family, just the two of us. But I couldn't be happier."

"Don't you wonder who she will be? I mean, where has she been, have we known her before (of course we must have) and why she chose to come to us instead of some other man and woman?" Faya pulled Rab to a bench and sat in his lap, leaned her head on his shoulder and twined her arms around him. He held her close, and both dreamed for a moment about the coming soul who had been entrusted to their care. Benai, from his room, could see the two and he murmured a short prayer that their lives would be as happy in coming years as it was at this moment.

Rab finally pushed Faya off his lap, got up, stretched and announced that he was hungry enough to eat almost anything set before him. "Oh, Rab, I'm sorry! You did say you were hungry and I was so anxious to tell you about Mai-dwar that I forgot! I have some fruit inside. Will that do until the evening meal? It won't be long," she said and squinted up at the low sun. "It's almost time for the Blessing. You will join us, won't you? I know you're tired, but please come. I'm supposed to play one of my own compositions tonight."

Rab hugged her. "Of course I'll come. When did I not? And the fruit will be just fine. But tell me something. Why Mai-dwar? Is that a family name?" Faya shook her head. "No, it isn't. But since it means 'beloved', I have always wanted that for our daughter. Do you mind?"

Rab smiled. "No, Faya, I think it is a lovely name. And she will be beloved by us both. Now let your starving husband eat, or I won't be much of a father or anything else. I'm famished!"

Chapter Twenty-four

The days that had once seemed to creep now flew by quickly. For the first time in her life, Faya was permitted to go into the City alone, although she preferred having her husband along for company. She found shopping a new but quite interesting experience. Rab indulged her desire for spending hours in the shops that lined many of the streets, and in a very short time she had become first acquainted with, then friends with many of the men and women who sold everything from food to the luxuries she had never had.

Somewhat to Rab's surprise, Faya didn't seem to care so much about buying; she was simply fascinated with the incredible amount of goods available. Benai had told her about the markets in his far country, but here in her own City were the same kinds of merchandise: gossamer shawls, beautifully embroidered bed covers, gold jewelry set with precious stones, figurines, scrolls, so many items she had never dreamed existed.

She spent a great deal of her time in the markets where all kinds of foods were sold. Some of these she did buy, taking back to her friends at the Temple exotic fruits, and little sweet cakes shaped like birds, fish or flowers. Krola and Shaleen received them with glee, sitting up until all hours, making themselves a bit unwell from overeating, but enjoying almost as much the stories Faya told them about the people she had met. Faya had a knack for meeting someone, and in a short time, knowing quite a lot about him. She had for so long been confined to the comparatively small Temple area, and here was a great City waiting to be explored. There were people, both men and women, who were friendly and willing to talk to one whose smile was so genuine, and who took a real interest in what they had to say. Rab was very proud of his young wife, and would introduce her to the shop keepers he had traded with, knowing they would give her the best bargains and the fairest prices.

She did not neglect her duties at the Temple. She spent three mornings a week with Ranoi and three afternoons with Benai, but she had been allowed to have the rest of the week to herself, so she chose to spend most of her free time with the children. Ceki had finally accepted the fact that Faya would not be at her beck and call, and was again her happy, exuberant self. Faya loved the time she spent teaching the little ones the ways of the plants and flowers she had tended for so long. She looked forward more and more to those hours when she could be with them, when her harp still charmed them and she could take the place of the mothers who could not always be there.

But Rab was the most important person in her life. He taught her a game he had learned in one of the countries he had visited, played with small stones on a board, and she delighted in trying her best to win, although she seldom did. Patience had never been one of her better traits, and she invariably would play too fast and lose to Rab's more cautious technique.

Several months passed, and Faya was beginning to know that Mai-dwar was a real entity, not just a dream child. Straightening up one afternoon, she realized that crawling about in the garden was something she would have to forego one day soon. Her back was beginning to ache, and as she stretched to ease the discomfort, Benai grinned at her.

"Well, my dear, it seems I shall soon lose my prize pupil. I've been wondering just how long you thought you could go on acting as though you were still twelve years old."

"Oh, Benai, I'm all right! After all, Mai-dwar isn't due to put in an appearance for about three months. I have lots of time, and there is still so much to learn."

“And let that man of yours take me to task for allowing his wife to hurt herself and maybe even the baby? No, thanks! You will not be handling any dangerous herbs from now on, nor will you grub in the dirt. You will act like a proper matron and take care of that little miracle you have growing inside you. Now come sit on the porch and we’ll have some of my special wine; I think there are a few cakes left from last night, so we can eat them while we talk. Now remember, a glass of wine, just one small one, will not hurt you, but only one!”

Faya laughed. “Just like my birthday, remember? I wanted more and you wouldn’t give me another glass.” She sighed with pleasure as she sank into the chair he offered, and had to admit to herself that she really was getting a little tired. Rab had been busy talking with some of the groups of priests who were visiting the Temple, so she had not taken the usual lunch time rest.

The morning had been a difficult one, having to work with a demanding patient, who was not nearly as ill as he thought he was, and carry her harp up and down the stairs. She was a healthy young woman, but the baby was making her own demands, and Faya finally had to acknowledge it.

She and Benai had spent many pleasant hours talking after their day’s work was finished. He had become more than a teacher to Faya, almost taking the place of her father. The man she had once adored seemed to have forgotten that he had a daughter, and Faya could go for months without even a thought of him. She still missed her mother and the talks they had at night before she slept, but the sharp agony of grief had eased.

Faya and Rab were so closely attuned that each could almost read the other’s thoughts. She had learned to block off unwanted intrusions of her mind, a technique Benai had taught her; she had even learned to keep Asorum from reading her thoughts, which amused him mightily. In his many long years as a priest, he had never met anyone just like Fayasas. As he told Dohnnie one day, “she keeps me young, just trying to find a way to stay a step ahead of her sharp mind.”

Rab, on the other hand, was almost never blocked. He and his young wife shared their interests, their hopes for the future, their beliefs and above all, their common devotion to the work they were both determined to do - to keep their beloved country from the ravages of greed, and their children under the blessings of the Power - but he never quite learned the technique of talking mind to mind as Faya and her mother had done.

Although Faya had been relieved of the heavier work she had been used to doing, Rab sometimes treated her as though she was a fragile child who needed supervision. When his solicitude became a little too much for her, she would slip away and go to her beloved rock. There, for a few short hours, she could feel the warmth of the sun, smell the earthy scent of the moss that was creeping more and more over the rock, and dream about the coming child. It was a time for reflection, for decision making, for silent praise and thanks to the Happy Spirits, and for just being herself again. Eventually Rab always found her, and by then, Faya was happy to feel his arms around her, reminding them both of the day Rab had come back and they knew they loved each other.

The months passed more quickly than Faya had thought they would. One bright spring morning, after she had been in the Children’s Garden teaching them a new song, and letting Ceki show her the dance step she had learned, Faya felt a sudden sharp pain in her back. She wriggled around to ease it, but instead, the pain moved with her, now striking across her abdomen. Then she felt a gush of fluid that wet her legs. With a gasp of disbelief and recognition, she asked Ceki to call Dohnnie, soothing the frightened child by saying that she merely wanted someone to walk back to the Temple with her. Ceki refused to budge, fearing her dearly loved friend was in trouble. In her own imperious way, she ordered one of the other children to go, and as the child hurried away, Ceki patted Faya on the shoulder.

"Don't be scared, Faya. I'll stay with you. Is Mai-dwar coming soon?"

Faya looked at her little charge, then shook her head. "Ceki, how do you know these things? But yes, I do believe Mai-dwar will be here very soon. So I think we should start back. Will you let me hold your hand?"

Ceki, very serious, nodded. "You can put your hand on my shoulder and I'll hold you up. I'll go very slow so you won't stumble."

Faya, between pain and laughter, put her hand lightly on the child's shoulder and they started up the broad lawn toward the Temple. Twice Faya had to stop, the perspiration breaking out on her forehead. She, who had never been sick a day in her life, had not realized that sudden pain could be so humiliating. Then she remembered her long weeks of training from Asorum and Ranoi. The pain eased and she and Ceki walked a little faster up the broad white steps.

"I do think, dear, that you should go and tell Dohnnie I will be needing her. I'm perfectly all right now. Please, go ahead, Ceki. I'll just sit here by the fountain and wait."

As the child ran off, she eased her unwieldy body down on the broad rim of the fountain, letting the sound of the water falling into the pool soothe her. The light reflected on the water, shimmering and sparkling, breaking into myriad colors from the thin stones set into the circle above the pool, brought a serenity she had not expected. The contractions were there, but coming in slow rhythm and she was not at all apprehensive. She only wished Rab was with her, but he had been away for several weeks, leaving with reluctance, knowing that her time was getting closer.

When Dohnnie came hurrying in, followed by Asorum and Ranoi, she smiled serenely at them. "Don't look so worried. Mai-dwar is coming, just a few days before I thought she would. Shall I go down to the birthing room now?"

Ranoi looked at her closely, put his hand on her bulging belly and nodded. "Yes, Fayasas, I think it is about time. She won't be here for a while yet, but it is just as well to be prepared. Haindohnne," he turned to the other woman, "will you please go ahead and let my assistant know we will be needing her soon? And Asorum, you come with me, and we'll see Fayasas safely down the stairs. Ceki, it's time for you to leave us now." As the child reluctantly left them, he held out his hand to Faya who was still sitting on the pool rim. She heaved herself up and again smiled at them quietly. Asorum looked closely at her face, then smiled himself. "You have been practicing, I see."

"Of course I have. I don't like pain any more than anyone else, and your instructions were quite clear." A bit of the old imperious nature asserted itself again, and the two men looked at each other. Asorum bowed to Ranoi with a satisfied smirk on his face, and Ranoi grinned back. The two were close friends and had no hesitation in trying a little one upmanship. Faya had been close to them both and each had taught her what they could. Asorum had seen that she learned pain control, using her mind to block off unnecessary discomfort. Ranoi had taught Faya to keep her body in the best condition, and how to breathe properly. He was the most skilled healer in the Temple, Asorum the wisest of men, and between them, they would make certain nothing untoward would happen. Faya, herself, had the utmost confidence in them both, and was eagerly awaiting the baby she knew would soon be in her arms.

As they walked slowly down the stairs to the birthing room, Faya was humming a tune she had just composed, and Asorum cocked his head to listen. "A song for your baby?" he asked.

The girl nodded. “I just thought of how she would look, so I wrote a song for her. When she is here, I’ll sing it to her and she will know me.”

Both men felt that Mai-dwar already knew her mother quite well, having been talked to, sung to, and played for through the long months of waiting. Even Rab had felt he could also talk to his baby, and had done so, much to Faya’s amusement.

When they reached the birthing room, they found Dohnnie and Ranoi’s assistant ready and waiting. The two women shooed the men back, undressed Faya and made her comfortable in a clean short robe. When she was seated on a chair, the men came back in and the waiting began. When a pain struck, Faya managed to keep the discomfort away, at the same time allowing the contractions to follow their natural course. Asorum had taught her well, and she had no fear of the labor that would bring her beloved child into the world. She was a young, healthy, happy being, and followed Ranoi’s instructions without hesitation, walking around the room, doing the exercises he had taught her, and willing her baby to come when it was the proper time.

Dohnnie was perhaps the most apprehensive of the group, wiping Faya’s face and whispering words of encouragement. “Dohnnie, I’m perfectly all....” a deep breath stopped her for a moment as a contraction took all her concentration, ”.... right,” she continued. “Don’t fret,” she went on. “Mai-dwar will soon make her appearance.” Several hours had passed since she had started labor, and the baby was coming faster than even Ranoi had expected.

When it was time for the birthing stool, Faya took her seat, the assistant behind her and Dohnnie ready to catch the baby as it was pushed out. Ranoi had his hand on her belly, making sure the baby’s head was in the proper position, and helping the contractions do their work.

An hour later, Faya looked for the first time on the face of her baby.

Dohnnie laid her in Faya's arms seconds after her birth, and as she cradled the new being, Asorum stooped beside her and put his hand on Mai-dwar's head. He murmured a blessing, then a prayer to the Power to ask that both the baby and her mother would continue safe and well.

Faya smiled at her baby, then turned to Asorum and asked, "My dear teacher, will you read my baby?"

"Of course, if you wish. When she is washed and wrapped, I will come back and together we shall find where she came from, and why she chose you and Rab to be her parents. Now let Dohnnie have your precious child, while you finish the job. The afterbirth must be delivered so your womb will be clean with no infection. You know the body must be cared for as well as the spirit. You have been through an ordeal. Yes, you handled it extremely well," he said in answer to her look of impatience, "but even you have limits, my dear Faya. Now let Ranoi help you, and I will be back this evening." He motioned for Dohnnie to take the baby, which Faya gave up reluctantly. Fifteen minutes later as she struggled up off the stool, Ranoi caught her as she almost staggered toward the bed that had been prepared for her.

"Here, child, lie back and we will do all that is necessary," he said soothingly. She was suddenly grateful for the soft pallet and the warm cover Dohnnie laid over her. Dohnnie again laid Mai-dwar on Faya's breast, and as the little mouth made mewling noises, the baby found a nipple and Faya sighed in utter contentment.

Chapter Twenty-five

When Rab came home three days later, he found Ceki waiting in the great hall. She had been there every day whenever she could get away from her classes, watching for Rab to come back. When she saw him, she ran over and took his hand, tugging and pulling, impatiently hopping on first one foot and then the other.

"Ceki, whatever is the matter?" he asked. Since the tiny child had never quite forgiven him for taking Faya away from her as she thought, he was surprised by her actions. She didn't answer, just pulled harder.

"Ceki, what's wrong? What do you want?" He put down the small package he was carrying and swung the girl up in his arms. To his astonishment, she snuggled her head on his shoulder, planted a kiss on his cheek, then said quite clearly, "I've come to take you to Faya."

"Take me to Faya?" Rab asked. "Why, Ceki, where is she? Is she all right? Is anything wrong? The baby - is the baby - has Mai-dwar come?" He set her down gently as she nodded happily.

"She is here, Rab, and we waited and waited for you to come see her. Faya said I could meet you. So please hurry. She is so pretty, Rab, all pink and soft, and she knows me. I think she does. She can cry real loud when she's hungry. And she can hold on to my finger if I put it where she can reach. Oh, do hurry, Rab. You are so slow!"

The man picked her up again and this time there was no need to tell him to hurry. His long legs made short work of the distance to his wife's side. She was sitting on the porch of the herb garden, the baby asleep in her arms, and the picture they made brought a jolt to Rab's heart. She turned toward him as he almost ran the last few steps, still carrying Ceki who was thoroughly enjoying the fast trip.

"Here he is, Faya. I told you I would bring him," the little girl cried, her excitement making her voice shrill. Rab set her down and went to Faya who held her face up for his kiss.

"Oh, Rab, I'm so sorry we couldn't wait until you got back, but Maidwar was in such a hurry!" Faya smiled at her husband. "But isn't she beautiful?"

Rab looked at the tiny bundle in his wife's arms. "Well, I can't say I am able to see much of her. Could you undo some of those things you have wrapped her in so I can get a proper look?"

"Things indeed! These are absolutely the most beautiful gowns a baby ever had! Dohnnie brought them back from that lovely shop where we went once before, remember? You know, the one that had such exquisite embroideries." While she was talking, she was removing the baby's outer wrappings. When Rab could finally see his daughter, her eyes were closed, her breathing even and quiet, and she gave no indication that her sleep had been in the least disturbed. Rab was looking first at her, then at Faya, when the baby, without moving her head at all, suddenly opened her eyes. She looked squarely at her father. Just days old, she seemed to focus her gaze on him, then her eyes closed and she resumed her serene sleep. Rab's voice was husky as he spoke softly.

"Faya, she looked at me. She knew me! I swear, she knew me." He reached out a finger to touch her cheek. "Did you see her?" he asked his wife.

"Yes, Rab, I did, and I think you are right. Who knows how much a baby can see, or hear, or know. They are so helpless, so tiny, and yet their souls are so old, so wise. I've often wondered who she has been, and why she came to us. Asorum was going to read her the day she was born, but I thought you might like to be here, so he waited. We will ask him this afternoon."

Rab smiled at his wife. "Thank you, Faya, I would indeed like to hear what he can tell us. Don’t you think she looks a little like me?”

Faya laughed. “At this age, who can say? But she does have enough hair to see that it will be golden-red like yours, thank all the Happy Spirits! I would have been sorry to see her hair as dark as mine.”

“Oh, darling, I am so glad yours is dark. There are enough like me around, and yours is so lovely, especially when you let it fall loose like it is now.”

She smiled. “One more thing, Rab....when do you want to have the Ceremony of Acknowledgment? It should be within the first week.” Ceki, whom they had almost forgotten, had been standing back but now came to Faya’s chair and put one arm around her shoulder.

“Faya, what is that Ceremony? Is it like a party? And can I come?”

Both Rab and Faya laughed at the intense little face. “Yes, Ceki, you most certainly can come, but it is not what you think of as a party. But on the other hand, why shouldn’t it be? Rab, let’s make it a real party . We will ask everyone to join in our happiness.” Faya’s eyes sparkled at the thought of the entire Temple helping with the naming of her baby.

“With the two of you determined to do this, how could I say no?” Rab’s own face reflected the satisfaction of the two facing him, his beloved wife, and the child who had come to mean so much to her. Ceki suddenly remembered where she was, and that she had promised not to come to this part of the Temple without permission. But hadn’t Faya told her she could wait for Rab and bring him here? Maybe if she was very quiet they would forget she should be sent back to her own part of the building. She tiptoed to the bench set along the wall, the bench where Faya and Benai had sat so many times talking about everything and nothing.

Rab and Faya were so wrapped up in their new baby that they neither saw nor cared that Ceki was still there, until Benai came out on the porch from his own room and spoke to her. He was quite aware that she was being a mouse in order not to be sent back, but he knew also that she had accomplished what she had been allowed to do, and now should go back to her classes.

"Well, Ceki, what do you think of Faya's and Rab's baby?" he asked, sitting down beside her. He smiled at the child, and she forgot she was being so very quiet, and started to tell him what a lovely baby it was, how she had been allowed to let Mai-dwar hold her finger, how long she could suckle, and how very misty blue her eyes were. At the sound of her voice, Faya turned, realizing Ceki was still there.

"Ceki! You are supposed to be in class now, aren't you?" she asked.

"Yes, but I thought - I mean maybe I could - oh, couldn't I just stay here for a while? Please, Faya. I'll be very quiet so I won't wake Mai-dwar, and anyway, classes are almost over for today. Please let me stay?"

Rab laughed then sobered. Putting on a very solemn face he turned to his wife. "Please, Fayasas, may Ceki stay for supper? I'll take her back afterwards, and she really did lead me here when I was going to stop and talk to Asorum before coming to you."

Faya just as seriously considered her answer, then they both broke into laughter. "Yes, you little scamp, you may stay for supper. And Rab, you are just as incorrigible as she is. How do you think we will ever be able to teach Mai-dwar her responsibilities if this is allowed to go on!" Even Benai chuckled, and the three grown-ups decided to hold an impromptu picnic in the herb garden.

Ceki was in ecstacy. Not only was she going to be allowed to stay, but she was being accepted into the world of the people she adored and looked up to. Before she could stop herself, she whirled around on one foot, knocked over a small table, spilled a container of milk that Faya had half drunk, and woke the baby. In sudden shock at what she had done, she stared at Faya, then Rab, then Benai, and burst into tears. The baby began to cry, Rab stooped to pick up the broken container, Faya got up too suddenly and almost stumbled, and Benai caught Mai-dwar before Faya could lose her hold on her baby.

Rab, looking up from the floor where he was still kneeling, he remarked rather wryly that while he had been on picnics before, never had he been on one that started as badly as this one, but a bad start made a good ending, and he, personally, was so hungry he didn't care who broke what, and it was probably time for Mai-dwar to have her supper, too. Ceki hurled herself into his arms, catching him off balance and they both went down flat on the floor. He gathered the still sobbing child into his lap and simply held her, rocking gently back and forth. Faya looked at him with gratitude and tenderness, Benai went to ask if they could have the evening meal here in the garden, and the baby stopped crying and began to nurse.

"See, Ceki, everything is all right now. No harm done to anything or anyone. Now stop crying, and when Benai comes back, we'll still have that picnic." Rab hugged the little girl and set her on her feet. Getting to his own feet, he leaned over Faya, who had settled back in her chair, and watched his daughter as she contentedly had her own picnic.

"Faya, my darling Faya, she is the most beautiful thing I've ever seen, and so are you," he whispered. As Ceki came to his side, he put one arm around her, the other around his beloved wife, and no man was ever happier or more at peace with the world than Rabithi the priest.

Chapter Twenty-six

The Ceremony of Acknowledgment was set for two days later. Rab and Faya had asked permission of Asorum to have the entire Temple, including the children, present. They had chosen Ianera to be the one who presented the baby to the Priest, and Dohnnie, of course, stood in again for Kadah, as she had done at Faya's wedding. Rab's friends were away in another part of the land, so he asked Benai to help in his part of the naming ceremony.

Mai-dwar was dressed in the finest clothes Dohnnie had brought her from the City. The package Rab had dropped when Ceki met him was retrieved, and when Faya opened it, she found a robe the color of new fonta flowers, the soft grey-blue of a lake at dawn. She wore it with a darker blue sash, whose tassels fell to the floor, and around her throat, she wore the blue beads Rab had given her, beads she loved and was seldom without. The great Hall was filled with flowers; the incense, faint and sweet, rose from the braziers, and the soft breeze that stole in from the open entrance brought yet another scent from the fruiting trees.

As the Ceremony started, Asorum stood at the foot of the great stairs, the musicians behind him on the steps, and the singers on either side, forming a half circle of happy faces. Rab, in a wine colored robe trimmed with silver, faced Asorum, and Faya stood beside him. Dohnnie, as stand-in for Kadah, walked into the Hall carrying Mai-dwar. She kissed and blessed the baby, then handed her to Ianera, who in turn held her up to face Asorum."Who is this child?" asked the priest.

"She is the daughter of Fayasas, who stands before you, and Rabithi, who acknowledges her," Benai answered.

Asorum turned to Rab. "Do you, indeed, make claim that she is your daughter? Will you care for her, and for her mother? Will you honor them both with your name and with your blessing?" The priest smiled at Rab, who took Mai-dwar from Ianera's arms.

"I am Rabithi, a priest, and I will do all these things. I give this child her name in accordance with her mother's wish, and I will care for them both, and honor them both. She is my child. I sired her. I acknowledge her to be mine." Rab put his hand on the baby's head in blessing.

"Give this child a name." Asorum took the baby, who had not stirred since she was brought into the great hall.

"Her name is Mai-dwar, the Beloved. The daughter of Fayasas and Rabithi." Rab stepped back as Asorum turned toward the assembled people.

"You are all witness to the naming of this new soul, Mai-dwar. From this moment, no one shall question her parentage, nor shall she ever become outcast because of doubt." He turned back to Faya and Rab. "I call upon the Happy Spirits, the Singing Ones who stand in the presence of the Power, to bless this child, Mai-dwar. Her name shall be written on the scroll you, Fayasas, hold; and on your scroll, Rabithi, so the generations will be complete. I give her back to you with the sure knowledge that she will bring joy to you both, and a great comfort to all who know her. In her days to come, she will be the relief of many who seek sanctuary, and one who eases the pain of those who suffer. I have read her shining soul, and it is a brilliance beyond anything we can imagine. Faya," here he dropped from the formal into the informal, "take this precious child and raise her according to the teachings of the Temple and in obedience to the commands of the Power we all worship. She is truly a beloved gift."

"Thank you, Asorum. I also have a gift for her." Taking off the blue beads, she carefully wound them around the baby's throat. "These I treasure above anything I have ever had. I give them to her now, with the wish that someday she will find a man to love as I love her father who gave the beads to me."

Mai-dwar finally opened her eyes, yawned, and her tiny star- fish hands clutched at the finger Rab extended to her. With that, then entire assembly burst into applause. The musicians struck their instruments, the chorus took up the song, and everyone joined in the Welcome Song. Ceki, who had been as solemn as a little owl, bounced forward, claiming Faya's attention, and said in her piping voice, "Is it time to have the party now?" If there had been any solemnity, it was shattered, and the people gathered around the mother and baby, laughing and chatting, piling the gifts they had brought into Rab's arms, and the rest of the day was spent in the enjoyment of the party Faya and Rab had promised Ceki.

Chapter Twenty-seven

When Mai-dwar was almost a year old her father was sent on a mission to the northern provinces. Upon his return, he and the men who had accompanied him were closeted with Asorum. The news they brought was grim. The country was in turmoil because of new laws recently put into effect. The Judges had grown stronger than ever. They had issued judgements against many of the smaller temples across the country, having taxed them beyond their ability to pay, and had forced them to close. Many of the teachers and priests who had lived in the temples the greater parts of their lives, found themselves homeless. Parents who had sent their children to the temples for schooling were now required to support the secular schools under the supervision of the Judges.

The most disheartening news was that many people did not know which way to go. They were denied their old beliefs, but were given nothing to replace them. Some were quite happy that they were no longer expected to pay tithes to the temples; others were bewildered at the intensity of feeling among their neighbors. Arguments flared between those who followed the old precepts of peace and justice, holding to their deep love and respect for the temples, and those who were now being incited to change their habits of prayer and devotion to the Power and join the 'new religion'.

Asorum spent several hours of discussion with Rab's group, trying desperately to find a way of holding the people in the City to their old beliefs. He could do nothing about the scattered cities across Atlantis, nor about the outlying farming communities. Atlantis was a large country, though smaller than it had once been, due to the many earthquakes that had destroyed much of the land and swept it into the surrounding sea. There was still volcanic action in the south, so far only smoke from the mountains, but still threatening. More ominous lately was the talk of increasing the output of the generators that supplied power to the country, and this worried Asorum, knowing as he did the potential for danger of overload.

The power came from a great crystal in the center of the country, placed there by the ancients, long before the memory of anyone now living. It was so finely tuned to the universe that it could draw energy from not only the sun, but the stars themselves. Very few in Atlantis had ever seen this crystal, and it was held in almost superstitious awe by many. It was said to pulsate, and this alone would have made it a thing of great mystery. It sat on a high mountain, guarded by priests whose knowledge of the mighty stone's power was passed down from father to son over many generations.

What Rab reported to Asorum was the rumor that the Judges had somehow managed to acquire access to the site of the crystal, and were beginning to give orders as to how the power it generated was to be used. Instead of being distributed among the provinces as needed, extra generators being set up were to harness the energy for quite another use, thus depriving the people of what many considered their birthright, freely given since the dawn of their history.

Asorum paced the floor of the great library where the meeting took place. "Rab, have you ever actually seen the great crystal?" he asked.

"No, Asorum, I have not. Nor has anyone I know. We are only reporting the rumors that are sweeping the country. Rumors that seem to have a solid foundation, since we have heard them from so many different sources. Of course, I know that it is just a rumor, so far, but I am disturbed and fear what reaction even a rumor may have." Rab paused and looked at his companions. "We have been forced to dress, not as priests, but as travelers, in order to avoid confrontation with men who would like to see the temples closed permanently. The Judges are unbelievably powerful in certain parts of the country. I only hope that Faya never learns what her father has become," he added.

"I, too, share that hope," answered Asorum. "Not only Faya, but several of our older students have seen their families divided by this. So far, we have managed to keep the worst of the rumors from the younger children, but even they are beginning to understand that something is wrong. Those allowed to go into the City come back with questions. They can't help hearing people talk when they are in the shops. Another problem is the parents. They come here for visits and they, of course, talk. Then the children begin to wonder what's going on, and at the moment I have no answer." He shook his head. "It is a great evil that has fallen upon us."

"What should we do next?" asked one of the priests. "Can we forbid contact with the people in the City?"

"You know the answer to that," said Asorum wearily. "We could no more close our doors than close our hearts. When one comes to us for help, we give help. When we are asked for food or shelter, we give food and shelter. When a man is sick, we call our Healers, and our prayers go to the Power. No, my friend, we cannot and will not forsake our ways just because we are fearful. Whatever we must do, we will find a way of doing." He was to regret those words bitterly in the days to come.

Rab finally had a chance to see his wife and daughter. Faya was torn between the joy of having her husband home again, and her dismay at the way he looked. Rab was tired and it showed more plainly than ever before. It was a bone weariness that had little to do with physical exertion. After an almost perfunctory kiss, he dropped down on a chair with a sigh that seemed torn from his heart. Faya was frightened. Rab had never come back even from a few days away from the Temple without making his return a small celebration, in which she had joined happily.

This time, he had been gone for more than ten days, and there was no joy, only weariness.

She knelt down beside him, and gently removed his sandals. They were dusty and almost worn through. When he smiled his thanks, her breath caught in her throat.

"Darling, what has happened?" she asked, trying not to sound as apprehensive as she really was. "You were gone so long this time, and I know Asorum has been watching for you for several days. We both have," she added.

"Faya, please don't ask me just now. I've spent too many hours giving our report, and all I want to do is have a quick bite of something - anything - .and then sleep for a week." He grinned weakly, then sighed again and put out his hand to pull her into his arms. "I'm sorry, darling. I'm just so tired. I didn't mean to be short with you."

Faya leaned forward to kiss him again, and then stood up. "I'll get you something. Would you like some wine first? Benai always leaves some here so we can have a glass in the evening while we talk over the day's work."

She moved to a table and poured a glass for her husband and one for herself. "Here, darling, as he always says, 'one small glass but only one'. Then I'll fix you a light supper and you can...."

She bit off the sentence as she looked down at her husband. Rab's eyes were closed and he was breathing evenly. Faya set the two glasses back on the table, picked up a light shawl to cover him and then quietly pulled a stool beside his chair. She sat there for almost an hour before he stirred. When he did, he muttered some words under his breath she could not understand. She gently stroked his forehead, willing him to wake, but unwilling to disturb him.

He finally opened his eyes, yawned and sat upright. "Was I asleep,

Faya? Sorry. I didn't mean to black out like that. I guess I was more tired than I realized. What time is it?"

"It's not so late, Rab. We could be in time for the Blessing and the evening meal if you feel up to it. Or I could have something brought in here for us. I'm sure Asorum knows how tired you and your friends are."

"I'm perfectly able to go to the meal with you; but first, I want to see my daughter. Where is she? I haven't heard a peep out of her. Is everything all right?" He looked around the room, really seeing it for the first time tonight, and realizing that Mai-dwar was not there.

"Of course she is all right. I would have told you if there was anything wrong. Ianera has her. When I knew you were home, I asked if she would take her until you had a chance to rest a bit. She has just learned to 'sing' along with the harp. At least she thinks she's singing, and once she gets started, there's no stopping her until she wears herself out."

Rab grinned. "Takes after her mother."

Faya glanced at him obliquely. "Oh? And who is always pestering me to play? Who says my harp is one reason he married me? Who says my fingers are enchanted? And who says...."

"Stop! Stop! I plead guilty." Rab laughed and pulled her into his arms. She came willingly, raising her face for a kiss and running her fingers through his hair.

"Rab, I have missed you so much. Ten days seemed like ten years. You won't have to go again for a while, will you?"

"I don't think so, Faya. We pretty well got all the information we need at present, but what we'll be able to do with it is anyone's guess." He looked so suddenly serious that Faya's heart skipped a beat.

"What, Rab? What information? Can you tell me?" "I think Asorum might want to talk to us all, and we'll wait and see what he has to say first. Right now, I need a quick wash up and then supper. I'm starved! Could you ask Ianera to bring Mai-dwar back? I haven't seen my child in ten days and I don't want her to forget me."

"No chance of that! But I'll go get Mai-dwar and then feed her while you get cleaned up. She will probably be sleepy by now, since Ianera has had her out in the Children's Garden almost all afternoon. Did I tell you that Ceki is now the official baby-sitter? She loves Mai-dwar, and Mai-dwar loves her."

Rab stared at his wife. "Do you mean you let that little rascal take care of a baby? She's not much more than a baby herself!"

"She's perfectly capable of watching her sleep, and really, Rab, that's about all she has to do. She knows to call me if there's anything she can't handle."

"Call you? You mean, she would leave Mai-dwar and run to find you? By that time, it might be too late. I can't believe you would allow that child...."

"Rab, listen to me, I have taught Ceki to call me the same way I used to call Mother. She learned very easily. I could ask her right now to bring Mai-dwar back, and she would do it. She has learned to be responsible because she loves both of us. Don't worry, my dear, I would never ever do anything that would put our baby in jeopardy."

Rab sighed. "I have never understood why you and I can't communicate that way."

Faya laughed. "But you almost always know what I am thinking, and that is sometimes more that I bargained for! I can never really fool you. Why don't you just relax while I go get our remarkable child and introduce her to her father, whom she knows perfectly well." She blew him a kiss and walked swiftly out of the room. Rab picked up the glass of wine he had not drunk, and drank it and then drank Faya's as well. "Thanks, Benai," he murmured under his breath.

By the time Faya came back with Mai-dwar, Rab had removed most of the dust and changed his clothes. The baby was chattering away at a great rate, although only Faya seemed to know what she was saying. To Rab it was entirely unintelligible. When she saw her father, though, she crowed with delight and held out her arms to him. As he took her from Faya, she gurgled happily and settled down in his arms, still talking a mile a minute.

"What is she saying?" He asked his wife. "Can you understand her?"

"Of course I can! She is telling you how much she liked being out in the garden, how sweet the air smells, and how very happy she is to have you back home."

"Of course. Why didn't I understand that! Now really, Faya, she hasn't formed any words yet, has she? How old must babies be before they can really talk? Do you suppose she is slow for her age?"

Faya laughed at his anxious face. "Oh, Rab, babies take their own sweet time learning to talk. She's just where she should be. Give her a few more months and she will talk your arm off! Slow, indeed! She's a very intelligent child, as anyone who wasn't half drunk on Benai's wine could plainly see. Give her to me, it's past time for her to be in bed, and Ceki will be here in a few minutes."

She took Mai-dwar, who was at first reluctant to leave her father. Fretting for a second or two, she was almost instantly drowsy. Ianera had already fed her, and as Faya laid her down on her little pallet, she murmured sleepily and her eyes closed. Faya had barely started the same sleep song her own mother had sung to her before the baby was asleep. She leaned over and kissed her, then motioned Rab to step outside while they waited for Ceki.

Chapter Twenty-eight

The peace that had been so much of Faya's inheritance in the Temple now seemed to have been shattered. Students came and went, the daily life was the same as before, but the feeling of unease grew. When the time came for the yearly Ceremony of Seeing, the Temple was as usual scrubbed, fresh flowers brought in, and everyone had a happy air of expectancy. When the morning finally came, two young students, Marchi and Alia, took their places on the wide porch, as Faya and Krola had done years before.

The visiting priests who attended the Ceremony walked slowly around the small lake on the front lawn, holding the glowing balls in their hands, then forming a semi- circle, placed them on the ground and waited for Asorum to look into the golden basin.

When he had looked for what seemed much longer than usual, he raised his face and the priests picked up their own orbs and looked deeply into them. Asorum was looking at them as though he was willing them to disagree with what he had seen. But each bowed and nodded his head. There was no smile on any face, and Asorum looked grim. Everyone there knew the outlook for the coming year was not what they had hoped, but no one knew exactly what Asorum had seen.

Instead of forming the lines back to the great entrance and being greeted by the children, the priests broke the circle and surrounded Asorum. Faya, who was watching the Ceremony from just inside the entrance, lost sight of her old friend. She turned to Rab, who suddenly put his arm around her. "Rab," she whispered, "what did he see?"

"I don't know," Rab answered slowly, "but whatever it was, he certainly didn't expect it, nor did the others."

Asorum finally walked away from the other priests, toward the herb garden, his head bowed and his eyes on the ground. Haindohne, who was keeping her eye on the younger girls, had a worried look, and seemed undecided just what to do.

The two youngsters, Marchi and Alia, who for weeks had been practicing the customary greeting, found themselves with nothing to do. "What do you suppose has happened?" asked Marchi. "Asarum always comes back here and we sing the Joyous Song."

"I don't know," answered Alia, "but I'm scared."

"Me, too. Asarum looked so - so - so stern. Do you think we did something wrong?" Marchi always assumed the worst when there was anything out of the ordinary.

"Of course not," said Alia. "We did just what we were supposed to do...didn't we, Haindohne?" She tugged at the older woman's sleeve. "Didn't we?"

Haindohne seemed distracted. "Yes, of course - you were just fine. I must go - no - you children must go back to your rooms and wait there until I call you." Haindohne gave Marchi a little shove and hurried off. Alia stared after her in puzzled concern. Dohnnie had never before been so abrupt and had always answered her questions.

Later that morning, just before lunch, Haindohne came for the girls, explaining that she had not meant to leave them so long, but things had been going rather badly. Most of the priests who had come so far were leaving, as though there was a vital reason to get back to their own temples.

Naturally the children wanted to know why, what had happened, why was Haindohne so worried, w here was Asarum, and why didn't they finish the day as they had done every year before? Haindohne said quietly,"I can't tell you anything more right now, but I'm sure Asarum will explain when he gets back."

Lunch that day was unusually quiet. There was no laughter among the younger children, and the older girls ate quickly and without any talking among themselves as had always been customary. After the Thanksgiving, one of the teachers came in and asked the children to remain in the dining hall. Asarum wished to speak to them. A surprised and worried murmur softly filled the room, before Asarum entered and stood for a moment as though unsure of what to say.

"As you all probably know by now, this morning brought some unexpected and disturbing information. I'm sure you all looked forward to this day, which has always been one of great joy. I am sorry it was so different this year. We will wait just a minute for your teachers to join us. I want everyone here before we discuss what has happened."

The students waited quietly for the priests and teachers to come in. When everyone was assembled, Asorum motioned for two of the older visiting priests to join him at the table. Then he introduced them, saying that they were among those who had learned to look deeply into the crystal balls they carried and by their efforts, enabled him to see clearly the pictures formed in the golden basin of water. What he had seen was not reassuring for the coming year. The pictures that formed had shown an upheaval little short of chaos in the laws governing Atlantis, and a great unrest among the people. The visiting priests affirmed what he said, adding that they had been talking to people in many of the different provinces, and had found the same feeling of disquiet. The King was no longer the ruler. The Judges had seized control, and were changing laws as they pleased, leaving the populace in total confusion. Their greatest worry, the two visitors said, was the lack of concern about the energy source, the great crystal. It's power was now being used to probe deeper and deeper into the earth, searching for the precious metals so valued for their ability to buy goods of all kinds. People were looking forward to being wealthy beyond their wildest dreams, due to the promises made by the Judges, who knew very well how to play on the greed that seemed to be inherent in so many people. Asorum and many of the older priests who had studied the planets, the stars and the earth itself, knew of the danger this deep probing could bring. Kwali, the oldest of the visitors, rose and asked to speak. Asorum bowed his permission and took his seat. When the old man stood, Faya noticed how bent his shoulders were, and how deeply veined his hands and neck. His voice was slightly husky, as though speaking was not something he was used to doing, but his words were clear .

"I do not know if my honored host, Asorum, has ever discussed with you the condition of the land we are now living on. This has been my life-long study. This fragile planet we call home is just that, fragile. If we use it unwisely, if we dishonor it, we must take the consequences, and those consequences may be bitter. We have, as you all know, a country that has much volcanic action. In the past, part of Atlantis has been lost because of this. The sea also has reclaimed much of what once was home to many. My friends, we are perched on a very unstable part of the earth. Beneath our feet are great pockets of natural gas, which we can and have tapped for our use. But under the guidance of the thinking men of our time, it has been used wisely, drawing what amounts to a minuscule part of the gas that is actually available, and being very careful not to upset the delicate balance by drilling too deeply and taking too much." He paused and coughed lightly.

"Now I understand that the new laws give certain people," here he paused and looked around, then continued, "the right to drill as they please, and the worst part is their attempted use of the great crystal for power. So far, they have not been able to harness this energy. But they will. They will. And when they do, may all the spirits of the Universe protect us." He looked at Asorum, bowed, and took his seat. For a long moment, there was no sound in the room.

Finally Asorum rose from his seat and again addressed his people. "What our elder, Kwali, has said, I know to be true. I, too, have been greatly concerned over the misuse of our power source, but up until now it seemed there was no immediate danger. Now, I am afraid there may be. What we have to do is something we all must decide. Please, go back to your own rooms and spend the rest of this unhappy day in prayer to the great Creator. Ask for wisdom, for understanding, and for the best way to right what is becoming a terrible wrong. Ask for guidance, and tonight, in your dreams, ask for an answer. Perhaps the Power will tell you what you need to know."

The old priest bowed his head as the people quietly repeated the Thanksgiving. Faya was in tears, Haindohne's hands were trembling so badly she knocked over a cup as she tried to tried to pick it up, and even Ceki was solemn. When they reached their own room, Faya turned to Rab. "Why did Asorum let the children hear that?" she asked in anguish. "They are too young to be frightened in this way. I don't understand how he could have done such a thing!"

Rab put his arms around her. "Faya, I don't know, but I rather guess Asorum had his reasons. He never does anything without a lot of thought, so obviously he knows what he is doing. If he feels the young ones need to know about this, I'm sure there is a plan in that wise old head."

"But did you see Ceki's face? I've never seen her look like that, not even when she is having a tantrum. I just don't see any reason why he had to frighten them so!" Faya began to pace the floor; Mai-dwar, who had been quietly playing with her blanket after her nap, started to fret; Rab wheeled around to pick her up, and as he reached her pallet, he stumbled over a low bench that was not in its usual place. For the first time since she had known him, Faya heard Rab let out a string of words that, while she could not understand them, she knew quite well what they meant. "Oh, Rab, what's happening to us?" she moaned in despair. "I've never seen you so upset, and I feel as though the rug has been pulled out from under my feet."

"Faya, I'm sorry I spoke as I did." He grinned rather sheepishly. "I'm just glad you don't speak that language! I feel that with Asorum and Kwali in control," he sobered as he picked the baby up and rocked her in his arms, "we will come out of this all right. We have all had a harrowing day, but here in our own room, just you and Mai-dwar and I, things don't look quite so bleak. When I have you two, I can face anything."

His wife laid her head on his shoulder, and felt his kiss on her hair. "I know, darling, it's just that everything seems so out of kilter today. Let me take her," she reached for her daughter, "it's time she had her own lunch."

Rab handed the baby to Faya, who slipped her robe off her shoulder to give her breast to the baby.

"When will she be completely weaned?" he asked. "She's eating almost everything in sight. Never saw such an appetite in anyone so small." He smiled down at the two, so alike and so different, one light and one dark.

"She could be weaned any time, but I still like the feeling of her taking my milk; it is such a bond that I hate to break it." "Well," Rab said slyly, "if you were to wean her, perhaps she might like to have a brother - or maybe a sister. What do you think?"

Faya sighed, then broke into a laugh. "Rab, you demon, with everything that is going on right now, I really don't think it is the right time for another child. But," she added hastily, "I'll keep it in mind!"

"Isn't she about through nursing right now? Faya, all of a sudden I have a great need to feel my wife in my arms." Faya looked down at her baby, then gently pulled away from her. Mai-dwar was content enough not to give more than a token whimper, so Faya laid her back on her little pallet and gave her a favorite doll to play with. As she started to pull her robe back up to cover her breasts, Rab's hands covered them, and her answering passion was enough to make them both forget the request to spend the rest of the day in meditation and prayer.

Later, Rab gently pulled a light cover over his wife's nakedness and gathered her close. With his arms pillowing her head, he murmured, "Faya, if the Power has given us such a gift as this, is it not a form of prayer when you give yourself to me as I give myself to you?"

"When love is shared, not in lust, but in the passion that comes from two bodies and two hearts in joy and trust, then yes, I do feel it is a gift that we should be thankful for. But we must also remember that more then just our family is riding on the prayers we offer. If we both try to sleep now and dream, maybe we will come up with something that could be useful." She snuggled more deeply on his shoulder and closed her eyes. In a very few minutes her breathing deepened and she slept.

Rab could not, though, and lay for an hour just thinking about the things he had heard and seen, what they might mean to his own family and to the rest of the country. He had traveled widely, looking for places that could be settled if the need should arise; places in the rest of the vast world where people from Atlantis could find new homes, keeping their beliefs, and raising their families without the fear of being forced to follow precepts that were untenable. He finally moved restlessly and Faya opened her eyes and sat up.

"Oh, darling, I did go to sleep! I'm afraid I didn't dream, though. Did you?" She yawned and stretched. "What did you dream, Rab?"

"I haven't been asleep. I was just lying here thinking about the places I've been, and how much I would like you to see them. Asorum wants the priests to find other lands for our people in case it becomes necessary to leave Atlantis, and this might be a good time to combine the reasons for going right now. Couldn't we leave Mai-dwar with Ianera and take a short trip together? We never have, and I did promise you I would show you some of the countries I've visited. It really is time to wean her, and since Ianera and Ceki take such good care of her...."

Faya sat up suddenly. "Rab, do you suppose it would be all right? We have never left her before, and I don't know how she would take being here without me."

"I don't know how much time we have, Faya, not with the state Atlantis is in right now. Couldn't you wean her in just a couple of weeks?" He stood up and slipped a light robe on. "I know this isn't much time to prepare anything, but I believe it could be done if we made our plans right away."

"Is there really so much hurry, Rab? She's just a little past two years, and I really hate the thought of leaving her, even for a short trip. Maybe we could take her with us. Would that be so impossible?"

"I never thought of that," Rab said slowly. "Wait - what about asking Ianera to go with us to help take care of Mai-dwar?"

"Rab, what a great idea! I'll ask her tonight after the evening meal. Where do you want to go?" Faya threw on her own robe that she had dropped earlier, and as she tied the sash and slipped into her sandals, she was thinking about some of the countries she had only heard of. "Do you suppose we could go to the country Benai lived in when he was a child? How far is it? And how would we get there?"

"I think that would be a possibility, we could ask him about it. I've never been there, myself, but I'm sure it would be an interesting place to visit, and we are still looking for new lands to settle in. We will need them soon."

"Rab, is there honestly so much danger? Is it because of the new laws? Or is there something more I have not been told?"

Her husband looked steadily at her for a moment, then making up his mind, he said quietly, "My dear, we are almost out of time. The drilling Kwali spoke of is a very real danger. Have you any idea what could happen if we broke through the crust that holds back the enormous gas pockets we are sitting over? The very few wells we have drilled are merely surface wells. They don't pose any problem, but we don't really know the thickness of the layers of earth protecting us; and if by reckless use of the great crystal's energy we broke through, no one could be sure what would happen. Perhaps an eruption of natural gas that would choke most of us before we knew what hit us. Or more likely, the earth might cave in to fill the space suddenly emptied, and the surrounding sea would destroy Atlantis before anyone had time to get away."

Faya stared at him in disbelief mingled with horror. "Oh, Rab, no! That could not happen! Please, tell me you are making this up. What have we done that the Power would allow such a calamity?" She put her hands on his shoulders, looking beseechingly into his face. "Rab, please..."

"Darling, I'm sorry I told you. I would give anything to say that I am seeing a mountain where there is only a little hill, but I'm afraid the possibility is real. For now, though, let's concentrate on taking the trip with Mai-dwar and Ianera, and perhaps we will find a place for our people to live in peace."

Faya nodded. "Yes, Rab, we will do that. If the Power is willing, we will find a land that will allow us to build another Atlantis, if that's what we must do. I will go with you and we will find it." She looked out at the garden, now glowing in the late afternoon light. The soft colors of the herbs were struck with the last rays of the sun, tipping the plants with gold.

How can I leave this, she thought. What would it be like living in a totally strange place, with no Atlantis to come back to? What of the Temple, the home she loved so devotedly? What of the friends she had made? Who would be able to go, and who would have no choice but to stay and face destruction? And what of Asorum? Would he leave, too?

Another thought crossed the chaotic surface of her mind. What of the Judges? Suppose they were no longer able to control Atlantis, would that make any difference, or had things gone too far already? Everything seemed to fall back on the Judges, and her father was one of them.

She seldom thought of him any more, but he was still a part of her life, and even though he had made no attempt to see her, not even when her mother died, she could never quite forget the man she had once loved and admired.

She finished dressing, slipping the string of blue beads over her head, and adding a bracelet Rab had brought her, also the blue sky stone, set in silver. It hugged her slender wrist and finished off her costume. Her husband looked critically at his wife. “Do you know, I believe I have the most beautiful woman in Atlantis ready to accompany me to the dining hall.”

Faya drew herself up to stand with eyes cast down. “Thank you, kind sir, I am appreciative of your remarks, but my mother told me never to be taken in by a man’s flattery. Do you by any chance have any ulterior motives?”

“Why, certainly, madam. And after the meal I shall be happy to explain each and every one. I will even be glad to demonstrate.”

“Oh, sir, you should not say such things to a young, innocent and inexperienced girl.” She looked up and fluttered her eyelashes at him.

"My heart is all a'quiver!" Then her lips twitched and she exploded into laughter. "Rab, you demon, wasn't this afternoon enough for one day? Come on, let's go eat. I'm starved!" They walked out, arm in arm, meeting Ceki on the way. Faya had 'called' her young friend, who would stay with Mai-dwar until they got back.

They spoke to Ianera that evening, and she agreed to accompany them wherever they went. She dearly loved the child who had brought so much joy into her life, and she was eager to explore the world she had never seen. Plans were made, re-made and re-re-made. Faya, as every woman has always done, laid out far too many robes, sandals and cloaks. Rab had to explain that they would be better off with half the number she wanted to take.

She agreed to travel light, but insisted that the blue beads would accompany her, no matter what else she had to leave. They had become a symbol of her love for both Rab and her daughter, and she was hardly ever seen without them. Mai-dwar loved playing with them, winding them around her neck as she had seen her mother do, and even chewing on the beads when she had begun cutting her teeth. Faya had taken them away from her more than once, after finding that even a baby's tiny teeth could mar the soft stones. Oh well, she thought, happiness has its price. They agreed to leave in six days. Asorum looked both apprehensive and pleased at their decision. He gave detailed instructions to Rab, who had been closeted with him and Benai for several hours. Asorum's meaning was clear: find a land where there are already people living, where the soil is fertile and where there is no strife. Groups had been sent out before, and had come back with reports of several possible areas, but the old priest wanted to be sure that they had covered all possibilities. There were so many people who would have to leave Atlantis forever, and they would be needed to teach the necessary techniques of survival, if it came to that.

Chapter Twenty Nine

Fayasas and Rab, with Ianera and Mai-dwar, took first a small boat down the river Kadah had once taken, to the place where it emptied into the sea. There they boarded a great ship that would stand the possibly rough waters they would encounter, especially going through a narrow pass that led into the Blue Ocean. The water in the sea that surrounded their country was uncomfortably boisterous, but in a few days, Faya found her sea legs and began to enjoy the motion. Mai-dwar seemed to have been a sailor all her life, and chuckled her way into the hearts of everyone on board.

Ianera wanted first to die. Then she wanted Faya and Rab to die with her for having suggested this would be a pleasant trip. When Rab wanted to take her up on deck to get some fresh air, she would gladly have gone if she could have pushed him overboard.

Finally, seasickness gave way to a sort of truce with her stomach, and she reluctantly sat on deck for a few hours before deciding she might not die after all. She still glowered at Rab when he walked past her with Mai-dwar, who by now was really talking like the little animal one of the sailors kept on a leash. Faya had made friends with some of the other passengers and many of the crew. She was interested in everything and everybody, and kept her new friends busy answering question after question.

When they finally reached the land they had been sailing toward, the ship turned south and entered the mouth of a wide river. The people who lived along the bank were different from any Faya had ever seen. They were dark complected, with black hair, and eyes, and although they did not seem hostile, there was really no warmth in their faces. This country was new to Rab, and he was a little apprehensive about his commission to find a place for the Atlanteans to settle. They sailed up river for a day, then moored at a rather marshy landing.

The swampy area was not to Rab's liking, and he asked Faya and Ianera to stay on board while he talked to some of the people there. When he returned some hours later, he explained that this area was not a healthy place, and they would have to go on further up river before a hospitable country could be found. The ship they had sailed on was too large to continue, so the captain made arrangements for them to transfer to a smaller boat.

Both the women were happy to leave the area. Even Mai-dwar fretted in the steamy heat. Rab paced nervously, not really liking this country, but hoping they would find another area that would suit them better.

The following day the heat was just as fierce, but the swampy area had been left behind. There were many mud huts along the river bank, and the people here seemed much more cheerful, waving at the boat and shouting what Rab assumed to be their wares for sale. They docked late that afternoon. For the first time in what seemed to Ianera to be simply an eternity, they left the ship and went ashore for a brief walk around the small village. The people were preparing their evening meals, and food was readily offered to the strangers. Children stared, then hid behind their mothers, but Faya had a way of drawing them out, and soon everyone was happily talking, not one word of which was understood by either group. Smiles worked their magic, though, and when Rab and his little family returned to their ship, they felt as though they had made at least a start. When they arose, the morning was cool, but as soon as the sun was well up in the sky, the heat again hit them. Neither Rab nor Faya were sure this country was suitable, but they had no doubt that the people would remain friendly. There seemed to be little if any industry; most of the villagers they had seen so far depended on their meager crops and on fish that they caught in the river. There were no large houses that they could see, nor were there any shops such as they had been used to in the cities of Atlantis.

For the first time in her life, Faya was almost happy with her looks. Her dark hair and eyes were the norm here. Rab and Ianera were the exception, with their blue eyes and red-gold hair, and of course Mai-dwar seemed almost an elfin child. The children in this country were almost afraid to look directly at her. Faya wound a scarf around her daughter's head, covering as much of her as possible, while Ianera and Rab covered as much of themselves as they could, not only for protection against the intense sun, but in order not to frighten anyone. There was nothing they could do about their light eyes. They were simply strangers in a strange land.

The one thing Faya had wanted so see was the huge statue of the human-headed lion that Benai had told her about. Rab agreed that they should see it, but just the two of them. There was no way to get there except on foot, or by donkey, and it would be too exhausting for Mai-dwar. A guide had agreed to take them after they had managed to draw a rather crude picture in the sand, illustrating what they wanted to see. Ianera stayed on the small boat with the baby, and Faya and Rab started off to the most desolate part of the earth they had ever seen. Sand was everywhere. It blew in their faces, got into their teeth and since they were facing into the winds, even seeing was uncomfortable.

When they finally neared the great monument, Faya gasped. Benai had told her it was a huge statue, but she had no real conception of the immensity of the lion that lay majestically on the sand, its human face serenely gazing at the skyline of eternity. They could see it from far off, and the closer they got, the more awe-inspiring it became.

"Rab, what do you suppose it is?" Faya asked.

"I haven't any idea. It looks old, but almost alive. It's his face that puzzles me," he answered.

"Not his face," his wife replied, "but her face. It's a woman."

"No. It can't be. Why would anyone carve a woman with a lion's body? Lions are supposed to be very fierce and protective" He winced when Faya suddenly chuckled. "Well, maybe you are right. At any rate, whoever it was supposed to be looks very wise, and almost as though he or she were waiting for something. I wonder what."

"Or who," said Faya."

They noticed their guide had drawn as far away as he could without actually leaving them. Rab motioned for him to come back to where they were, but the guide stubbornly stood his ground.

"Faya, it's a long way back. I suppose we should start. Old sour face is not going to be happy here any longer. Wonder if there is some superstition about this statue. We can't talk to the people here to ask who built it, so I guess we had better leave it to the desert."

After several more weeks of exploring the country, Rab felt they had enough information to take back to Asorum. They could honestly report that the country was beautiful in places, that the soil would probably respond to more intensive farming practices, and that the people were not unfriendly. It was a very good possibility that this far land would support many of their own people so long as they did not deprive the native population of their own way of life.

When they got back to the mouth of the river and again boarded their ship, Faya heaved a sigh of relief. She had not expected to find herself in such a primitive country; but in spite of the heat, the flies and the lack of very many things to buy to take back to her friends, she enjoyed the actual travel. Feeling for the first time in her life a sense of freedom, she began planning the next trip she and Rab would take. Then, she told herself, she would go to a country where there were the bazaars Benai had spoken of, where she could dress as she was used to dressing, without having to cover every inch of her body to avoid sunburn, where she would find the exotic cities she had dreamed of.

Ianera was determined never, but never, to leave Atlantis again, if it meant bouncing over an ocean that threw one from side to side, and where one could not stand up and walk properly without hanging on to a rail.

Rab teased her all the way home, but she was adamant. No, she would absolutely not go on board a ship again, not even if it meant she would lose Faya's love forever! Not one foot would she ever again take toward a sea voyage.

When their ship met again the great river that circled Atlantis, they were happy to get back into the smaller boat that would take them home. By now Mai-dwar was entirely comfortable being on the water, and ran all over the boat, keeping Faya and Ianera constantly wary of her getting too close to the rail and falling overboard.

Rab was writing his impressions of the country they had just left, readying it for Asorum and the other priests to read and decide if this was a place for Atlantean settlers to go. It was a time to stop and take stock of what might lie ahead, each of them asking the Power to guide their decisions, and lead them in the right choices.

Chapter Thirty

They were met at their own small dock by Asorum, Krola, Shaleen and Dohnnie, the welcoming smiles and hugs bringing answering smiles and a few happy tears. After the travelers had been given time to go to their own quarters and rest an hour or so, they were summoned to the great entrance hall. As they walked toward the pool in the center, Faya looked around for something she felt was missing. Ceki. Where was Ceki? Was she so unhappy at being left that she refused to come and meet them now?

That was the first question Faya asked Asorum. “Where is Ceki?”

His face was somber as he looked first at Haindohne, then back at Fayasas. “I wish I did not have to greet you with this news, Faya, but Ceki has left the Temple. Her parents came for her seven days after you left. She has been gone since then, and we can not persuade her father and mother to bring her back.”

“But why, Asorum? She seemed so happy here and I thought her mother was pleased at the progress she was making.”

The old priest sighed deeply. “Yes, she was. You know Ceki’s father is a contractor, one of the better ones from what I’ve heard. He was re-doing a school building, and he was promised a promotion at a much higher wage if he would transfer Ceki from the Temple to that school. He said it would look better politically, if the daughter attended the school her father built. Of course, the school is one that is monitored by the Judges. So Ceki was taken away and is now being taught the better way of life.”

Asorum’s voice was bitter, and Faya’s heart went out to him. She knew how deeply it hurt when even one child was turned in the wrong direction, and Ceki had been a very special pupil. The little girl had become very dear to Faya as well. Her first impulse was to go to Ceki’s mother and try to talk her into letting her daughter return to the Temple, but she knew it would be futile. She remembered only too well how cold her own father had been to her mother because she had defied him, and she was afraid that Ceki's father would react in much the same way. The touch of greed put a powerful tool in the hands of the Judges, and they knew well how to use it.

Faya decided to let Rab do the talking to the assembled priests. She simply wanted to go back to her own room and hold Mai-dwar. The very thought of anyone's influencing her daughter was a horror that she was determined never to allow.

The loss of Ceki was only the beginning. Several other students left the Temple, and rumor began to circulate that soon the Judges would close temples all over Atlantis. Haindohne, whose love of teaching was the best thing in her life, was distraught. She began to guard the smallest students as though she feared abduction, particularly when they had their play time in the Children's Garden. She trusted no one she didn't know personally, and even the older students noticed how she had suddenly become almost paranoid. Finally Ranoi took her in hand and explained that such fear was unhealthy, reflecting upon the children she was trying to protect as much as on herself.

"Fear breeds fear," he said, "and I don't wish to see any child taught to be fearful."

Haindohne bowed her head. "I know," she answered. "It's just that I am so afraid the little ones will be taken away from all we have tried to instill in them, and then where will they be? What will they have for support if they may no longer call upon the Power? The Prayer is outlawed everywhere. How are our children to be taught values? How will they know right from wrong? Who will give them the incentive to become good citizens? To help other people? To try and make our world better for their having been here?" Her eyes filled with tears as she looked out at the beautiful garden where she had spent so many happy hours with the children.

"Dohnnie, if I may call you that, the Judges will not last forever. Greed feeds upon itself, too, and soon they will begin to squabble among themselves for the right to have just a little more than the next one has. Already, the king is no long really king, and he simply doesn't care. He has all the precious metals, the jewels and the women he can possibly want, and he's quite content to leave any decisions to someone else - anyone - .so long as he is not disturbed. It's a sad thing to watch. When he was young, he had such potential; but over the years, he has become totally uninterested in his country, and even less in its people, if that were possible."

"Yes, I know that," replied Dohnnie. "It has been said that he is never seen in public, and many people wonder if he is still alive."

"Oh, he alive," said Ranoi. "He is to all effects a prisoner in his royal palace, which suits him very well. Promise me, Dohnnie, that you will not let the children see or feel your fear. Remember what you have been taught about Shadows...."

"Face them, and the Shadows turn to Light? Yes, Ranoi, I will remember. Thank you for talking with me." She bowed and left, feeling a little less apprehensive, but still determined not to let the children stray far from her sight. She was to find out later how dangerous a decision that could be.

Chapter Thirty-One

Surprisingly, matters stood pretty much the same for over a year. There were of course all sorts of rumors, and much credence was given to some of them. Others were so absurd that no one took them seriously. There were so-called prophets who foretold everything from great wealth to great destruction. The king was dying. No, the king was going to make a royal journey throughout his kingdom to see how his people fared. Atlantis was to become a republic. Certainly not, it would stay as it was except for the Governors who would act as co-rulers with the king, and the Judges would take their places governing the provinces. Great deposits of precious metals were discovered in a remote area of the country and there would be a frantic rush to get it out of the ground. No, it was not metal, but precious gems that had been discovered.

So the stories grew and faded, grew and faded. No one knew exactly how such tales had started, but everyone was sure they were true. Well, some of them must be, mustn't they?

Asorum went back to his precious manuscripts hoping to find some solace in history. Faya worked at her herbs, learning more every day under the watchful eye of Benai. She helped Ranoi when she was needed, and of course her music was still a great part of her life. Mai-dwar was growing fast, her mother hard put to keep up with her. Rab was away more than he liked, going around the country with a small group of priests, trying to put the people's minds at ease about the rumors flying, and keeping an ear to the ground for what was really happening.

A sort of truce had settled on the temples; no more had been closed in the past year, and Asorum was almost beginning to relax. Not quite, though. He did not trust the Judges' sudden withdrawal from actively persecuting those who supported the temples. And he wondered. Why had they suddenly kept their distance? Why were they less antagonistic toward the priests? More than once the thought crept into the wise old priest's head, where was Fayasas' father, and what was he doing? He had made no effort whatsoever to see his daughter, or even ask about her. In the years Faya had spent in the Temple, she had never heard from her father, except for the brief message that he would not attend his wife's funeral.

Asorum simply did not believe that any man as ambitious as Faya's father would ever completely give up what any man would have considered an asset to his position, a child who was one of the best loved Healers and musicians in Atlantis. He was hopeful, of course, but having lived a very long life, he had seen too much of human nature to be convinced that a thacasca could change into a fonta leaf. The day soon came when he realized how right he had been.

Faya had just finished her bath in the late afternoon, shortly before she would join the others at the evening meal. Mai-dwar had been bathed by Ianera, who had taken over quite a bit of her care, and was ready to go with her mother to the dining hall. A message was sent that Faya was wanted in the library, where a visitor had asked to see her. She hastily re-braided her hair and smoothed her robe before walking swiftly through the passages that led to the entrance hall, and from there into the library. I wonder why the library, she thought. Usually visitors were met in the entrance hall, or if they needed treatment, they were taken directly down to one of the healing rooms.

She stopped in the doorway of the library, looking intently at the man who stood with his back to the window. Although his face was in shadow, she could see he was tall, slim and slightly grey. Dressed in tight leggings and a flared leather tunic over an undershirt of some glossy blue material, he looked every inch a man who was used to command. He stood quietly, waiting for the woman to enter the room. When she did, it was with hesitant steps. Something about the man held her interest far beyond mere curiosity. She was sure she did not know him, so she made the customary bow given to strangers who were always treated with courtesy. He bowed in return, but his lips twitched as though he held back a laugh, but laughter that did not reach his eyes.

Faya was puzzled. Something about the man seemed almost familiar, but she could not remember ever having met him. “You asked to see me, sir?” she said.

“Yes, Fayasas, I did. You don’t recognize me, I see. But then, why should you. It has been, let’s see, perhaps seventeen years?”

“Seventeen years, sir? I was a child then. How could you have known....” She stopped with a gasp.

“Yes, Faya?” the man smiled.

“You are...you aren’t my...father?” she asked, her knees suddenly threatening to give way. She sank down on a low bench. “Father,” she repeated. “Why?”

“Is it so unusual for a man to want to see his daughter, my dear?” He walked over to her and took her hand. It was limp in his. “Have you no greeting for me?”

Faya stood up, her anger suddenly flaring at the way he took for granted her acceptance of his coming to the Temple. The bitterness and grief he had caused her mother, and his abandonment of her, gave her the strength to answer. She withdrew her hand and stood facing him. “No, Father, I certainly do not. I have no greeting for you now or ever. Nor do I wish to prolong this conversation. You will excuse me; it is time for the evening meal, and my daughter is waiting for me.” She turned to go but stopped when he laughed.

“Yes, I heard that you were married and had a child. She must be, what, three or nearly four? Just about the age you were when Kadah took you away and brought you to this...this place. Sit down, Faya, I have something to say to you, and it concerns your child."

As she turned to face him, Faya felt a clutch of fear at the way his eyes went over her as though she was some specimen he was not particularly pleased with. He was taller than she by almost a head, and she noticed for the first time the richness of his costume; the several rings on his fingers and the shining metal headdress that held back the greying hair. Then she saw the badge on his left sleeve.

"So, you are now a Governor. Asorum always said you were ambitious." She was determined not to show her anxiety, but she could not help asking, "What of my daughter? You have no claim on her. No married woman in Atlantis may be forced to surrender her child. You know that, even though my mother had to bring me here to keep you from making a mockery of the law." "For which, my Faya, she paid dearly," he said softly. "But that is not why I am here. I would like you to meet two of my friends who will be staying on here for a while." He turned, and motioned to two men Faya had not seen when she entered the room. They had been standing beside one of the cases that held the scrolls and the shadows of the late afternoon had hidden them.

Her bow was barely an indication of their presence. The men returned it, but were silent. Her father sighed as if to reprove a bad mannered child. "Faya, I'm sure your Asorum has taught you that any guest is to be treated with respect and courtesy. These men are my friends, and have sought lodging here at the Temple for a time. I will, of course, not stay. I have much work to do and I cannot take the time away from my province, even for you, my daughter." He laughed again gently, and Faya shuddered.

Worried about his earlier remarks, she asked, "What did you mean, you had something to say to me that concerned my daughter?"

"Oh yes," he replied. "I did say that, didn't I? Well, never mind, it wasn't important, at least not at the moment. We will no doubt talk more at a later time. Oh yes," he said, understanding the look on her face, "I will be back, one day. Perhaps soon. Perhaps not. In the meantime, my two friends will help you in any way they can, any way at all. Now I really must tear myself away, even though this meeting has been all too short." He went to the young woman who by now was shaking inside so badly she could hardly stand, and again took her limp hand.

"Goodbye, Fayasas. You really do look somewhat like your mother," he said as he eyed her critically. "But if I remember correctly, you never liked your looks, did you? Pity. You are really quite attractive." He nodded at the two men and left the room.

Chapter Thirty-Two

Faya stood for a moment, then ignoring the two, she followed him out. He had already walked the short distance to the entrance hall and by the time Faya reached it, her father was going down the steps of the porch. She watched him for a minute or two, her thoughts whirling, and the fear rising in her throat until she thought she would choke. He did not look back.

Her first thought now was for Mai-dwar. She almost raced back to her own room, only to find Ianera and Mai-dwar walking calmly along the passage, chatting away like a pair of parrots. The child grinned at her mother, but did not stop. Ianera stopped short, seeing the look on her friend's face.

"Faya, my dear, what is it? You look as though you had seen a spirit!"

"I did, Ianera. One I had hoped never to see. My father was here and wanted to talk to me."

"Your father," she gasped, "but I thought - well, I don't know what I thought. You never mention him. Why was he here? Or do you want to talk about it?" The older woman was so concerned that Faya decided she had to calm herself and her friend so Mai-dwar would not hear and understand what they were saying. She put her finger to her lips and spoke in almost a whisper. "I really don't know what he wanted, but he frightened me, just being here. Let's go on to the evening meal; I want to talk to Asorum, and I don't want her to hear this just yet." She indicated her daughter, who had gone on ahead.

Ianera nodded and they continued walking slowly to the dining hall. Faya went immediately to Asorum and asked if she could see him after the meal.

"Yes, Fayasas, I think we should have a talk. I knew who your visitor was, although I had never met him. Are you all right now?" The old priest was as concerned for Faya as Ianera had been, and the anxiety shone in his face.

"Yes, my dear friend, I am all right, but all of a sudden, I don't seem to want anything to eat." She looked at the table where the youngest children were, saw that Mai-dwar was seated with her own friends, and was already reaching for her milk. Wait, Mai-dwar, she said silently, wait for the Prayer. The child withdrew her hand and looked around to find her mother, who was at the far side of the room. Faya turned back to Asorum.

"Where are the two men who came with my father?" she asked.

"We have put them in one of the guest rooms for now. I haven't decided just yet what to do about them. They asked for lodging, and you know we never turn anyone away. However, this time, I am getting an uncomfortable feeling about those two. Well, please take your seat and we'll talk later, after the meal; and Faya, try to eat just a bite or two. An empty stomach is not the best help when one needs all one's strength." He smiled at her, as she turned to go to her own part of the dining hall. "Yes, I will. I promise." She knew she could choke down only a morsel of food, but perhaps Asorum was right. She decided to forego most of the meal and eat only a piece or two of fruit. That should carry me pretty well, she thought .

As she joined the others and raised her arms in the Prayer, she thought of her mother. Kadah, who had taught her so much in such a few years. Kadah, who had been so cruelly treated by the man she had chosen to live with, and whose child she had borne. Kadah, who had been stripped of all she held most dear, and had been forced to endure a stony silence until she died. The mother she had loved so devotedly, and whose spirit still walked with her daughter every day of her life.

Mother, she thought, how could you stay as loving and kind as you did, after the way Father treated you, and how can I be expected now to welcome him? She shook her head as a plate was passed to her, and the tears that were so near the surface ran down her cheeks. She hastily wiped them away, but not before Haindohne had seen them.

Dohnnie left her seat and came to sit beside the young woman. “Faya, what is it? Why are you crying? Are you ill?” Faya shook her head again. “No, Dohnnie, I’m quite all right. Just tired, I think.”

“Just tired indeed! I’ve known you too long to believe that, my girl. Now what is it? Can’t you tell me?”

Faya looked at the woman who had become almost a mother to her, and again shook her head. “Later, Dohnnie, I’ll tell you everything. But right now, please don’t ask me, or I’ll disgrace myself and start howling right here and now.”

“Of course, darling. When you’re ready. Now dry those eyes and at least pretend you’re eating. Krola is already staring at you, and pretty soon she’ll come over and demand to know what’s wrong. She will probably jump to the wrong conclusion, that you and Rab have had a quarrel. You haven’t, have you?” Dohnnie asked. “Rab isn’t even here, Dohnnie, and you know we don’t have quarrels. I”m all right. You go back and eat.” Dohnnie watched Faya for a moment, then nodded and went back to her own seat. Faya never knew how she got through the rest of the meal. She did take a piece of fruit, but it had no taste, and the small glass of wine went down without her noticing which vintage it was. After the Thanksgiving, she hurried over to Mai-dwar, who was happily prattling with some small friends. Taking the child up in her arms, much to the surprise and dismay of her daughter, who promptly let out a shrill howl of anger at being so suddenly deprived of her normal play time with her friends, Faya carried the still protesting little girl back to her own room. When she set Mai-dwar down, the child just stared at her mother, her lower lip thrust forward and a storm arising in her eyes.

Faya knelt beside her before there was time for the storm to break. “Listen, darling, I have something to tell you, and you must understand what I am going to say. Look at me, Mai-dwar. This is important, so please, don’t turn your head away from me. Listen to me. I want you to promise something.”

“What?” The storm was still very near the surface, and the child glowered at her mother.

“Mai-dwar, I want you to promise that until I tell you differently, you will never, ever, leave this room without holding either my hand or Ianera’s. Not to go to school, not to go to the dining hall, not to go to the gardens. One of us must be with you. Will you promise me that?

“I’m not a baby! I can find my own way wherever I want to go. And I don’t have to hold your hand. I’m almost four.” “Yes, Mai-dwar, I know you are, and that’s one of the reasons I want to be with you. I can’t tell you anything else right now, only please, promise me you won’t go anywhere unless I am with you. Or Ianera,” she added.

Faya was close to tears, herself, and her daughter began to be puzzled. She had never seen her mother so upset. The anger left her face, and she put her head on Faya’s shoulder.

“Mother, what’s the matter? Did I do something wrong?” The same old question she had asked so many years ago now echoed in her mind. Did I do something wrong? Is that why I had to be sent here instead of staying at home with you and father? The tears broke and ran down her cheeks. She gathered the now whimpering child and rocked her, feeling the soft little body melting against her.

“No, Mai-dwar, no, you have done nothing wrong. You are my own sweet daughter whom I love more than anything in this world. It’s just that there might be some trouble here at the Temple and I want to know that you are safe. So will you do as I ask, and promise to stay with either Ianera or me? Always?"

The child nodded, then reached up and patted her mother's face. "Don't cry, Mother. I'll be good; but when Father comes back, may I go with him?"

Faya managed a weak laugh. "Yes, of course, darling, when Rab comes back he will protect you even better than I can. Now, let's get a cloth and get these tears washed off, shall we? And remember, my sweet, you are and always have been a good girl. I'm so proud of you."

She washed her daughter's face, put her to bed and sat with her until she saw the girl's eyes start to droop. "Mother, sing me the sleep song, please." Mai-dwar turned over on her side facing her mother, and Faya sang softly, "sleep, little Mai-dwar, sleep. Grow in wisdom, grow in happiness. Sleep, my daughter, sleep." The old lullaby worked its magic, and before Faya had finished singing the song and humming the tune once more, the child was asleep.

Faya sat silently, her head in her hands; then remembering that Asorum was probably waiting for her, she got up softly and left the room. She looked back once at her sleeping child, and murmured under her breath, "I will never allow anyone to hurt you, no one!"

She walked swiftly back to the dining hall where the old priest was indeed waiting.

"Is Mai-dwar all right?" he asked.

Yes, she is asleep, and I will know if she even stirs. Oh, Asorum, what do you suppose is going to happen? Why did my father come here, and why did those two men come with him?"

The old priest paced back and forth for a moment. Then with a sigh, he shook his head. "Faya, I haven't the faintest idea what is in his mind. He is totally unpredictable. I did know that he had been made a governor of one of the eastern provinces; perhaps I should have told you, but you seemed to have put him out of your mind, and I didn't want to bring up an unhappy memory." She chewed on a fingernail while she thought over the scene with her father. She had been so frightened. He was still the man she had obeyed without question when she was very young; the man she had adored, but who had been the reason she had been brought here by her mother. Her feelings were torn, but deep in her heart she knew she had no choice to make. She looked up at Asorum.

"I cannot believe my father was here just because he wanted to see me. He spoke of Mai-dwar, but never really told me what he meant, and that was the worst of it. Just a hint of something I felt would be unpleasant, and he knew how I felt. I could see it in his eyes. He was amused that he could upset me." Asorum shook his head again. "How could any man, any father, treat a child that way? It is as if he was taking out his resentment against Kadah on you, and of course, you really had nothing to do with it. You were only four..."

"Mai-dwar, is nearly the same age," she broke in. "Is that just a coincidence, or does he have something planned that would involve my daughter? Asorum, I'm so frightened." She sat suddenly as though her legs would not hold her. The priest stood beside her with his hand on her shoulder.

"Faya, don't anticipate something that may be no more than a test to see how or if you can stand up to him. No harm can come to Mai-dwar here, you know that. Even a governor may not come into a Temple and take anyone by force. They can try to close us down, but the people still want and need us, so I don't see how anything can come of this meeting with your father. I think he is just showing his authority."

Neither Asorum nor Faya believed a word of what the priest had said, but the woman was grateful for his attempt to calm her fears. She smiled tremulously at him, and rose from her seat.

"Thank you, dear friend; you are right, and I should stop worrying. I'll feel much better after I have prayed for guidance. Perhaps my dreams will tell me what do." She stopped as a thought struck her. "Those two men - they looked vaguely familiar, but I'm sure I have never seen them before. Oh well, probably just my imagination. Good night, Asorum. May your sleep be deep and sweet."

"Yours, too, my dear. Kiss Mai-dwar for me." They both left the room, she to her own bedroom and Asorum to the garden where he could think things out in peace and quiet among the sweet herbs he loved so well.

Faya sat for a long hour watching her child asleep, and praying over and over to the Power for protection. She was not sure what she feared, but she knew in her heart that whatever came, she must be prepared. "Oh, Mother," she said silently, "I would give the world if I could only talk to you again."

She buried her face in her hands, leaning against the wall back of the child's small pallet, only to wake with a start several hours later, surprised that she had fallen asleep. This will never do, she thought. Nothing will be gained by my sitting here all night. She rose and undressed, finally lying on her own bed, eyes fixed on the ceiling of the room, and her heart thudding in her breast. Rab, she thought, please come home. I need you so!

Chapter Thirty -Three

Morning finally came, and a puffy-eyed Faya got up to go about her usual duties. After taking her daughter to the bathing room and getting her dressed, they joined the others in the dining hall. At one of the far tables the two strange men were seated, both of them looking her way as she came into the room. They whispered to each other, making Faya feel as she had years ago when the girls teased her about her dark hair and eyes. She felt like checking to see if her robe was smooth and her hair was braided correctly. She noticed that neither man joined in the Prayer, but stayed seated when Asorum rose and lifted his arms. That was an insult. Even visitors who may not have believed in the Prayer always stood out of respect. Faya looked over at Shaleen, who was staring at the two men in utter disbelief. She poked Krola in the ribs and pointed to the visitors. Krola was as astounded as her friend. When the Prayer was ended, Asorum motioned for everyone to be seated, while he remained standing. He looked long and hard at the two men who had never left their seats. One of them had the grace to look down at his empty plate as though he realized he had overstepped the bounds of good taste. The other arrogantly stared back at Asorum. The priest simply gave the signal for the food to be served, ignoring the usual custom of introducing guests. Faya was ashamed that she was part of the reason for their being there, although she did not understand it at all. Fortunately, very few knew that Faya's father had brought the two men into the Temple. While she knew in her heart she had nothing to do with them, it was her own father who was really responsible, and she was her father's daughter.

The meal was quiet; even the younger children seemed to know this was something out of the ordinary, and ate without much talking. When they all arose for the Thanksgiving, Faya noticed one of the men rose with them, bowing his head slightly, but not moving his lips. The other kept his seat, staring coolly around the tables. All at once some memory stirred in Faya's mind. Those two men, no wonder they had looked vaguely familiar. She had seen them in the Children' Garden years before, the two men Haindohnne had asked to leave. They had been dressed as priests then, but now they wore robes of office. The older one, who had at least made a token of bowing his head, was still standing. He looked at his companion, who was staring fixedly at Fayasas. When the students and teachers began to leave the room, the men remained at their table. Faya turned to go, catching up with Dohnnie at the doorway.

"Dohnnie, wait. I need to ask you something. Did you ever see either of those two men before today?" "No, Faya, I don't think so. Why?"

"Remember the two men who said they were priests and tried to question us about the children? Years ago? In the Garden?"

Dohnnie stopped suddenly, the memory flashing through her own mind. "Oh - yes, I do remember. I thought then there was something peculiar about them. In fact, I told Asorum I didn't like them. Are you sure these are the same two?" Dohnnie turned to look back at the table where the visitors sat. "I think you may be right, Faya. Does Asorum know?"

"I just recognized them a minute or so ago. Remember, he did not see them then, so I'm sure he wouldn't know they were the same. But I am certainly going to tell him now!" She took her friend's arm and pulled her rapidly away from the dining hall. "I think Asorum has gone to the herb garden. He usually does when he's worried about something, and I know he was upset at the way those two ignored the Prayer."

The two women hurried out to the herb garden, where they did indeed find Asorum pacing back and forth as he usually did when something was upsetting. Faya went to him and put her hand on his arm as he turned to look at her. “Yes, Faya? Did you want me?”

“Asorum, do you remember the two priests who were not really priests who came here several years ago, asking how and what we taught the children? Dohnnie said she told you about them, and how she had asked them to leave the garden and go into the Temple properly before looking around.”

Asorum stood in thought for a moment. “Yes, I do, child, but I never really saw them. Why do you ask?”

Dohnnie broke in. “Because those two men who were at the guest table are the same ones. They were not priests, nor did they even act like priests then. Now they make no attempt to pretend they are. But why are they here? Asorum, I'm worried.” “Dohnnie, so am I,” he replied. “But at the moment, I don't see what we can do. They have done nothing wrong, except ignoring our Prayer and the Thanksgiving. I can't ask them to leave because of that, even though I'd like to take the toe of my foot to their backsides. Faya, you met them. What did they say to you?”

Faya hung her head. “Nothing, Asorum. My father merely said they would stay here for a while, then he would come back. Oh, why?” she burst out. “Why does that man have to come here after all these years, and what did he mean when he said it concerned Mai-dwar?”

Asorum put his arm around her shoulder. “My dear child, nothing will happen to your daughter. Even a Governor can't just walk in and take a child away from a Temple. Only her parents have that right.”

“Yes, I know, but I'm so scared. I don't know what to do.”

“You will do nothing, Faya. Just go back to your own room and see that Mai-dwar is kept as far away from those men as possible. If and when your father comes back, I'll deal with him.” The old priest looked grim as he said this and Faya felt reassured. She and Haindohnne went back into the Temple, where Faya left her friend and went back to her own room. "Oh Rab," she murmured under her breath, "where are you? I need you!"

She slept fitfully that night, but when she awoke, everything seemed as normal as usual. She kept a close eye on her daughter that day, and the days following. When a few more days passed and the two men had made no move to contact her or her child, seemingly keeping to themselves, she began to relax a little.

She didn't know until a few days later that the men had gone to Haindohne, asking all sorts of questions which the woman simply refused to answer. They followed her during the day, when she moved from class to class, and persisted in questioning her. What classes were the children taught? Did they all have to learn that ridiculous Prayer? What did their parents think about the way the priests influenced the young minds? Didn't that old head priest ever recognize the real power in Atlantis? Why weren't the children allowed to go to the City where they could learn the ways of the real world? And why did Fayasas keep her daughter away from her father? It was his right to see his granddaughter. Didn't she know how important he really was?

Trained in the polite manner of those who taught in the Temple, Dohnnie avoided them as best she could, but when they began to insinuate that they could and would get the answers they wanted from the children themselves, Dohnnie lost her temper. She faced them both one day and told them in no uncertain terms that if they didn't stop bothering the children, she would call a meeting of all the priests and have them thrown out. Then, she said, she would let the entire City know just what they were doing.

Even the Judges would find such a scandal hard to live down, she told them. The idea that they thought they could come into the Temple and upset things that way, without a real reason, was unheard of, and she would see to it that they were stopped. With that she stormed out, turning in the doorway to remind them again that she meant exactly what she said.

One of them smiled cruelly. “Do you threaten us, lady? Be careful. We have ways of getting what we want.”

Haindohne made no answer. She looked fully at them, then gathered her robe up as if stepping over something that smelled, and left.

At the evening meal, neither man was present. For the first time in days the entire community felt a sense of relief. Dohnnie sat with Fayasas, Mai-dwar was at the small children’s table, and the meal was unhurried and peaceful. Even Asorum unbent more that usual and told stories of his earlier days before he came to the Temple. That was always a treat. The old priest was a marvelous story teller, and the children were delighted. Faya remembered how he had told her about the little bird on her first harp, how he had so patiently taught her to play it, and how much his unwavering support had meant to her. When the final Thanksgiving was said, Faya was asked if she would play for them before bedtime.

She brought her harp into the dining hall, and the next half hour was a fitting end to the first unhurried meal they had known in some time. When she stopped, Dohnnie went up to Faya, kissed her, and thanked her for making the evening so beautiful. Faya smiled at the woman she loved so well. “Good night, Dohnnie,” she said. “May your dreams be happy ones.”

“And yours, too, my dear. May your tomorrow be bright.”

Some hours later, Faya found herself restless, unable to close her eyes. Mai-dwar was sleeping soundly, and the entire Temple was quiet, but she just couldn’t relax. She turned from side to side. Finally accepting the fact that she simply wasn’t sleepy, she got up. Throwing a shawl around her shoulders, she slipped quietly out to the porch. The moon was casting a soft glow over the garden, and the scent of the herbs was soothing. This garden was her pride and joy, where she had worked so hard and learned so much; but the other herb garden was where she really wanted to be, just sitting by the quiet pool, inhaling the odors of the fonta underfoot, and the thacasca that was in full bloom.

Walking swiftly but silently, she went down the long passage that led to the great entrance hall, and from there into her favorite garden. Stepping just outside the doorway, she took a deep breath, drawing the night air into her lungs, tasting the delicious scents that floated over the peaceful scene. The moon was hidden for a moment behind a small cloud, then it sailed out in all its splendor, lighting the garden and turning the shadows into silver.

The pool, reflecting the moon's light, caught her attention and she started to walk over to the shining water, when she realized there was something on the surface. Someone had dropped a shawl or a robe on the water and it swayed with the soft movement caused by the light breeze that moved the thacasca leaves. When she stooped by the pool and started to reach for the material, her hand froze in mid air. One long shuddering breath was wrenched from her throat before her scream split the silent night. "Dohnnie, Dohnnie, no...oh help me, somebody, please help me!" Her cries brought one of the priests who had been working late in the library. He ran into the garden.

"What is it? Why did you scream? Are you all right?" He tried to raise the shaking woman up from her crouch on the edge of the pool before he saw what she was pointing at. For an instant he hesitated, disbelief holding him back. Then he pushed Faya aside and plunged up to his knees in the water. As he turned Dohnnie's body to lift her from the pool, Faya saw the open eyes and the look of stunned surprise frozen on the woman's face. She did not see the knife buried in Dohnnie's back, but the water had a soft tinge of pink where her blood had stained its purity.

By the time the young priest was able to carry the dead woman to the edge of the pool and lay her gently on the grass, Asorum and three other priests as well as several women teachers had arrived breathless, hastily gathering their robes that they had thrown on when they heard Faya's screams. Asorum knelt beside the body of the woman who had meant so much to him as well as to the Temple itself, and gently closed the staring eyes. When he looked up, his lips were trembling and his own eyes were filled with tears. Faya stood like a statue, looking at the body lying in the silver moonlight, her hands clenched at her sides, her face stony. The tears would come later. Now all she felt, after that first awful moment, was a coldness inside, a lump in her throat that forbade speech, and a numbness in her mind. This was a bad dream. It would go away. She would wake and find it was only a dream. Only a dream. Only a dream. She turned like a sleep walker and went out of the garden, into the entrance hall and down the long passage to her room. I am dreaming, her mind kept repeating. I am dreaming. I will wake up and tell Dohnnie what a strange dream I had. When she reached the porch that surrounded the wing of the building where her room was, she did not go in. Instead, she sat on one of the benches and began to rock herself back and forth.

Asorum found her there a few minutes later, still rocking back and forth, her arms wrapped around her body, her bare feet flat on the cold marble floor, and her eyes looking at nothing at all.

Chapter Thirty-four

In the days that followed, Faya was locked into a grief so deep she was almost an automaton. Even Mai-dwar could not break through the stony silence. Ianera tried to talk to her, but there was no answer to any question. Asorum knew he had to find out what Faya might have seen, so he and Ranoi took her down to one of the healing rooms, where Ranoi put her into a deep sleep.

"Can you hear me, Fayasas?" he asked.

"Yes, Ranoi, I can hear you," she answered, her eyes closed and her breath coming evenly.

"Do you remember playing the harp for us the night before last?"

"Yes, of course."

"Where did you go after you stopped playing? Can you tell me that?"

Faya sighed deeply. "I went back to my own room. Mai-dwar was asleep, but I could not get comfortable." "What did you do then?"

"I got up, wrapped a shawl around my shoulders and went out onto the porch." She stopped, took another deep breath, and then relaxed again.

"Yes, Faya, you may relax even more deeply. Now, do you remember where you went after that?" Ranoi did not want to hurry her, but they simply had to know what had happened. "Yes, of course. I went back to my room and went to sleep." Faya had a brief smile on her lips. Ranoi shook his head at Asorum, and whispered, "she is blocking it out."

Asorum nodded. "I expected that. Can you get her to try and remember more, or should we let it go for now?"

"No," answered Ranoi, "It would be best to see what we can do now. The longer she keeps it in, the harder it will be for her to let it out." He turned back to the sleeping woman. "Faya, you did not go back to your room. You went to the herb garden, didn't you."

Faya murmured, "Did I? I don't remember." She turned her head and shrugged her shoulders as if trying to get in a more comfortable position.

"Faya, listen to me. What you saw you do not have to live through again. Just see the picture. Nothing can harm you; you are only looking at a picture. Tell me what you saw when you went into the herb garden."

Faya's eyes opened wide, although her mind was still in the grip of the hypnotic trance."Dohnnie...Dohnnie...Why are you in the pool? It's night, and you can't swim here. It's too small a pool. Dohnnie, come out of the water. Please, Dohnnie...."

"It's all right, Faya. We will help Dohnnie out of the pool. Just try to remember if there was anyone else there." The priest's voice was soothing.

"No," she answered, "just Dohnnie. But why is she in the water? Dohnnie, please come out of the pool." Faya's head began to thrash back and forth on the pallet, so Ranoi put his hand on her forehead, soothing her with words and a light pressure. "It's all right, Faya, it is only a picture you are seeing. You may sleep now, and when you waken, you will remember only what you want to remember." Faya's eyes closed again and her body began to relax.

"I don't think, Asorum, that there is much more she can tell us." said Ranoi. "Obviously there was no one else there. Whoever did this terrible thing would not have waited around. I had hoped she might have heard or seen something. I will let her sleep as long as she can. Her body and spirit need this time for rest."

Asorum nodded at his friend. "Tell me, Ranoi, will this session help her acknowledge the agony she has felt up to now? Will she be able to mourn, will she be able to cry? Grief locked in will simply eat away at her soul. I wish Rab would get here soon, but we don't even know where he is."

Ranoi sighed. "Yes, it would help if her husband could console her, but in answer to your question, I just don't know. I hope she will come back to us when she wakes. The way the mind works is not always known, and Faya had a great shock. But she is young and healthy, and I am hopeful that letting her sleep will start the healing." He picked up a light blanket and covered the sleeping woman. "I want my assistant to stay with her until she stirs, then I will come back and see if she will talk to me."

The two men left the room, leaving Faya with a young woman who had instructions to call Ranoi the minute Faya awoke. It was hours later when he was called. Faya was awake and crying soundlessly. The healer priest went to her and held her against his shoulder while the sobs wracked her slender body. He heaved a great sigh of relief, but did not take his arms from around her.

Finally Faya lifted her head, her eyes still swimming with tears, but the cold hard lump in her heart had dissolved. "Oh Ranoi, why? Why did this have to happen?" she cried bitterly.

"Faya, even the wisest of priests do not have the answers to all questions. We may think we know everything, but we find we do not. Why Dohnnie met such a death is beyond my knowledge right now, but I promise you, we will find out and the guilty one or ones will be punished." He continued to stroke her back, murmuring soothing wordless sounds.

"I know who did this," Faya said suddenly. "I know quite well who did this."

Ranoi looked at her in silence for a moment. "No, Faya, you do not know. You may suspect, but you have no proof of anything as yet."

"Yes, Ranoi, I do know. Even though I did not see it happen, I know. And I am to blame."

The priest looked hard at the woman who had just made such a statement. "Why do you think you are to blame, Fayasas? Certainly you had nothing to do with this."

Faya sat up, wiping her eyes with the back of her hand. "Yes, Ranoi, I am to blame. My father brought those two men here, and they are the ones who," her voice shook for a moment, " who killed Dohnnie."

"My dear, how do you know this?" asked the priest .

"Dohnnie didn't know that I had heard a little of what they were asking. She tried to keep them away from me, and wouldn't tell them anything about me or Mai-dwar. They wanted to know about the other children, too, and she wouldn't tell them anything. But I knew what they were asking. The same things they asked when they were here several years ago."

Ranoi decided it was time to call Asorum. He asked the assistant to find the priest and bring him to the healing room. When Asorum arrived, Faya threw herself in his arms, accepting the steady love he had always shown her.

"Are you all right, my child?" he asked.

"Yes, dear Asorum, I am all right now. Only," she stopped and looked at Ranoi, " I am certain I know who killed Dohnnie." Her voice still quivered as she said the name of her beloved friend, but she continued. "The two men that my father left here...they are the ones who did this. I told Ranoi but he says I have no proof. I never asked how she was killed, but I saw blood in the water." "She was stabbed. In the back," Asorum said sadly.

"Of course," answered Faya. "They would never have had the courage to face her. The knife...may I see it?"

"Why would you want to, Faya?" asked Ranoi.

"Because I will know if it is theirs," she said simply. "It will carry their evil and I will feel it." He was suddenly sure that this gifted woman could do just what she said. He asked that the knife be brought to them. When Faya saw it, a great shudder ran through her body. She looked at it steadily for a minute, then closed her eyes, took a deep breath and let her mind reach out to the cold metal.

Asorum and Ranoi were silent, allowing Faya the time she needed to pick up the knife's vibrations. When she finally looked at the two priests, her eyes were hard and her mouth was a straight grim line.

"This knife belongs to the younger of the two men. He has carried it for many months. It was given to him by a much older man who had come from some far off country. He was alone when he struck Dohnnie. His companion was not there. She had gone to the garden after the evening meal, and he followed her. He was taunting her about how easy it would be to take the children away from the Temple if he really tried, and she told him she would see that the City knew what he was trying to do and they would relieve him of his position - I don't know exactly what he does - but Dohnnie turned her back on him and he suddenly lost control and struck her. He didn't want to lose his knife, but he heard me coming toward the garden and had to leave it. In her back. I missed seeing him by seconds." She said this calmly, without emotion, but Asorum knew how much strength it had taken for her to allow that picture to form in her mind. It was a picture she would never be able to forget.

When she finished talking, her face crumpled and she moaned. "Oh, Asorum, Asorum, why did I have to be born of such a father? Why? Why?" She pounded on her knee with a doubled fist until the priest reached over and held her hand.

"Faya, listen to me. When you were born, your father was so proud of you, and both he and your mother gave you every bit of love they had in their hearts. It was only later when he became first a lawyer, then a Judge that ambition took over his life, and he would allow nothing to stand in the way of his rise toward an even higher position. He is now a Governor. Where he will go from there, no one knows. He aims high.

"When your mother removed you from his influence, he took the final step toward losing what humanity he had. It was never anything you had done. The pattern was set when Kadah insisted on living with him, even without a true marriage, because he was handsome, charming and very persuasive. We tried our best to dissuade her, but when a woman is in love, all the arguments in the kingdom will seldom change her mind. For a while, we thought things might work out, especially when we knew you were on the way. Kadah asked me to read you when you were born, and I knew that she had been given a very special gift. I told her and your father much about you, and they were so happy that I chose to believe they would become a true family, even though your father simply would not allow it to be blessed as Kadah wished." He stopped for a minute to gather his thoughts.

"Little by little, your father let the sweetness go out of his soul (and yes, he was a loving husband in many ways) until there was little left but the desire to become more and more important. But Faya, it was not your fault. Please believe me. You are not in any way to blame for what has happened. If there is blame here, it is mine for not having seen how dangerous those two men were. I didn't believe that anyone could ever come into our Temple and defile it in this manner. I didn't want to believe such a thing could happen. No, child, you are not responsible. I am." Faya looked at the old priest in dismay. "Asorum, how can you say that? No! I won't accept that." She shook her head, got up and paced the small room back and forth. Asorum caught her arm and pulled her down beside him on the bench.

"Faya, right now it really doesn't matter whose fault it was, or who should take the blame. What we must decide now is what to do about this terrible crime that has been committed here in these sacred grounds. Without definite proof, we have very little to go on."

"But Asorum, we know who did this! I told you!"

"Yes, Faya, and I believe you. But would others? How many of the City people can or would accept the fact that one of the officials acted in this way? Remember, the Judges have grown stronger every year, and many of the people are firmly behind them. We in the temples are having a hard time keeping our students, and something like this could have the opposite effect if we talked openly against their misuse of power." He rose and looked down at her, noticing for the first time the set of her jaw and the almost opaqueness of her eyes. Always before, when she looked at him, her eyes were clear and her soul shone through. Now, he was alarmed at the way she was closing herself off.

"Faya, my dear child, don't let your pain and anger destroy the beautiful being you are inside. We are all so devastated by this that it is difficult to think clearly, but it is necessary that we do, perhaps more now than ever before." He laid his hand on her head and she smiled at him, but the smile was forced.

"All I can think of," she said slowly, "is my father's remark about Maidwar; that she was about the same age I was when Mother brought me here, and how cold he looked when he reminded me that she had paid dearly for doing that. If I thought for one minute that my child was in danger from him or anyone else, there is nothing I would not do to protect her. You know that, Asorum. And," she added grimly, "those two men are still here."

The old priest felt a chill as she spoke, knowing her as he did, her determination to get what she wanted, her stubbornness when she set her mind on doing something, her way of working through a problem until it was solved to her satisfaction.

“Faya, we cannot dismiss them without proof. You know our laws. A guest is to be respected and allowed to stay as long as he or she is in need of anything we can give them. These two have not, so far as I know, asked for anything; and except for the disrespect shown when they refused to honor our Prayer, they have behaved as anyone else would.”

“Even when they questioned Dohnnie the way they did? I don’t call that decent behavior.”

“I know, child. I promise you, I will see that they leave here. One way or another, we will be rid of them. There is nothing more we can do.”

“Yes,” Faya replied, “one way or another.”

Asorum smiled at her. His own pain and the feeling of responsibility that was such a weight on his heart, plus the deep weariness he felt, were so great that he failed to catch the veiled meaning behind her words.

Chapter Thirty-five

Faya lay awake for hours that night. Oblivion was something her mind craved, in spite of the earlier sleep. For the first time in her young life, she had a headache, her eyes burned, and she felt as though her body belonged to someone else. Tossing restlessly from one side to the other, her thoughts went over and over that horrible night. Dohnnie floating face down in the water. Dohnnie's staring eyes and frozen face when she was laid on the grass beside the pool. Dohnnie, the woman who had befriended her when she first came to the Temple, the one person she could talk to as she had talked to her mother. She remembered the smiling eyes when Dohnnie gave her to Rab at their wedding, the proud carriage when she faced down the men who had been the cause of her death. Dohnnie.

Time after time Faya got up and looked down on her daughter as she slept, and time after time her mind went back to Asorum's words, assuring her that there was no danger for her child. Toward dawn, she did sleep fitfully. When she awoke, it was to find Mai-dwar sitting beside her, patting her face and murmuring words of comfort. She knew she must have frightened the child, so she reached up and pulled her down to snuggle beside her for a few minutes.

"Good morning, darling. Did you sleep well?"

"I did, mother, but you were crying. Does you head hurt?" Mai-dwar was still stroking Faya's face.

"Yes, it did...but how did you know?"

"Because when you hurt, I do, too, and it doesn't feel good. Will it make it better if I rub it a little bit?" Faya sighed. She knew that Mai-dwar was an exceptional child. What mother doesn't think that? She had also known since Asorum had read her child, that her daughter was a sensitive, one who could feel another's pain, but she did not know that

Mai-dwar would find this rare gift so early in her life, a gift that could carry a heavy responsibility.

"Thank you, darling, I would like that." She rolled over so the child could reach the back of her neck where most of the pain was located. In a very few minutes, she felt the relief that only a sensitive's touch could bring so quickly. I must tell Asorum about this, she thought. He will know how to train her to best use this ability.

When they had bathed and eaten, Mai-dwar went to the classes she enjoyed with the other very young students, only this time, there would be no Dohnnie to take them out to the Children's Garden, tell them stories, and play with them. Ianera took over as monitor, and the morning passed quietly.

When Faya came in from her work in the herb garden later that afternoon, she found Mai-dwar in her own room, busily sorting out clothes.

"What are you doing, dear? And where is Ianera?" The older woman was supposed to be with her daughter at all times since Faya could not be there during the time she was working with either Ranoi or Benai.

"She had to go to the City. Somebody was sick, I guess." Mai-dwar didn't look up from folding a short shift.

"Oh, I'm sorry to hear that. But why are you playing with your clothes? They will get wrinkled." The question beating in her brain came out suddenly. "Mai-dwar, who brought you back here?" It was not like Ianera to leave without telling Faya.

Mai-dwar finally looked up at her mother. "Nobody brought me. I can find my own way. Which one do you like the best?" she asked, holding up two short dresses.

"What do you mean, nobody brought you back? Don't you remember you promised never to go anywhere without one of us with you? Mai-dwar, I'm disappointed in you. When you make a promise, you must keep it."

"But I only came back to get my new dresses. I'm going to visit my grandfather." The little girl looked up at her mother. "And may I wear the blue beads? You said they were really mine, and they would look so nice with this dress." She smiled up at Faya. "I didn't know that I had a grandfather, but he wants to meet me." Faya's face was white. Her knees gave way and she sat down hard on the floor beside her child. She had been pretending to herself that the man who had sired her would not really do anything to hurt either her or her daughter. Now she knew he would stop at nothing to make her pay for the humiliation he felt in having lost his only child. Her refusal to have anything to do with him must have broken the final link of affection he had once felt for her.

"Mai-dwar," she said quietly, "I think you had better put your clothes away for now. It is nearly time for the evening meal, and we can talk about this tomorrow. Here, let me help you hang these up again. You don't want them to look as though you slept in them." She managed a smile which took more effort than she could afford, but she was determined not to frighten her daughter.

"I have an idea," she went on. "How would you like to have a picnic here in the garden with me tonight? We could ask Benai to join us; would you like that?"

Mai-dwar looked first at the dress she was holding, then at her mother. She was not easily fooled, and she was quite sure the picnic was intended to take her mind off the planned visit to the City where her grandfather lived. Well, the man had said they would not go until tomorrow. "All right, Mother. Could we have some of those honey cakes, you know, the kind we have on special occasions? And will Benai tell me stories about when he was a little boy?"

"I"m sure he will, and yes, I'll see if there are honey cakes. Now help me fold these up properly, and I'll let you wear the blue beads tonight, just for special."

A quick knock on Benai's door, and his agreement that a picnic was the very thing he wanted settled the matter. Food was sent for and the porch became their dining area. After the light meal, Benai took the child on his lap and the rest of the evening passed with his stories, Faya's singing, and finally a very sleepy Mai-dwar, who still had honey cake crumbs on her mouth when Benai carried her to her own little pallet.

Faya decided not to say anything to Benai, although the young priest was aware that something was upsetting her. He did not press Faya to tell him, for which she was grateful. She had much thinking to do that night, thinking that was best done alone.

She knew suddenly and surely what she was going to do, what she had to do. It was against everything she had been taught, everything she believed in, but there was no hesitation, no wavering in her mind. She knew what to do. As long as she herself was available there would be no peace. Wherever she was, her father could and would find her, and there would never be safety for Mai-dwar.

When she was sure everyone in the Temple was asleep, she put on a pair of gloves that she wore when working with dangerous plants, and crept silently out into the garden. Stooping down beside the plant she wanted, she carefully pulled away the soft dirt that covered the roots, and with a gently tug, pulled it out of the earth. Working swiftly, she shook the loose dirt off and carried it to the porch. She had ready a bowl and a grinding stone which she used with a practiced hand. Making a paste from the roots, she mixed it with a sweet smelling oil and then poured the mixture into two small bottles. Corking them carefully, she set them on a high shelf in the room that no child could reach. Then she went back out to the garden.

Falling on her knees beside the loosened dirt where she had removed the plant, she first patted it back into place; then still on her knees, she lifted her face to the sky. Her prayer that night was not to the Power. It was to her mother, a plea for understanding, for help in doing what she felt must be done, and for forgiveness for the pain she would cause to those who loved and trusted her.

She thought of Rab, the man she adored and who would be anguished at her betrayal of the laws they lived by. When she thought of Asorum she almost wavered, seeing in his eyes the disbelief that would come, the agony of the part he would have to take in the final outcome.

Mother, she cried silently, help me. Help me do what I simply must do to save my child and the children here whom I love. Can I do anything else? Mother, help me, help me! She stayed on her knees, her face buried in her hands, until a pale dawn started to lighten the garden. The moon had long since quit the sky, the few stars she could still see were dim, and the first song of a bird tentatively broke the silence. When she tried to rise, her knees were so stiff from the long unaccustomed kneeling that she staggered. Catching herself, she went quietly into her room to lie down for a few hours. Sleep eluded her, but for once she was glad to stay awake. She had plans to make, and this was to be the only time she would have entirely alone. Again she thought of Rab, wishing with all her soul that she could communicate with him in the old way as she had with her mother. When would he come back? Where was he now? Would her action forever break the close ties they had forged from their love? She turned over on her face, the tears finally released, and she gave herself the luxury of once again being a child who silently cried and could not stop.

When she had finally wept until she could weep no more, she got up, bathed, dressed and woke her daughter.

"Come on, little sleepy-head, it's time to get up." Mai-dwar rolled over, smiled at her mother, yawned and stretched.

"Mother, can I get my dresses out now?" Like the child Faya had been, she seldom forgot anything she wanted. "Can I, Mother?"

"Later, darling. Now you must have your bath and get dressed so we can eat with the others."

"Mother, you never told me about my grandfather. Why, Mother? Has he been away for a long time? Didn't he ever want to see me before?" The little girl was busily washing her face and her speech was rather muffled, but Faya heard every word and each one went through her like a sword.

"Yes, he has been away, in the City, and I'm sure he has wanted to see you, but maybe he has been so busy helping run the country that he hasn't had much time." Faya felt as though the words would choke her, but she had to keep Mai-dwar from finding out the kind of man her grandfather was. It would serve no purpose to hurt the child, and if her plans could be carried out, she would never know.

"Just remember, darling, your own father will be back soon. Don't you remember, he promised to take you on another trip with him. Wouldn't you rather do that?"

Mai-dwar sat on the floor, one sandal on and the other still in her hand. "Well," she said slowly, "I could do both. Go see my grandfather first and when Rab comes back, we could go on a trip. Where will we go this time, Mother?"

Faya thought her heart would break as she looked at the happy face of her daughter. Oh, Mai-dwar, if I could only know where you will be, she thought. I must trust Rab to take you so far away that no one will ever find you.

"I don't know where we will go this time, dear, but I rather suspect it will be some place you haven't seen. This is a very large world and there is so much to see. You liked the last trip, didn't you?" she asked.

"Well, almost all of it. I didn't like having my head wrapped up, though."

"That was to keep you from getting sick from being too hot. Perhaps this time it will be a cooler place. Ready? Then let's go and have our first meal." She took the child's hand and they walked down the long passage, past the school rooms, into the dining hall.

The two men were just sitting down at their table, and Faya gave them a quick look, then turned away. She knew she could not eat anything with them in the same room. Food would just not go past the lump in her throat when she thought of what they had done. Again, they ignored the Prayer, remaining seated. And again, Asorum made no comment. At the end of the meal the older of the two stood for the Thanksgiving, while his companion remained in his seat. Faya knew it was sheer defiance, to see how long the priests would overlook their insulting manner. She wondered if the older man knew just what had happened, then she thought, oh of course he would know! They have probably already managed somehow to get word to the man who sent them. Well, I have words to get to you, too, my father, and mine will not please you nearly as much.

Immediately after the meal, Faya saw Mai-dwar into the classroom, then went to look for Ianera. She still could not understand how the older woman could have left Mai-dwar without even a word to her mother. She found that Ianera had just come back, having been in the City overnight. When she faced Faya, it was with tears and an almost hysterical outburst. "Faya, I'm so sorry! I don't know how I could have been so stupid as to believe them."

"Them, Ianera? Who?"

"The two guests we have here at the Temple."

"What did they tell you, Ianera?" Faya's voice was quiet but the look on her face brooked no hastily trumped up story. "The older one told me he had just had a message from my aunt, who said my father had been in a bad accident and was dying. I didn't even stop to wonder why the message came to him, I was so upset and frightened. My father is an old man, and he's all the family I have left. I just forgot everything else, and went as fast as I could to my old home."

"And found your father completely all right and probably surprised to see you?" asked Faya.

Ianera nodded, the tears still streaming down her face. "Faya, I'm such a fool! And after what happened here two nights ago, why, oh why did I believe him!"

Faya put her arms around her friend. Ianera didn't know that Faya had identified Dohnnie's killer, and this was no time to tell her. "Don't, Ianera. Mai-dwar is all right, I'm all right, and there was no harm done. Stop crying now, no one is blaming you for...."

"For being such a stupid idiot," Ianera broke in. "Will you ever forgive me, and trust me again?"

"My dear, we have been friends ever since that first day when you came to show me the way back from Benai's quarters. A story like that could make anyone forget their own name. Those men can be very persuasive. They should be; my father has taught them well."

"Your father, Faya?"

"Yes, my father. He brought them here. I believe his idea is to punish me for what my mother did to his ego when she brought me here. But don't worry; he won't get far. It was just a trick to see how much they can rattle me." She hugged her friend and the two walked back to the herb garden together. "I'm going to leave you here, Ianera. There are some plants I need to make more salves. I'll see you later, and please don't continue to blame yourself. Everything turned out all right." Ianera gave her friend a rather watery smile, but went to her own work with a lighter heart.

Faya worked in the garden until it was time to meet Mai-dwar for the noon meal. She took the child to her table, then went to her own. When the meal was half over, she rose, made an excuse to those at her table, and left the room. She had made sure that the two men were eating, and paying her little attention. Walking swiftly back to her room, she picked up the two bottles she had filled the night before, wrote directions for their use on a piece of paper, and tucked them into the sleeve of her robe, then made her way to the great entrance hall and on to the guest room wing. Entering the room that the two men had been given, she placed the bottles on a small table and left as quickly as she had come.

It was not unusual for the priests to leave a guest oils for the bath, or rubbing lotions for tired feet after a traveler had come far. Faya was quite sure the men would take the oils as their due, and use them according to the directions she had placed with them. Now she could only wait, hoping and praying that Rab would come back soon.

Chapter Thirty-six

Faya spent another sleepless night. The two men had eaten the evening meal as usual, and afterwards, Faya had again been asked to play her harp. For the first time, her fingers fumbled on the strings, and she excused herself, saying she had a bad headache. Asorum gave her a hard look, but said nothing. To his knowledge, Faya had never had an ache or pain in her life, except when her baby was born, and the wise old priest knew something was in the wind; but he felt it was probably the strain of the last few days, Dohnnie's death and her burial ceremony which Faya had not attended. Her mind had been too blanked out even to understand what was going on.

When she arose the following morning, she asked Ianera to see that Mai-dwar got to the dining hall. She, herself, was late for the meal. When she walked in, she first looked toward the table where the two men usually sat. She had not expected them to be there, and indeed they were not.

She took her own seat, but shook her head when food was passed to her. At the end of the meal, after the Thanksgiving was said, Asorum came to her table.

"Faya, I noticed that you did not eat this morning. Child, are you not well?" he asked.

"No, Asorum, I am not. Will you excuse me for a minute? I want to ask Krola to take Mai-dwar to her first class. Then I must talk to you." Before he could reply, she turned and walked rapidly to the door. When she came back, he was still waiting at her table. He looked steadily at her.

"Faya, what has happened? My dear, I know you so well, and yet lately I have felt you are shutting me out. If you are in trouble, let me help you."

Faya's own eyes filled with tears. "My dear friend, you cannot help me. Not now. Not ever again. For whatever I have done, the consequences are mine to take." She stopped for a moment, trying to find a way to soften the agony he would feel when he found she had betrayed everything he had taught her over the years. There was no easy way.

"Asorum, the two men who were responsible for Dohnnie's murder did not come to the first meal today. They will not come to any other. By now, they are both dead. By my hand." It was said simply, but the meaning of the words did not register for a minute. Then Asorum paled, and for the first time since she had known him, Faya noticed how old he really was. His hands shook as he blindly reached out for her, his body swaying as his knees gave way. She caught him as he fell toward the table.

There were no words. He simply sat with his hands over his face, his breath coming in ragged hoarse rasps. She let him have the time to wrap his dignity around him again, then gently took his hands and drew them down so she could see his face.

"Asorum, I know quite well what I have done, and how I must pay for such a sin. You told me long ago that before one may take a life, one must be able to create a life. This I cannot do. I have broken a sacred law. I have done the unforgivable, I have committed a crime as great as the one that took Dohnnie's life. I know this. And I tell you now, I am ready to pay the price. I would do it all over again if it would keep my child safe from the kind of life my father and the other Judges would have her live.

"Oh, yes," she went on as he started to speak, "I know where this all started, and who is really the instigator. I never thought, though, that he would strike at me through my daughter. There is no love, no compassion in that man, and if he were here instead of the two he sent, I would have done the same. He killed my mother, even though he may never have laid a hand on her. He had Dohnnie killed, and I don't know how many others have and will suffer at his hands. But at least, those two who are lying dead in their room will not try to seduce another child away from the true path of life."

Asorum looked at her with such heartbreak in his face that she felt ill, but the steel in her spirit stood her in good stead.

"Faya, why did you not come to me? I would have done anything within my power to help you. I told you that no man had the right to take a child from the Temple. Were you so afraid that they would try to take Mai-dwar away?"

"They worked more subtly than that. They had convinced her that she should go meet her grandfather who wanted so much to see his only granddaughter, and she believed them. Why would she not? She's not quite four years old, and they were very persuasive. They tricked Ianera into leaving the Temple by telling her that her father was dying. Do you think they could not have found a way to get my daughter out of the Temple? Once out, I would never have found her. My father would have seen to that!" she said grimly.

"But child, child, do you really know what you have done? And what will have to be done now? Have you any idea what this will mean to us here? To the Temple? And what of Rab and your daughter, what will it mean to them? Do you really know what this will do to us all?"

"Yes, Asorum, I do know. I spent the entire night thinking about it, and there was just no other way. I had to protect Mai-dwar, and I also had to show the Judges that our people will no longer stand for their treatment of people who are trying to live a life of peace."

"Do you call killing two men a peaceful way of life, Faya?" Asorum asked bitterly.

"No, I do not. But sometimes one must fight fire with fire." she replied. "I remember the terrible vision I had some years ago. Do you remember,

Asorum? You and Ranoi tried to wipe it out of my memory, but once these men came, I saw it again. All I could think of was what would happen to Atlantis, to the children, to the people, if it was not stopped. I know now that nothing can stop the fate that hangs over us, but we can, we must, take steps to save those that we can."

"You saw the vision again, Faya? When?"

"I have not been able to sleep since I 'read' the knife. I've had plenty of time to think, and at night when the hours were so long, I could see it all over again, the fire, the people running, the screaming, the utter devastation. Asorum, if things go on the way they are going now, Atlantis will be totally destroyed; nothing and no one will be left. That's why you must see that at least some of our people get away to other lands. Rab and I found at least one place. There are more."

The sudden urgency in her voice for a moment dulled the shock and pain gnawing at the priest's heart. He had seen the same vision, as had Kwali. There was so little time left, time that he had hoped he could use to see the people of Atlantis on journeys to distant lands where they could pick up the lives that were so soon to be shattered.

Right now, though, there was Faya, the daughter of a woman he had taught, loved and prayed for, the child he had watched grow up here in his Temple, with a brilliant mind and a compassionate heart, a musician and a healer. A girl who had in one short night destroyed everything he had worked so hard to give her. What would happen to her now? He knew the answer even before the question formed in his mind. 'Until you can create life you may not take a life.' That was the law, not to be broken, save at the peril of your soul. And the punishment was the same for anyone who broke that law, man or woman.

The old man rose to his feet. He looked at the woman he loved with all his heart, and his face was set in a mask of grief that would never, in this lifetime, be lifted. He had no choice. He was the priest who must administer justice as well as wisdom.

"Faya, you will come with me now. You will be required to stand before the entire Temple and I will repeat what you have said to me, then you will be judged. And I think you must know what the judgement will be." He held out his hand.

Faya took it, and kissed it. The tears rolled down her cheeks as she looked him squarely in the face. "Asorum, I am so sorry, so very sorry that I have hurt you like this. I have done a thing that is reprehensible in your eyes; something that can never be undone." She took a deep breath and continued. "I have no pity in my heart for the two who lie dead now. Nor for the man who brought them here. I can only say again that the hurt in your eyes is the one thing I shall never be able to forgive myself for. I am ready. Tell me where to go."

Asorum turned and led the way out of the dining hall, across the great entrance, to a small room on the far side of the Temple, a room Faya had never seen. It was tiny, just large enough for a chair and a single pallet.

"Here, Faya, is where you will stay until you are called." He turned to the door.

"Wait, please...may I see Mai-dwar and tell her I will not be with her for a while?"

"No, Faya. I will see that Ianera cares for her until Rab returns. You will not see or talk to anyone until judgement has been passed. Now I must prepare the others for what has happened, and I must also send word to your father. They were his friends and he has the right to hear how they met their death." When the door closed behind him, Faya dropped to the small pallet. She put her hands over her eyes, trying desperately to shut out the picture of Asorum's grief filled face and the thought of her child being told her mother was not going to be with her.

That was the one thing she had not taken into account, separation from Mai-dwar.

"But why should I have thought anything different," she asked herself. "Oh, Rab, Rab, where are you? Please come back and take Mai-dwar far away from Atlantis while there is still time." She rocked back and forth, the anguish in her soul too deep for tears.

For the rest of that day and the following night, Faya saw no one, heard from no one, except for the woman who brought her a tray of food, and left without a word.

The next morning, the summons came as she knew it would. She was asked to come into the great entrance hall, where she found everyone assembled, everyone but Mai-dwar and Ianera. All eyes were on her as she walked slowly to the foot of the staircase and took her place beside a priest who had motioned for her to stand by him.

Asorum, in his capacity as chief priest of the Temple, spoke in a ragged, rough voice, telling the people what had occurred, and why it had happened. He made no excuses for Faya, but he did explain the circumstances and her fear at losing her only child. A murmur of disbelief rose like angry bees swarming. The priest raised his hand for silence and continued.

"Since the death of our beloved friend, Haindohnne, this young woman, Fayasas, has been in a constant state of fear. Instead of coming to me or to one of you," here he looked at the priests assembled, "she chose to take matters into her own hands and take the lives of two guests. Whether they were evil is not the point. We know their intentions were certainly without justification. The man who brought them here was this woman's own father, and he, as much as anyone, must share the blame. But not all of it. While a guest in this Temple is to be treated with honor, we know now that at least one of these two was responsible for

Haindohnne's death, a crime that would certainly justify the strongest punishment, but not without a fair trial. This he did not receive.

"The laws of our Temple, of every temple in Atlantis, are specific. The one law we are concerned with here was given to us centuries ago, and it must be honored by us all. 'Until you can create life, you may not take life.' The Power that we all worship creates life. We do not. We are mortal, and no matter how long our lives, we all must die someday. That death is reasonable, a gift from our Creator, so we may return in another body after we have used this one as long as necessary. It is the same as putting on a clean fresh robe after the one we have been wearing has become ragged.

"We believe that life is continuous, that nothing ever really dies. We change, as the seasons change. We either grow, or we go backwards, but we return until we learn the lesson each particular lifetime has to teach us. When someone destroys the life of another, that person will have been denied the right to live out his or her days until the needed lesson has been learned, or until such time as the Power decided that the life is no longer useful.

"Fayasas has done the one thing that can never be undone. It is up to you all assembled here to judge whether she may live with us, or suffer the punishment our laws demand." Asorum gave Faya one long look then walked out of the hall, the mask of grief etched on his face. He would never see her again.

Chapter Thirty-seven

Faya was taken out of the hall while the priests debated. There was really no choice, and they all knew it. Krola and Shaleen were so shaken they could barely speak. Ranoi, who had worked with Faya in the healing rooms, and Benai, who had taught her to use the herb that brought her ruin, asked to be excused from speaking. Both men loved the woman and were reluctant to hear the words they knew would seal her fate. Ianera was still with Mai-dwar, who had been confined to her room while the priests debated her mother's punishment.

It was over in a less than an hour. The laws governing the Temple were few but strict. The punishments meted out for serious transgressions had been set down centuries before, and never changed. Faya was sentenced to banishment, which sounded less stringent than it really was.

It meant she would be taken to the high cliffs overlooking the Temple, where the dead were buried. There she would remain for the rest of her natural life, shut away from any contact with the people she had known, from the daughter she had tried to protect, and from her husband, whom she had not seen for several weeks. She would not be harmed physically. Food would be brought to her once every five days, enough to sustain her body, but she would never again see the light of the sun, nor hear a human voice. There would be no words spoken to her.

She was only twenty-two years old. Banishment meant long years of nothingness. It meant an eternity of thinking of the consequences of her actions. If Atlantis survived, she would grow old wondering what was happening to her daughter, to her husband, to the people she had worked with and for all her short life.

She was brought back into the hall. When the punishment was read out by the priest who had taken Asorum's place, a long shuddering wail went up. Krola, Faya's closest friend from the earliest days, the girl who had shared her room until marriage separated them, stood in total shock, too stunned even for tears. Shaleen, with whom Faya had played, traded secrets with, helped in the Children's Garden, was devastated. Her mouth was trembling so hard she could not form any words. The only person in the hall who showed no sign of emotion was Faya herself. With the courtesy she had always shown to an elder, she bowed to the priest. "I accept my punishment. I would, however, ask one favor, if it maybe given."

The priest looked at her inquiringly, but made no reply. Faya continued.

"I would like to see my daughter one more time, and I must write a letter to my husband, who has been gone for several weeks and is not yet returned. Will this be permitted me?"

The priest consulted two others who stood with him. They nodded in agreement.

"You will have this one day with your daughter. Your letter must be read and approved by us before it can be delivered to Rabithi when he returns. Tomorrow you will go to the cliffs. You have what remains of today."

She bowed again and one of the women motioned for her to follow her. They went back to Faya's own room, a favor she had not expected. Mai-dwar ran into her arms.

"Mother, where have you been? I've waited and waited for you, but you were gone so long!"

"I know, honey, I left you much too long. But now I must get ready to go on an unexpected journey. Will you help me get ready?"

"Where are we going? Is Father going with us? When will he get back here? Will it be a nice place, not hot like that other place?" Mai-dwar was so full of chatter she did not notice how silent her mother was. "And Mother, will I get to meet my grandfather before we go? I wonder if he will like me."

Faya smiled gently. "Yes, my dear he would like you, I am sure of that. But Mai-dwar, I have to leave a few days early, just to get things ready for you and your father. You will wait for Rab to come back and get you, then you and he will leave Atlantis on a nice long trip to some very wonderful place."

She was not sure how much more to say. She need not have worried. The little girl was still too full of her own plans to be concerned about Faya's.

"That's all right, Mother. But what about my grandfather? Will I have time to see him before we leave?"

"No, darling, I don't think so. Perhaps when you come back. Right now he is so busy helping the people of our country that he probably doesn't have much time. But I'm sure he will understand that you want to see him, too."

Faya hated the lies she had to tell. Mai-dwar was much too young to understand the enormity of her mother's actions, and to be told now that she would never see her again, would be unnecessarily cruel.

"Mai-dwar, would you do something for me? Go get the box on my table over there and bring it to me, will you please?" The child obediently brought it to her mother and put it in her lap. It was not a large box. It was made of some wood that was foreign to Atlantis, and when the lid was raised, the sweet scent it still carried filled the room. The carving on the outside was curious, and Faya had never quite decided what the symbols meant. Benai had given it to her years ago, telling her that the trees it was made from grew in one of the countries he had visited, and were considered sacred by the people living there. She had loved it, and it was one of the few things her daughter had never been allowed to play with.

She kept a few treasures in it, a stone she had picked up at the foot of that great human-headed lion on her trip with Rab, a white feather that had drifted down one day when she was sitting on her beloved rock, seemingly from the heavens themselves, as she had seen no bird then, and the small red slippers she had worn the last time she had seen her own mother. Finally, wrapped in a piece of a fine material, were the blue beads.

She lifted them out and slipped them over her daughter's head. "Maidwar, I want you to keep these now for your very own, and you may wear them whenever you wish. You don't have to ask me for permission. They are yours to keep."

The child looked down at the beads resting lightly on her chest, then up at her mother. Delight spread across her face. "My very own? For always? Oh, thank you, Mother. But I'll let you wear them whenever you ask me," she said generously." Faya had to laugh. It stretched the muscles that had suddenly grown unaccustomed to mirth. She hugged Maidwar, then set the box back on the table.

"Honey, I must write a letter now. Will you ask Benai if you may stay with him for a while? I will call you when I have finished writing."

The little girl gave her mother a flashing smile and was out the door as if with wings. She and Benai were the closest of friends, and she loved the stories he could tell. Faya sat there for a minute longer, then got out the writing material and began her letter.

It was to Rab, of course, and always before she had found it easy to put her thoughts down. This time the words just wouldn't flow. They were scattered, almost unintelligible. How could she tell the man she adored that he could never see her again? That she had destroyed their life together? That she had left her child without a mother? That so long as she lived, there would be no peace for her family? Worse, she knew that Rab would never leave if there was the faintest chance she could ever be released from her confinement. Mai-dwar must leave Atlantis, now, while there was still time. Faya's father was an immediate cause of worry, but the deeper reason lay in the terrible visions she had seen, the destruction of her beloved country which she knew was inevitable. Rab and Mai-dwar must get out while there was still time.

Sighing, she put everything away. She left the room and went to Benai. Asking Mai-dwar to leave them alone for a few minutes, she spoke rapidly and with emphasis. He listened closely, then nodded.

"Faya, I'm sure you know how dear you have become to me, and to most of us here at the Temple. I can understand what you did, perhaps better than the others. I, too, have felt the overwhelming anger that had to find its expression in action. If I could have found the man who sold me into slavery, I would have done the same as you. I only wish...." He stopped, then took her in his arms. "I only wish I could have helped you more." His face rested against her hair, and the tears she had been holding back streamed down her face.

"Benai, you who have been more than a friend and teacher, how can I ever ask your forgiveness for what I did to hurt you and the others? Please, see that Rab follows what I ask of him. Mai-dwar must be taken away from here at once, before my father has time to act. If my banishment does nothing else, perhaps it will make him see the necessity for speed, and for secrecy. No one must know where they go. Please, Benai, promise me?"

"You know I will Faya." He released her and gently wiped her face. "Now don't let your daughter see your pain and grief. She will be hurt soon enough. Smile with her, Faya. You are a strong woman, and I know how great your heart is. Call her back. You have so little time. And Faya, be assured I will do exactly as you ask. In fact, I believe I shall be going with them."

Her sudden radiance was thanks enough. She took his hand and kissed it, then went out to the porch and called her daughter.

Chapter Thirty-eight

Early the next morning, Fayasas, daughter of Kadah, walked slowly up the steep slopes behind the Temple. Behind her came the priests, led by Benai. When they reached the top, Faya stopped and waited while the men opened a grille that covered the face of a small cave. This was to be her home for the rest of her life. Around her were the graves, ancient and new, of those who had died while serving at the Temple. Her mother's grave was here, too, although Faya did not know which it was. Each one was a sealed cave; hers alone had a grille covering the entrance.

She was motioned toward it. Instead of obeying as they had expected, she went to Benai and knelt before him. Her face, framed in the unusual dark hair which was now loose around her shoulders, was white; her dark eyes enormous.

"Sir," she said, "I know I have no right to ask a favor. But would you allow me one last look at the world I am so soon to leave forever?"

Benai did not consult the other priests. His eyes looked deeply into hers, reading her soul, then he nodded. Faya rose, walked away from the caves toward the edge of the high cliff. She stood for one long moment, then she raised her arms in the beginning of the Prayer.

"To the Power I send my spirit." She did not finish the words. Instead she crossed her arms over her chest and bowed her head. Then she stepped forward into space. As her body hurtled down toward the sharp rocks below, her heart sang a blessing to Benai for his compassion; but her last inward vision was the smiling eyes of her daughter above the string of blue beads.

END